11/14

SPIT DELANEY'S ISLAND

BOOKS BY
JACK HODGINS

Spit Delaney's Island (1976)

The Invention of the World (1977)

The Resurrection of Joseph Bourne (1979)

The Barclay Family Theatre (1981)

The Honorary Patron (1987)

Left Behind in Squabble Bay (1988)

Innocent Cities (1990)

Over Forty in Broken Hill (1992)

A Passion for Narrative: A Guide to Writing Fiction
(1993, expanded 2001)

The Macken Charm (1995)

Broken Ground (1998)

Distance (2003)

Damage Done by the Storm (2004)

The Master of Happy Endings (2010)

SPIT DELANEY'S ISLAND

SELECTED STORIES BY

Jack Hodgins

RONSDALE PRESS

SPIT DELANEY'S ISLAND
Copyright © 1976, 2011 by Jack Hodgins
First published 1976, Macmillan of Canada

RONSDALE PRESS
3350 West 21st Avenue, Vancouver, B.C.
Canada V6S 1G7
www.ronsdalepress.com

Typesetting: Julie Cochrane, in Granjon 11.5 pt on 15
Cover Design: Cyanotype
Cover Photo: "Scene at Tofino" by Aimin Tang
Paper: Ancient Forest Friendly "Silva" (FSC)—100% post-consumer waste,
    totally chlorine-free and acid-free

Ronsdale Press wishes to thank the following for their support of its publishing program: the Canada Council for the Arts, the Government of Canada through the Book Publishing Industry Development Program (BPIDP), the British Columbia Arts Council, and the Province of British Columbia through the British Columbia Book Publishing Tax Credit program.

Library and Archives Canada Cataloguing in Publication

Hodgins, Jack, 1938–
    Spit Delaney's island: selected stories / Jack Hodgins.—2nd ed.

ISBN 978-1-55380-111-5

    I. Title.

PS8565.O3S6 2011   C813'.54   C2010-906438-0

At Ronsdale Press we are committed to protecting the environment. To this end we are working with Canopy (formerly Markets Initiative) and printers to phase out our use of paper produced from ancient forests. This book is one step towards that goal.

Printed in Canada by Marquis Printing, Quebec

for Dianne

ACKNOWLEDGEMENTS

Some of these stories first appeared in *Journal of Canadian Fiction*, *Capilano Review*, *Northwest Review*, *Descant*, *Wascana Review*, and *Canadian Fiction Magazine*. "At the Foot of the Hill, Birdie's School" was read on CBC's "Anthology."

CONTENTS

I

Separating

People driving by don't notice Spit Delaney. His old gas station is nearly hidden now behind the firs he's let grow up along the road, and he doesn't bother to whitewash the scalloped row of half-tires someone planted once instead of fence. And rushing by on the Island highway today, heading north or south, there's little chance that anyone will notice Spit Delaney seated on the big rock at the side of his road-end, scratching at his narrow chest, or hear him muttering to the flat grey highway and to the scrubby firs and to the useless old ears of his neighbour's dog that he'll be damned if he can figure out what it is that is happening to him.

Hitch-hikers do notice, however; they can hear his muttering. Walking past the sheep sorrel and buttercup on the gravel shoulder, they see him suddenly, they turn alarmed eyes his way. Nodding, half smiling at this long-necked man with the striped engineer's cap, they move on through the shade-stripes of trees, their own narrow shadows like knives shaving the pavement beside them. And all he gives back, all they can take away with them, is a side-tilted look they have seen a hundred times in family snapshots, in the eyes of people out at the edge of group photos unsure they belong. Deference. *Look at the camera, son, this is all being done for you, it has nothing to do with me.* He does not accept their attention, he admits only to being a figure on the edge of whatever it is they are really looking at: his gas station perhaps, or his rusty old tow truck, or his wife piling suitcases into the trunk of her car. He relocates his cap, farther back on his head; his Adam's apple slides up his long throat like a bubble in a tube, then pushes down.

Spit Delaney cannot remember a time when he was not fascinated by the hitch-hikers. His property is close to a highway junction where they are often dropped off by the first ride that picked them up back near the ferry terminal. On these late-summer days, they line up across the front of his place like a lot of shabby refugees to wait for their second ride. Some walk past to get right out beyond the others, but most space themselves along the gravel, motionless, expressionless, collapsed. In pairs or clusters they drape themselves over their canvas pack-sacks and their sleeping bags. Some stretch out level on the ground, using their gear as head-rests with only an arm and an upright thumb to show that they're awake, or alive. They are heading for the west coast of the Island, he knows, the Pacific, where they have heard it is still possible to live right down on the beach under driftwood shelters and go everywhere naked from morning until night. The clothes they are so eager to shed are patched jeans and wide braces and shirts made to look like flags and big floppy hats. There is a skinny boy with a panting St. Bernard tied to his pack with a length of clothes line; there is a young frizzy-haired couple with a whining baby they pass back and forth; there is a grizzled old man, a hunched-over man with a stained-yellow beard, who must be at least in his seventies though he is dressed the same as the others. Stupid old fool, thinks Spit Delaney, and grins. Sitting on his rock, at the foot of the old paint-peeled sign saying B/A, he isn't afraid to envy.

There are ninety miles of road, of this road and another, between the rock at his road-end and the west-coast beaches they are heading for. It runs grey-silver over hills and along bays and through villages and around mountains and along river banks, and is alive already with traffic: tourists set loose from a ferry and racing for campsites, salesmen released from motels and rushing for appointments. Beginnings are hard, and endings, but the long grey ribbon that joins them runs smooth and mindless along the surface of things. In his head Spit Delaney can follow it, can see every turn, can feel himself coming over the last hill to find the ocean laid out in the wide blue haze beneath him. The long curving line of sand that separates island from sea and man from whale is alive with the quick flashing movements of people.

Behind him the trunk lid slams shut. His wife's footsteps crunch down the gravel towards him. He can tell without looking that she is wearing the crepe-soled shoes she bought in a fire sale and tried to return the next day. Spit Delaney's heavy brows sink, as if he is straining to see something forty miles across the road, deep into brush. He dispatches a wad of throat-phlegm in a clean arc out onto a stalk of dog-daisy, and doesn't bother watching it slide to the ground.

She stops, a few feet behind. "There's enough in the fridge to last you a week," she says.

He ducks his head, to study the wild sweet-pea that twists in the grass between his boots.

She is going, now.

That is what they have agreed on.

"Sit down when you eat," she says. "Don't go standing up at the counter, the way you will."

The boy with the St. Bernard gets a ride at this moment, a green GMC pickup. They leap into the back, dog and boy, and scramble up close to the cab. Then the boy slaps his hand on the roof, signal to start, and settles back with an arm around the dog's neck, laughing. For a moment his eyes meet Spit's, the laugh dies; they watch each other until the pickup has gone on past the other hitch-hikers, on up the road out of sight behind trees.

I am a wifeless man, Spit tells the disappeared youth. This is the day of our separation. I am a wifeless man.

In his fortieth year Spit Delaney was sure he'd escaped all the pitfalls that seemed to catch everyone else in their thirties. He was a survivor.

"This here's one bugger you don't catch with his eyes shut," was his way of putting it.

And wasn't it obvious? While all his friends were getting sick of the jobs they'd worked at ever since they quit high school and were starting to hop around from one new job to another, Spit Delaney was still doing the same thing he'd been doing for twenty years, the thing he loved: operating Old Number One steam locomotive in the paper mill, shunting up and down the tracks, pushing flatcars and boxcars and tankcars off and onto barges. "Spit and Old Number One, a marriage made in heaven," people joked. "Him and that machine was made for each other, a kid and his toy. That train means more to him than any human could hope to." Only it wasn't a joke, it was true, he was glad to admit it. Who else in all that mill got out of bed at four o'clock in the morning to fire up a head of steam for the day's work? Who else hung around after the shift was over, cleaning and polishing? Roy Rogers and Trigger, that's what they were. Spit and Old Number One. He couldn't name another person whose job was so much a part of himself, who was so totally committed to what he did for a living.

In the family department, too, he was a survivor. While everyone else's kids in their teens seemed to be smashing up the old man's car or getting caught at pot parties or treating their parents like slaves or having quiet abortions on the mainland, Jon and Cora looked as if they were going to sail right through their adolescence without a hitch: Cora would rather watch television and eat chocolate cake than fool around with boys or go to parties; Jon would rather read a book than do anything else at all. The two of them looked safe enough. It was a sign that they respected their father, Spit would say, though he admitted some of the credit had to go to his wife.

Stella. That was one more thing. All through his thirties it seemed as if every time he turned around someone else was splitting up. Everybody except him and Stella. Friends broke up, divorced, couples fell apart and regrouped into new couples. The day came when Stella Delaney looked at him out of her flat, nearly colourless eyes and said, "You and me are just about the only people we know that are still married." You couldn't count on the world being the same two weekends in a row. It was a hazard of their age, boredom was doing it, Stella told him, boredom and the new morality. People suddenly realizing what they didn't have to put up with. There was no sense inviting anybody over for Saturday night, she said, they could be separated by then. But, miraculously, by the time Spit reached his fortieth year, he and Stella were still married, still together. However, if they intended to continue with their marriage, she told him, they'd have to make some new friends. Everyone else their age was newly single or newly remarried or shacking up with people half their age; what would they have in common?

The secret of his successful marriage, Spit insisted, was the way it started. Stella was a long-legged bony-faced woman of twenty-two, already engaged to some flat-assed logger from Tahsis, when Spit came into the kitchen at the back of her father's store. She was doing peach preserves for her first married winter, and admiring the logger's dinky little diamond ring up on the windowsill in front of her. Her big hands, in the orange mess of peel and juice and carved-out bruises, reminded him of the hands of a fisherman gouging out fish guts. The back of her cotton dress dipped up at the hem, to show the tiny blue veins behind her knees and the pink patches of skin where she'd pressed one leg to the other. He touched. She told him "Get lost mister, I got work to do," and he said "That logger musta been bushed and desperate is all I can say" but stayed to win her anyway, and to rush her off to a preacher's house on the day before her intended wedding. With a start like that, he said, how could anything go wrong?

It couldn't. He was sure of it. Things that were important to him, things that were real—his job, his family, his marriage—these things were surely destined to survive even the treacherous thirties.

But before he had time to congratulate himself, things began to fall apart. He insisted later that it was all because the stupidest god-damned question he ever heard just popped into his head all of a sudden. He didn't look for it, he didn't ask for it, it just came.

He was lying on his back in the sand at Wickanninish Bay, soaking up sun. He'd driven over with the family to the west coast for the weekend, had parked the camper up in the trees above the high-tide line. Stella was lying beside him on her giant towel, reading a magazine, oiled and gleaming like a beached eel. The question just popped into his head, all of a sudden: *Where is the dividing line?*

He was so surprised that he answered out loud. "Between what and what?"

Stella turned a page and folded it back. Most of the new page was taken up with a photograph of a woman who'd increased her bust measurements in a matter of days and wanted to show Stella how to do the same.

"Wha'd you say?"

"Nothing," he said, and rolled over onto his side to face away from her. Between what and what? he asked himself. Maybe he was beginning to crack up. He'd heard of the things that happened to some men at his age.

Between what is and what isn't.

Spit sat up, cursing.

Stella slid her dark glasses down her nose and peered at him. "What's the matter with you?"

"Nothing," he said. *Where is the dividing line?* When the words hit him again like that he jumped to his feet and shook his head, like a cow shaking off flies.

"Sand fleas?" she said.

"It's nothing," he said, and stomped around to shake the sand out of the hair on his legs.

"Too much sun," she said, and pushed herself up. "We better move up into shade."

But when they had settled down by a log, cool in the shade of the wind-crippled spruce, she told him it might just be this beach that was spooking him. "This Indian Lady at Lodge," she said, "told me her people get uneasy along this beach." Spit knew Sophie Jim by name, but Stella always referred to her as This Indian Lady at Lodge. It was some kind of triumph, apparently, when Sophie was finally persuaded to join the Daughters, their first native. "She said there's a story that some kind of Sea-Wolf monster used to come whanging up out of the Pacific here to gobble up people. It came up to sire wolves for the land too, but went back into the sea to live. She says they're all just a little nervous of this place."

Spit's brain itched from the slap of the sudden question. He wanted to go home, but the kids were far out on the sand at the water's edge, and he could holler at them till he was blue in the face without being heard above the roar of the waves.

"She said all up and down this coast there are stories. About monsters that come out and change people into things. To hear her tell it there must've been a whole lot of traffic back and forth between sea and land."

"A whole lot of bull," he said, and put on his shirt. It was cold up here, and what did he care about a lot of Indian stuff? He knew Indians. When he was a boy the people up the road adopted a little Indian kid, a girl, and told it around that nobody, *nobody* was to dare tell her what she was. When she was ten years old she still hadn't figured out that she wasn't the same as everybody else, so Spit sat her down on the step and told her. He had to tell her three times before she believed him and then she started to howl and cry and throw herself around. But she dried out eventually and went Indian with a vengeance, to make up for lost time. He couldn't go near her without having to listen to a whole lot of stuff she'd got soaked up into her brain from hanging around the Reserve. So he knew all about Wasgo, Stella couldn't tell him anything new about that guy. He knew about Kanikiluk too, which was worse. That son of a bitch would think nothing of stepping out of the ocean and turning a man into a fish or making a piece of seaweed think it was human. He knew all about the kind of traffic she meant.

"They say we crawled up out of there ourselves," she said. "Millions of years ago."

"Let's go home," he said. "Let's get out of here."

Within fifteen minutes they had Cora and Jon herded up off that beach and pushed into the back of the camper and had started on their way back across the island to their little house behind the gas station. It wasn't really a gas station any more, though he had never bothered to pull the pumps out; the shed was a good place to store the car parts and engine pieces he kept against the day they would be needed, and the roof out over the pumps was a good place to park the tow truck. Nor was it a real business—his job at the paper mill was enough for anyone to handle—but he'd fixed up the tow truck himself out of parts and used it to pull people out of snowbanks in winter or to help friends when they got their tractors mired in swamp.

When he got home from the coast he did not go into the gas station to brood, as he might have done, nor did he sit behind the wheel of his tow truck. This was too serious for that. He drove all the way down to the paper mill, punched himself in at the gate, and climbed up into the cab of Old Number One. He knew even then that something was starting to go wrong. *Where is the dividing line?* He sat there with his hands on the levers deep into night, all the way through to the early morning when it was time to fire up her boilers and start getting her ready for the day's work ahead. *And what does it take to see it?*

And, naturally, that was the day the company picked to tell him what they'd done with Old Number One.

Sold her to the National Museum in Ottawa.

For tourists to gawk at.

Sons of bitches. They might as well have lopped off half his brain. Why didn't they sell the government his right arm too while they were at it?

The hundred-and-thirty-ton diesel-electric they offered was no consolation. "A dummy could run that rig!" he shouted. "It takes a man to put life into Old Number One!"

He ought to be glad, they told him. That shay was long past her usefulness, the world had changed, the alternative was the junkyard. You can't expect *things* to last for ever.

But this was one uncoupling that would not be soon forgiven.

First he hired a painter to come into the mill and do a four-foot oil of her, to hang over the fireplace. And unscrewed the big silver **1** from the nose to hang on the bedroom door. And bought himself a good-quality portable recorder to get the locomotive's sounds immortalized on tape. While there was some small comfort in knowing the old girl at least wasn't headed for the scrapyard, it was no easy thing when he had to bring her out on that last day, sandblasted and repainted a gleaming black, to be taken apart and shipped off in a boxcar. But at least he knew that while strangers four thousand miles away were staring at her, static and soundless as a stuffed grizzly, he would be able to sit back, close his eyes, and let the sounds of her soul shake through him full-blast just whenever he felt like it.

Stella allowed him to move her Tom Thomson print to the side wall to make room for the new painting; she permitted him to hang the big number **1** on the bedroom door; but she forbade him to play his tape when she was in the house. Enough is enough, she said. Wives who only had infidelity to worry about didn't know how lucky they were.

She was president of her Lodge, and knew more than she could ever tell of the things women had to put up with.

"Infidelity?" he said. It had never occurred to him. He rolled his eyes to show it was something he was tempted to think about, now that she'd brought it up, then kissed the top of her head to show he was joking.

"A woman my age," she said, "starts to ask what has she got and where is she headed."

"What you need is some fun out of life," he said, and gathered the family together. How did a world tour sound?

It sounded silly, they said.

It sounded like a waste of good money.

Good money or bad, he said, who'd been the one to go out and earn it? Him and Old Number One, that's who. Hadn't he got up at four o'clock every damn morning to get the old girl fired up, and probably earned more overtime that way than anybody else on this island? Well, was there a better way to spend that money than taking his family to Europe at least?

They left her mother behind to keep an eye on the house. An old woman who had gone on past movement and caring and even speech, she could spend the time primly waiting in an armchair, her face in the only expression she seemed to have left: dark brows lowered in a scowl, eyes bulging as if in behind them she was planning to push until they popped out and rolled on the floor. Watching was the one thing she did well, she looked as if she were trying with the sheer force of those eyes to make things stay put. With her in the house it was safe to leave everything behind.

If they thought he'd left Old Number One behind him, however, if they thought he'd abandoned his brooding, they were very much mistaken; but they got all the way through Spain and Italy and Greece before they found it out. They might have suspected if they'd been more observant; they might have noticed the preoccupied, desperate look in his eyes. But they were in Egypt before that desperation became intense enough to risk discovery.

They were with a group of tourists, standing in desert, looking at a pyramid. Cora whined about the heat, and the taste of dry sand in the air.

"It's supposed to be hot, stupid," Jon said. "This is Egypt." He spent most of the trip reading books about the countries they were passing through, and rarely had time for the real thing. It was obvious to Spit that his son was cut out for a university professor.

And Cora, who hated everything, would get married. "I can't see why they don't just tear it down. A lot of hot stone."

Jon sniffed his contempt. "It's a monument. It's something they can look at to remind them of their past."

"Then they ought to drag it into a museum somewhere under a roof. With air conditioning."

Stella said, "Where's Daddy?"

He wasn't anywhere amongst the tourists. No one in the family had seen him leave.

"Maybe he got caught short," Jon said, and sniggered.

Cora stretched her fat neck, to peer. "And he's not in the bus."

The other tourists, too, appeared uneasy. Clearly something was sensed, something was wrong. They shifted, frowned, looked out where there was nothing to see. Stella was the first to identify it: somewhere out there, somewhere out on that flat hot sand, that desert, a train was chugging, my God, a steam engine was chugging and hissing. People frowned at one another, craned to see. Uneasy feet shifted. Where in all that desert was there a train?

But invisible or not it got closer, louder. Slowing. *Hunph hunph hunph hunph.* Then speeding up, clattering, hissing. When it could have been on top of them all, cutting their limbs off on invisible tracks, the whistle blew like a long clarion howl summoning them to death.

Stella screamed. "Spit! Spit!" She ran across sand into the noise, forgetting to keep her arms clamped down against the circles of sweat.

She found him where in the shrill moment of the whistle she'd realized he would be, at the far side of the pyramid, leaning back against its dusty base with his eyes closed. The tape recorder was clutched with both hands against his chest. Old Number One rattled through him like a fever.

When it was over, when he'd turned the machine off, he raised his eyes to her angry face.

"Where is the line?" he said, and raised an eyebrow.

"You're crazy," she said. "Get a hold of yourself." Her eyes banged around in her bony head as if they'd gone out of control. There were witnesses all over this desert, she appeared to be saying, who knew what kind of a fool she had to put up with. He expected her to kick at him, like someone trying to rout a dog. Her mouth gulped at the hot air; her throat pumped like desperate gills. Lord, you're an ugly woman, he thought.

The children, of course, refused to speak to him through Israel, Turkey, and France. They passed messages through their mother—"We're starved, let's eat" or "I'm sick of this place"—but they kept their faces turned from him and pretended, in crowds, that they had come alone, without parents. Cora cried a great deal, out of shame. And Jon read a complete six-volume history of Europe. Stella could not waste her anxiety on grudges, for while the others brooded over the memory of his foolishness she saw the same symptoms building up again in his face. She only hoped that this time he would choose some place private.

He chose Anne Hathaway's Cottage in Stratford. They wouldn't have gone there at all if it hadn't been for Jon, who'd read a book on Shakespeare and insisted on seeing the place. "You've dragged me from one rotten dump to another," he said, "now let me see one thing I want to see. She was twenty-six and Shakespeare was only my age when he got her pregnant. That's probably the only reason he married her. Why else would a genius marry an old woman?" Spit bumped his head on the low doorway and said he'd rather stay outside. He couldn't see any point in a monument to a woman like *that*, anyway. The rest of them were upstairs in the bedroom, looking at the underside of the thatched roof, when Old Number One started chugging her way towards them from somewhere out in the garden.

By the time they got to Ireland, where they would spend the next two weeks with one of her distant cousins, Stella Delaney was beginning to suffer from what she called a case of nerves. She had had all she could take of riding in foreign trains, she said, she was sure she'd been on every crate that ran on tracks in every country of Europe and northern Africa; and now she insisted that they rent a car in Dublin for the drive down to her cousin's, who lived about as far as you get on that island, way out at the end of one of those south-western peninsulas. "For a change let's ride in style," she said, and pulled in her chin to show she meant business. She was missing an important Lodge convention for this. The least he could do, she said, was make it comfortable.

The cousin, a farmer's wife on a mountain slope above Ballinskelligs

Bay, agreed. "'Tis a mad life you've been living, sure. Is it some kind of race you're in?"

"It is," Stella said. "But I haven't the foggiest idea who or what we're racing against. Or what is chasing us."

"Ah well," said the cousin, wringing her hands. "God is good. That is the one thing you can be certain of. Put your feet up and relax so."

She knew about American men, the cousin told them. You had to watch them when they lost their playthings, or their jobs, they just shrivelled up and died.

Stella looked frightened.

Oh yes, the cousin said. She knew. She'd been to America once as a girl, to New York, and saw all she needed to see of American men.

Spit Delaney thought he would go mad. He saw soon enough that he could stare out this farmhouse window all he wanted and never find what he needed. He could look at sheep grazing in their little hedged-in patches, and donkey carts passing by, and clumps of furze moving in the wind, he could look at the sloping farms and the miles and miles of flat green bog with its brown carved-out gleaming beds and piled-up bricks of turf and at the deep curved bay of Atlantic ocean with spray standing up around the jagged rocks until he was blind from looking, but he'd never see a train of any kind. Nor find an answer. Old Number One was in Ottawa by now, being polished and dusted by some uniformed pimple-faced kid who wouldn't know a piston from a lever.

"We'd've been better off spending the money on a swimming pool," Stella told the cousin. "We might as well have flushed it down the toilet."

"That's dumb," Cora said. She buttered a piece of soda bread and scooped out a big spoonful of gooseberry jam.

"Feeding your pimples," Jon said. He had clear skin, not a single adolescent blemish, nor any sign of a whisker. Sexually he was a late developer, he explained, and left you to conclude the obvious: he was a genius. Brilliant people didn't have time for a messy adolescence. They were too busy thinking.

"Don't pick on your sister," Stella said. "And be careful or you'll get a prissy mouth. There's nothing worse on a man."

A hollow ache sat in Spit's gut. He couldn't believe these people belonged to him. This family he'd been dragging around all over the face of the earth was as foreign to him as the little old couple who lived in this house. What did that prim sneery boy have to do with him? Or that fat girl. And Stella: behind those red swollen eyes she was as much a stranger to him now as she was on the day he met her. If he walked up behind her and touched her leg, he could expect her to say Get lost mister I got work to do, just as she had then. They hadn't moved a single step closer.

I don't know what's going on, he thought, but something's happening. If we can't touch, in our minds, how can I know you are there? How can I know who you are? If two people can't overlap, just a little, how the hell can they be sure of a god-damn thing?

The next day they asked him to drive in to Cahirciveen, the nearest village, so Jon could have a look around the library and Stella could try on sweaters, which she said were bound to be cheaper since the sheep were so close at hand. Waiting for them, sitting in the little rented car, he watched the people on the narrow crooked street. Fat red-faced women chatted outside shop doors; old men in dark suits stood side by side in front of a bar window looking into space; a tall woman in a black shawl threaded her way down the sidewalk; a fish woman with a cigarette stuck in the middle of her mouth sat with her knees locked around a box of dried mackerel; beside the car a cripple sat right on the concrete with his back to the store-front wall and his head bobbing over a box for tossed coins.

The temptation was too much to resist. He leaned back and closed his eyes, pressed the button, and turned the volume up full. Old Number One came alive again, throbbed through him, swelled to become the whole world. His hands shifted levers, his foot kicked back from a back-spray of steam, his fingers itched to yank the whistle-cord. Then, when it blew, when the old steam whistle cut right through to his core, he could have died happily.

But he didn't die. Stella was at the window, screaming at him, clawing at the recorder against his chest. A finger caught at the strap and it went flying out onto the street. The whistle died abruptly, all sound stopped. Her face, horrified, glowing red, appeared to be magnified a hundred times. Other faces, creased and toothless, whiskered, stared through glass. It appeared that the whole street had come running to see him, this maniac.

Stella, blushing, tried to be pleasant, dipped apologies, smiled grimly as she went around to her side of the car.

If her Lodge should hear of this.

Or her mother.

The chin, tucked back, was ready to quiver. She would cry this time, and that would be the worst of all. Stella, crying, was unbearable.

But she didn't cry. She was furious. "You stupid stupid man," she said, as soon as she'd slammed the door. "You stupid stupid man."

He got out to rescue his recorder, which had skidded across the sidewalk almost to the feet of the bobbing cripple. When he bent to pick it up, the little man's eyes met his, dully, for just a moment, then shifted away.

Jon refused to ride home with them. He stuck his nose in the air, swung his narrow shoulders, and headed down the street with a book shoved into his armpit. He'd walk the whole way back to the cousin's, he said, before he'd ride with *them*.

She sat silent and bristling while he drove out past the last grey buildings and the Co-op dairy and the first few stony farms. She scratched scales of skin off the dry eczema patches that were spreading on her hands. Then, when they were rushing down between rows of high blooming fuchsia bushes, she asked him what he thought she was supposed to be getting out of this trip.

"Tomorrow," he said. "Tomorrow we go home."

Spit Delaney had never travelled off the Island more than twice before in his life, both those times to see a doctor on the mainland about the cast in his eye. Something told him a once-in-a-lifetime trip to Europe ought to have been more than it was. Something told him he'd been cheated. Cheated in a single summer out of Old Number One, his saved-up overtime money, the tourist's rightfully expected fun, and now out of wife as well. For the first thing she told him when the plane landed on home territory was this: "Maybe we ought to start thinking about a separation. This is no marriage at all any more."

He stopped at the house only long enough to drop them off, then fled for coast, his ears refusing the sounds of her words.

But it was a wet day, and the beach was almost deserted. A few seagulls slapped around on the sand, or hovered by tide pools. Trees, already distorted and one-sided from a lifetime of assaults, bent even farther away from the wind. A row of yellowish seaweed, rolled and tangled with pieces of bark and chunks of wood, lay like a continuous windrow along the uneven line of last night's highest tide. Far out on the sand an old couple walked, leaning on each other, bundled up in toques and Cowichan sweaters and gum boots. The ocean was first a low lacy line on sand, then sharp chopped waves like ploughed furrows, then nothing but haze and mist, a thick blending with uncertain sky.

There was no magic here. No traffic, no transformations. No Kaniki-luk in sight. He'd put ninety miles on the camper for nothing. He might as well have curled up in a corner of the old gas station, amongst the car parts, or sat in behind the wheel of his tow truck to brood. The world was out to cheat him wherever he turned.

Still, he walked out, all the way out in the cold wind to the edge of the sea, and met a naked youth coming up out of waves to greet him.

"Swimming?" Spit said, and frowned. "Don't you tell me it's warm when you get used to it, boy, I can see by the way you're all shrivelled up that you're nearly froze."

The youth denied nothing. He raised both arms to the sky as if expecting to ascend, water streaming from his long hair and beard and his crotch, forming beads in the hairs, shining on goose-bumped skin. Then he tilted his head.

"Don't I know you?"

"Not me," Spit said. "I don't live here."

"Me neither," the youth said. "Me and some other guys been camping around that point over there all summer, I go swimming twice a day."

Spit put both hands in his pockets, planted his feet apart, and stretched his long neck. He kept his gaze far out to sea, attempting to bore through that mist. "I just come down for a look at this here ocean."

"Sure, man," the youth said. "I *do* know you. You let me use your can."

"What? What's that?" Why couldn't the kid just move on? You had to be alone sometimes, other people only complicated things.

"I was waiting for a ride, to come up here, and I come into your house to use the can. Hell, man, you gave me a beer and sat me down and told me your whole life story. When I came out my friend had gone on without me."

Spit looked at the youth's face. He remembered someone, he remembered the youth on that hot day, but there was nothing in this face that he recognized. It was as if when he'd stripped off his clothes he'd also stripped off whatever it was that would make his face different from a thousand others.

"You know what they found out there, don't you?" the youth said. He turned to face the ocean with Spit. "Out there they found this crack that runs all around the ocean floor. Sure, man, they say it's squeezing lava out like toothpaste all the time. Runs all the way around the outside edge of this ocean."

"What?" Spit said. "What are you talking about?"

"Squirting lava up out of the centre of the earth! Pushing the continents farther and farther apart! Don't that blow your mind?"

"Look," Spit said. But he lost the thought that had occurred.

"Pushing and pushing. Dividing the waters. Like that what-was-it right back there at the beginning of things. And there it is, right out there somewhere, a bloody big seam. Spreading and pushing."

"You can't believe them scientists," Spit said. "They like to scare you."

"I thought I recognized you. You pulled two beer out of the fridge, snapped off the caps, and put them on the table. Use the can, you said, and when you come out this'll wash the dust from your throat. You must've kept me there the whole afternoon, talking."

"Well, nobody's stopping you now. Nobody's forcing you to stay. Go on up and get dressed." If all he came up out of that ocean to tell about was a crack, he might as well go back in.

Which he did, on the run.

Straight back through ankle-foam, into breakers, out into waves. A black head, bobbing; he could be a seal, watching the shore.

Go looking for your crack, he wanted to shout. Go help push the continents apart. Help split the god-damned world in two.

"There's no reason why we can't do this in a friendly fashion," Stella said when he got home. "It's not as if we hate each other. We simply want to make a convenient arrangement. I phoned a lawyer while you were out."

She came down the staircase backwards, on her hands and knees, scrubbing, her rear end swinging to the rhythm of her arm. Stella was death on dirt, especially when she was upset.

"Don't be ridiculous," Spit said. "This isn't Hollywood, this is *us*. We survived all that crap."

She turned on the bottom step, sat back, and pushed her hair away from her eyes. "Not quite survived. It just waited until we were off our guard, until we thought we were home-safe."

He could puke.

Or hit her.

"But there isn't any home-safe, Spit. And this *is* Hollywood, the world has shrunk, it's changed, even here." She tapped the pointed wooden scrub brush on the step, to show where here was.

Spit fingered the cassette in his pocket. She'd smashed his machine.

He'd have to buy a new one, or go without.

"Lady," he said, "that flat-assed logger don't know what a close call he had. If he'd've known he'd be thanking me every day of his life."

Though he didn't mean it.

Prying him loose from Stella would be like prying off his arm. He'd got used to her, and couldn't imagine how he'd live without her.

Her mother sat in her flowered armchair and scowled out over her bulging eyeballs at him as if she were trying to see straight to his centre and burn what she found. Her mouth chewed on unintelligible sounds.

"This is my bad year," he said. "First they take away Old Number One, and now this. The only things that mattered to me. Real things."

"Real!" The old woman screeched, threw up her hands, and slapped them down again on her skinny thighs. She laughed, squinted her eyes at the joke, then blinked them open again, bulged them out, and pursed her lips. Well, have we got news for you, she seemed to be saying. She could hardly wait for Stella's answer.

"The only things you can say that about," Stella said, "are the things that people can't touch, or wreck. Truth is like that, I imagine, if there is such a thing."

The old woman nodded, nodded: That'll show you, that'll put you in your place. Spit could wring her scrawny neck.

"You!" he said. "What do you know about anything?"

The old woman pulled back, alarmed. Her big eyes filled with tears, her hands dug into the folds of her dress. The lips moved, muttered, mumbled things at the window, at the door, at her own pointed knees. Then suddenly she leaned ahead again, seared a scowl into him. "All a mirage!" she shrieked, and looked frightened by her own words. She drew back, swallowed, gathered courage again. "Blink your eyes and it's gone, or moved!"

Spit and Stella looked at each other. Stella raised an eyebrow. "That's enough, Mother," she said. Gently.

"Everybody said we had a good marriage," he said. "Spit and Stella, solid as rocks."

"If you had a good marriage," the old woman accused, "it was with a train, not a woman." And looked away, pointed her chin elsewhere.

Stella leapt up, snorting, and hurried out of the room with her bucket of soapy water.

Spit felt, he said, like he'd been dragged under the house by a couple of dogs and fought over. He had to lie down. And, lying down, he had to face up to what was happening. She came into the bedroom and stood at the foot at the bed. She puffed up her cheeks like a blowfish and fixed her eyes on him.

"I told the lawyer there was no fighting involved. I told him it was a friendly separation. But he said one of us better get out of the house all the same, live in a motel or something until it's arranged. He said you."

"Not me," he said. "I'll stay put, thank you."

"Then I'll go." Her face floated back, wavered in his watery vision, then came ahead again.

"I'd call that desertion," he said.

"You wouldn't dare."

And of course he wouldn't. It was no more and no less than what he'd expect, after everything else, if he thought about it.

All he wanted to do was put his cassette tape into a machine, lie back, close his eyes, and let the sounds of Old Number One rattle through him. That was all he wanted. When she'd gone he would drive in to town and buy a new machine.

"I'll leave the place clean," she said. "I'll leave food in the fridge when I go, in a few days. Do you think you can learn how to cook?"

"I don't know," he said. "How should I know? I don't even believe this is happening. I can't even think what it's going to be like."

"You'll get used to it. You've had twenty years of one kind of life, you'll get used to another."

Spit put his head back on the pillow. There wasn't a thing he could reach out and touch and be sure of.

At the foot of his obsolete B/A sign, Spit on his rock watches the hitch-hikers spread out along the roadside like a pack of ragged refugees. Between him and them there is a ditch clogged with dry podded broom and a wild tangle of honeysuckle and blackberry vines. They perch on their packs, lean against the telephone pole, lie out flat on the gravel; every one of them indifferent to the sun, the traffic, to one another. We have all day, their postures say, we have for ever. If you won't pick us up, someone else just as good will do it, nobody needs you.

Spit can remember a time when he tried to have a pleading look on his face whenever he was out on the road. A look that said Please pick me up I may die if I don't get where I'm going on time. And made obscene gestures at every driver that passed him by. Sometimes hollered insults. These people, though, don't care enough to look hopeful. It doesn't matter to them if they get picked up or not, because they think where they're going isn't the slightest bit different from where they are now. Like bits of dry leaves, letting the wind blow them whatever way it wants.

The old bearded man notices Spit, raises a hand to his forehead in greeting. His gaze runs up the pole, flickers over the weathered sign, and runs down again. He gives Spit a grin, a slight shake of his head, turns away. Old fool, Spit thinks. At your age. And lifts his engineer cap to settle it farther back.

Spit cannot bear to think where these people are going, where their rides will take them. His mind touches, slides away from the boy with the St. Bernard, sitting up against the back of that green pickup cab. He could follow them, in his mind he could go the whole distance with them, but he refuses, slides back from it, holds onto the things that are happening here and now.

The sound of Stella's shoes shifting in gravel. The scent of the pines, leaking pitch. The hot smell of sun on the rusted pole.

"I've left my phone number on the memo pad, on the counter."

The feel of the small pebbles under his boots.

"Jon and Cora'll take turns, on the weekends. Don't be scared to make Cora do your shopping when she's here. She knows how to look for things, you'll only get yourself cheated."

He'd yell *Okay!*

He holds on. He thinks of tourists filing through the National Museum, looking at Old Number One. People he'll never see, from Ottawa and Toronto and New York and for all he knows from Africa and Russia, standing around Old Number One, talking about her, pointing, admiring the black shine of her finish. Kids wondering what it would be like to ride in her, feel the thudding of her pistons under you.

He'd stand at the edge of the water and yell *Okay you son of a bitch, okay!*

"It don't look like there's going to be any complications. My lawyer can hardly believe how friendly all this's been. It'll all go by smooth as sailing."

Spit Delaney sees himself get up into the pickup with the youth and the St. Bernard, sees himself slide his ass right up against the cab, slam his hand in a signal on the hot metal roof. Sees himself going down that silver-grey road, heading west. Sees himself laughing.

He says, "My lawyer says if it's all so god-damned friendly how come you two are splitting up."

"That's just it," she says. "Friends are one thing. You don't have to be married to be a friend."

"I don't know what you're talking about," Spit says. It occurs to him that he has come home from a trip through Europe and northern Africa and can't remember a thing. Something happened there, but what was it?

He sees himself riding in that pickup all up through the valley farmlands, over the mountains in the centre of the island, down along the lakes and rivers, snaking across towards Pacific. Singing, maybe, with that boy. Throwing his arm around the old floppy dog's ugly neck. Feeling the air change gradually to damp, and colder. Straining his neck to see.

"I got my Lodge tonight, so I better get going, it'll give me the day to get settled in, it takes time to unpack. You'll be all right?"

Sees himself hopping off the green pickup, amongst the distorted combed-back spruce, the giant salal, sees himself touching the boy good-bye, patting the dog. Sees himself go down through the logs, through the white dry sand, over the damp brown sand and the seaweed. Sees himself at the water's edge on his long bony legs like someone who's just grown them, unsteady,

shouting.

Shouting into the blind heavy roar.

Okay!

Okay you son of a bitch!

I'm stripped now, okay, now where is that god-damned line?

Three Women of
the Country

I

Mrs. Wright's first thought when she heard all the racket coming from somewhere over on Starbuck's farm was "Will it be something I can write up for the paper?" She was paid twenty cents an inch for sending all the news from Cut Off in to the weekly newspaper in town and nothing unusual missed her notice. More often than not her column was just a list of weekend visitors, but she hoped some day to write up a story so exciting they would print it on the front page under big black headlines, maybe even with pictures.

When the noise started she was down on her knees weeding the rose garden in front of her house. The July sun had just lifted itself above the fir ridge across the highway and she wanted to get the weeding done before it beat straight down on her out of that stainless-steel sky. It was no surprise to a woman like Mrs. Wright that the day was already the hottest one yet; her well was getting low and she couldn't turn the hose on the gardens or the front lawn without the risk of losing all her drinking water. What else could she expect?

Mrs. Wright went up onto her back porch to see if she could find out what was causing the noise, held a hand up to shade her face from the sun. Not that she perspired, mind you; there wasn't enough of her to produce a drop of sweat. But still, she suffered from the heat. A little stick of a woman, hardly taller than her porch railing, she wore a mop of white hair on top like an abandoned nest. Her skin, stretched tight over tiny bones, was mottled and dry.

Directly in front of her was the one field she still owned, its hay freshly cut and sold, and beyond the far fence there was one of Mrs. Starbuck's fields with a few of her white-face cattle grazing. She could see, through a gap in the trees, Mrs. Starbuck's house where Mrs. Wright had gone to live as a bride with her first husband. It was a tall solid-looking house with a huge poplar tree beside it and a rock pile not far away. The two high windows that faced this way were blank squares in the sunlight. And far on the other side of Starbuck's farm, right back against the jagged rim of timber, was the white gable of Mr. Porter's house.

But not a person in sight. She got her ladder and leaned it against the side of the house. Then she climbed up and stood on the red duroid roof for a better look. In the distance, beyond the farmhouse and the barn. Mrs. Starbuck was running this way, flapping her arms and carrying on, screeching sounds that weren't even words by the time they got as far as Mrs. Wright's ears.

My God, woman, Mrs. Wright thought. If you could only see yourself.

But of course she couldn't. Mrs Starbuck was not the type to wonder what kind of impression she was making. The first thing Mrs. Wright would tell anybody about Mrs. Starbuck was that she was more man than her husband ever was. Naturally, as long as he was alive she pretended to be feminine, wore dresses and nagged at him and kept the house clean enough (though not nearly as clean as Mrs. Wright had kept it when she was Mrs. Left and lived over there), but the minute he died she put on his old clothes, let her appearance just go, and started clearing land. In the year since his death she'd logged off fifteen more acres, burned up the stumps, and planted it all in hay and oats. She drove her tractor as if she was born on one. And looked, Mrs. Wright couldn't help thinking, as if she belonged on one.

Mrs. Starbuck had passed right by her own house and was starting down her nearest field. Those precious white-face cows of hers high-tailed it off in every direction to get away from her. Mrs. Wright was surprised she hadn't stopped running to tiptoe through the herd so she wouldn't disturb them. She always acted as if they were the only cows worth anything on this whole island, and nearly had a heart attack when Mr. Porter's Holstein bull got through the fence. "If that black bastard ruins my herd," she told him. "I'll have your hide. I'll sue."

Mrs. Wright judged people by what she saw. She had five good senses, she knew, and that was all anyone was given for judging what was real. And what she saw when she looked at Mrs. Starbuck was bohunk. She hated to say it, she hated even to think it, because it was the ugliest word she knew; but friend or not, it described Mrs. Starbuck. She was no immigrant (though Mrs. Wright had heard once that Edna Starbuck's parents were born in Norway, which would explain her height, and perhaps even her size—Scandinavians, Mrs. Wright had observed, often got heavy after fifty), but just the same she dressed and acted as if she came from another country where there wasn't much money around and no one had ever heard of a thing called good taste.

Just look at her. How many normal people would come screeching across the field like that in the middle of a July morning? She hadn't even thought of driving her car over, or getting Mr. Porter to drive her. It didn't even occur to her that the people going by on the highway—Americans mostly, in their campers—probably thought she was crazy. All Mrs. Wright hoped was that after so much commotion the emergency was worth while. She hated to see people get all upset over nothing.

She sat down on the roof and waited while Mrs. Starbuck got closer. She wondered what her first husband, Mr. Left, would think of the way that woman ran their farm. He would probably faint from shock. She already knew what Mr. Wright thought of it: "Nothing about that woman surprises me," he said. "If you told me she murdered her grandmother I'd believe you, she's that foreign to me."

And Mrs. Wright had to admit there were times when she thought the silly woman ought to be put away. Society should watch out for people like her, she said, but Mr. Wright just raised an eyebrow at the idea.

Everybody had had a good laugh when she changed her name from Mrs. Left. People said, "You did it on purpose. You chose Mr. Wright just because it sounded funny coming after Mr. Left and you probably don't love him at all." But they were wrong. Her maiden name was Baldwin and all the time she was married to Mr. Left, much as she liked him and thought he was a good husband, she still thought of herself as Milly Baldwin. And when her first husband was killed fighting a forest fire and Mr. Wright proposed, it didn't occur to her that the shift in names was a strange coincidence until someone at the wedding reception said "I guess your third husband will have to be Mr. In-between."

"Haw haw," she said.

Her first husband was a good enough man. She had liked him for his efficient masculine ways. But she had never been able to talk to him about the things she could talk to Mr. Wright about. Since she'd married Mr. Wright she'd learned how to balance the economy, reform the penal system, control foreign investment, and wipe out welfare. He'd taught her it all, and her greatest regret was that there was no one else she could tell it to. She couldn't think of a soul in Cut Off who would know what she was talking about.

Certainly, if she'd brought up foreign investment in front of Mrs. Starbuck the best she could expect to get was a blank stare. What did Mrs. Starbuck know about anything beyond farming? Words like economics or welfare recipient were lost on her, they were as foreign as the menu in a Greek restaurant. Mrs. Starbuck probably didn't even know *one word* of the other official language in her own country.

Mrs. Wright did. She wanted to help out the government and make all those people back in Quebec feel good so she borrowed a French text from the local school and started memorizing. She learned *un deux trois quatre cinq six* quite quickly and decided she had a flair for languages. *Je regarde autour de moi* (she could remember it even now). But she couldn't foresee an opportunity to say things like that, even if Mr. Wright ever got around to taking her Back East some time so she could try it out in a Montreal restaurant. She sent away for a LEARN FRENCH AT HOME record and it was in her stereo set right now, beside the Andy Williams album, waiting for her to have time to play it.

Mrs. Wright felt pity for Mrs. Starbuck. Imagine living in a bilingual country and not knowing one word of the other language! The worst of it was that Mrs. Starbuck wasn't even very good at handling English, let alone something else. And if Mrs. Wright ever got so silly as to offer Mrs. Starbuck her French book or record, the crazy old bat would probably say something like "There's no Frenchies in Cut Off. Where would I use it?" to show her ignorance and backwardness.

She climbed down off the roof and backed her pickup truck out of the garage, ran it up beside the house, and left it idling in neutral while she got out. The way Mrs. Starbuck was galloping across the field, waving her arms and ki-eye-ing like an immigrant, she was sure they would be heading off somewhere in the pickup and thought it wouldn't hurt to be ready. What would people do if they didn't have her to fall back on?

"What is the matter with you?" she called.

Mrs. Starbuck was halfway across the nearest field. She stopped running but, instead of answering Mrs. Wright, put her hands on her knees and stood still with her head down like that, breathing heavy, for a few minutes. Then she jerked upright and moved forward again, not running, dragging her feet through the hay stubble as if she were ready to drop.

Dress like a woman for a change and you could move faster, Mrs. Wright thought. But Edna Starbuck hadn't worn a dress in a year. Coming up towards Mrs. Wright's fence now, she had on a too-large pair of man's pants, heavy black gumboots, a plaid mackinaw, and a greasy baseball cap. Except for her broad hips and enormous thighs she could have been a man, somebody's old hired hand staggering across the field, drunk.

Mrs. Wright put her foot on the bottom strand of barbed wire and pulled up on the next so there would be a space for Mrs. Starbuck to crawl through without getting her clothes all caught up in the fence. Mrs. Starbuck fell through and lay panting on the grass at Mrs. Wright's feet. Her baseball cap fell off and Mrs. Wright could see pink scalp through the thinning grey hair, plastered by sweat to her head.

"What's wrong?" Mrs. Wright asked. "What's happened?"

Mrs. Starbuck got to her feet and put her hat back on. She put one hand on the chestnut tree and leaned all her weight into it. "One of my calves," she said, and paused a while to catch up on her breathing, "down the well."

"Down *what* well?" Mrs. Wright shouted.

"Way out back, the dried-up one."

It was proof to Mrs. Wright that Mrs. Starbuck, even if she could clear land, wasn't capable of running a farm by herself. A man would have checked that well to make sure it had a decent top on it. She knew the one. She could remember her first husband putting a good solid cap on the top, but you couldn't expect it to last for ever. That was a good twenty years ago and wood does rot.

"Why didn't you get Porter over to help? He's closer."

"I did," Mrs. Starbuck said. "He told me to get you too. It'll take all of us."

"Well that's a surprise," Mrs. Wright said. "I thought *he* could do anything. Why didn't you drive over?"

Mrs. Starbuck blinked. "I never thought of it," she said. "Do you have ropes?"

Mrs. Wright ran back to the garage and took down a coil of new rope from a nail on the wall. When she got back to the pickup Mrs. Starbuck was already inside, ready to go.

"Too bad my husband isn't home," Mrs. Wright said as she started the pickup moving down the driveway.

"Oh, I don't need a lawyer, just plain weight. Somebody to pull."

Thank you very much, Mrs. Wright thought. But that was typical of Mrs. Starbuck. She couldn't see that an intelligent person could figure out a better way of doing things. She thought when a thing had to be done the best way was always the obvious way—bull work. She probably couldn't see any sense in a man like Mr. Wright existing at all, sitting in an office thinking of ways to help people and never lifting a manure fork from one day to the next.

"If it's just more weight you want. I can't see why you came to me."

Mrs. Wright looked down at her little body perched like a child behind the wheel. Her legs were so short her husband had had to wire thick wooden blocks onto all the pedals so she could drive. Her arms were like the thin scaly legs of a Rhode island rooster.

"You always sound and act like you're bigger and heavier than you are," Mrs. Starbuck said.

There was admiration in her voice. Mrs. Wright was sure of it. Mrs. Starbuck, even though she was incapable of understanding a woman like Mrs. Wright or carrying on any kind of intelligent conversation with her, had always had a real respect. She'd always known, it seemed, that Mrs. Wright was no run-of-the-mill, that she was a person with depth and someone you could count on.

Mrs. Wright drove the pickup along the highway to the end of her property and then turned onto the road that led back to Mrs. Starbuck's. She tooted the horn as she passed the little cabin where the Larkin triplets lived, Percy, Bysshe, and Shelley. Shelley was at the door shaking mats when Mrs. Wright drove by, but the two brothers were nowhere in sight. Probably off on their motorcycles, she thought, seeing how many cars they could pass in an hour, burning up gas paid for right out of the taxpayer's pocket. If Mr. Wright's ideas were ever put into practice those two wouldn't know what hit them, the welfare cheques would stop so fast. They were twenty-four years old and perfectly capable of working at something, even if the three of them together didn't have as much intelligence as a Jersey cow. Mrs. Wright believed that people should be forced to contribute if they want to hang around breathing air and taking up space.

"At least," Mrs. Wright said, "you didn't ask *them* to help. They'd manage to get your whole herd down the well before they were through."

The road was shaded from the sun by the heavy alder trees that grew in close to the sides and made it almost like a tunnel. An old Model T Ford, abandoned years ago by someone who just drove it in and walked away, sat off to one side with bracken and alder shoots growing right up through it, as if it belonged there. Farther on, the road crossed the bridge over a little stream, so shallow in summer it barely moved, and then divided: left to Mrs. Starbuck's and right to Mr. Porter's. In the wedge of land between the two branches of road a half-dozen cars—stripped of everything but body and frame—sat as if dropped there at the same time by a giant hand to shoot off sparks of sunlight from pieces of broken glass. Mrs. Wright's first husband dragged them there years ago when she got fed up with seeing them around the yard.

Mrs. Wright cringed every time she got a close-up look at Mrs. Starbuck's house. When she and Mr. Left lived there they cared for the place, were proud of it. They bought it off an old Swede when they were first married, and for years had kept it up. She always said that if the house were closer to the highway it would be a showpiece. But Mrs. Starbuck and that husband of hers had never given two hoots about the place. That white handsome two-storey house had been covered over with cheap grey artificial bricks bought in rolls and hammered on in a single afternoon. Her beautiful gardens had been walked all over by cattle and never weeded; the only flowers still alive were those strong enough and determined enough to push up through weeds and not mind being trampled on by cows. Mrs. Wright could hardly bear to go inside. Whenever Mrs. Starbuck cornered her into an invitation she always encouraged her to serve tea in the sun porch so she wouldn't have to look at the way the inside of the house had gone downhill. Everything old was rotten; everything new was in bad taste.

"Turn here," Mrs. Starbuck said.

"I guess I know where we're going," Mrs. Wright said. And swung the pickup truck down the lane towards the barn. She let Mrs. Starbuck get out to open the gate, then drove through and waited for her to close it and get back inside the truck. Then they drove, bouncing and squeaking, over the grazing land—around stumps and blackberry bushes and over cedar rails piled up in shallow drainage ditches—down hill nearly to the still solid edge of the timber and pulled up alongside Mr. Porter who was trying to get the calf out of the well. His daughter Charlene was under a tree drinking from a quart jar of water.

Mr. Porter looked up when they got out of the pickup and pushed his hat back on his forehead. "Here's something for your column, Millicent," he said. He had been chopping away at the broken boards but laid his axe aside when she arrived.

"Don't be ridiculous," she said. "Nobody wants to read about calves."

"Well this one's stuck good. I hope you brought rope stronger than this piece I got here. It won't pull a thing without snapping."

The rope he had tied around the calf's neck was hardly thicker than binder twine. Mrs. Wright wondered if there was a man alive in this world, aside from her two husbands, who could do things right. It seemed every

Three Women of the Country / 31

time she turned around there was somebody else doing something the wrong way and needing her to set it straight.

"I don't know how you keep that place of yours from falling apart, John Porter," she said, "if that's the kind of equipment you use."

She took the coil of rope from the back of her pickup and walked over to the well. The calf, which was not really a calf at all but one of Mrs. Starbuck's Hereford yearlings (only half the size it could have been if it had been cared for properly and given good feed) was not even down the well. Only its back end had fallen in and got wedged; the head and front feet were above the ground.

"Judging by the racket I would've guessed this thing was down at the bottom at least, twenty feet down and wedged crosswise."

Mrs. Starbuck had run over and crouched down by the calf. She started running her hand down its forehead, between its white bulging eyes, and crooning soft words at it. "I just hope it's not hurt," she said. Her big florid face was down level with the calf's as if she were trying to hypnotize it. "I could kill the so-and-so who broke that well cover."

"You're looking at him," Mrs. Wright said. "That white-face beef there stepped right through the top."

"Don't be silly," Mrs. Starbuck said. "No cow is stupid enough to walk on a wooden well cover."

Shallow. That's all Mrs. Wright could say about her, just shallow. And she could have added "Is your cow so stupid it'll walk on a well cover that's *already* been broken through?" but she held her tongue. There were some people you just couldn't talk to, they knew it all. To set them straight only brought out the meanness in them.

And Mrs. Starbuck could be mean. Mrs. Wright had seen her catch a dog in the chicken run and beat it with a stick of wood until her arm ached. That Mr. Starbuck when he was alive had taught her meanness. It was because he was such a little man and so weak—he tried to make up for it by nastiness and he taught her to be the same way. To tell the truth, Mrs. Wright thought that, big as she was, she had been scared of that miserable little man and eventually took on some of his characteristics for her own protection.

Right now, though, she was looking at that calf as if she had never struck a living thing in her life, as if she were the kindest person in the world.

Talk about two-faced. Well, no, Mrs. Wright wouldn't call it exactly two-faced because Mrs. Starbuck never tried to hide it. She could love and hug that calf right now and then as soon as it was out of the hole, kick its ass for being so stupid as to fall in. Mrs. Wright had seen people treat their children like that but when she was bringing up her own two she tried to be consistent so they could always know what to expect.

"All right," Mrs. Wright said. "Get away."

She meant Mrs. Starbuck but they both moved. Mr. Porter and Mrs. Starbuck backed right up to where the girl was sitting at the base of the tree. They crouched down and watched her.

She made a lasso of the rope and dropped it over the calf's neck. Then she worked it under the legs until it cinched up around the chest.

"Okay John Porter, come here."

Porter lifted his hat and scratched, then walked up and took the coil of rope from Mrs. Wright's hand. "Tie it to the truck," she said. Make yourself useful is what she meant. She couldn't stand to see a man doing nothing while a woman worked. Even if a woman like her nine times out of ten could do a thing better, it still wasn't right.

She watched him uncoil the rope and walk with it over to the pickup. Moving fast just wasn't in him so she watched while he walked over and crawled under the truck and ran the rope around the axle. But before he could pull the rope taut, his hand slipped and banged against something. He came out from under that truck holding onto his hand and biting his lip shut as if he were afraid of what he might say if he once opened up.

"You're all right," his daughter said. She ran over to him and held the hand and muttered something to him that Mrs. Wright couldn't hear.

It's a good thing it's only skinned knuckles, she thought. What would you do if it was broken and you had to go to a doctor? Mr. Porter belonged to some religion (she could never remember the name) that didn't believe in going to doctors or getting inoculation shots or anything like that.

Mrs. Wright couldn't imagine herself not wanting to go to a doctor, they'd always done so much for her. And she figured there was only one reason for people like the Porters to refuse the benefit of modern medicine. No, there were two reasons. First, they were probably scared of what doctors could do, needles and knives and things. But more likely, it was just that they wanted to be different from other people, set apart. They were using religion as an excuse. Just wait until the crunch came, just wait until they were in real trouble; they'd be high-tailing it down to that doctor's office like anyone else, and be grateful for all the advances of medical science.

Mrs. Wright was a tolerant woman when it came to religion. She admired the Mennonites, sticking together in their little community up the highway a mile or so. She was careful, of course, not to wear a kerchief over her head or leave her apron on when she was outside working in the garden. Not everyone was as understanding as she was, and she didn't want them to think as they drove by that they were already in the Mennonite settlement. She knew a lot of Catholics, too, and they could cross themselves all they wanted as far as she was concerned, if they thought it would do them any good. And most of the Finns who lived in Cut Off were Lutherans but they never went to church so it didn't make any difference. No, you could have any religion you wanted and Mrs. Wright would tolerate it. The only thing she couldn't tolerate was stupidity and as far as she was concerned the Porters were stupid. There should be laws forcing them to go to doctors.

Mr. Porter hadn't straightened up yet when Mrs. Wright heard what sounded like two buzz saws running wild and turned to see what was happening. Percy and Bysshe Larkin rode down the hill on their motorbikes. They bounced over the bumps, yahoo-ing and grinning like a couple of drunks, their rear ends leaping off the seats a foot with every bump. At the truck they parted and roared two opposite circles around the whole lot of them, then skidded to a stop and put their legs out to keep from falling over.

"Just in case this poor calf wasn't scared enough already from being down a well," Mrs. Wright said.

They grinned at her from their two identical empty faces. She couldn't even be sure they knew what she meant.

Mrs. Starbuck moved up beside her and put her fists on her hips. "What you two doing on my place anyway? I bet you left every damn gate open for my cows to get out and run all over the country."

Bysshe Larkin examined the sky. Searching for birds or wind. "Heard a lot of racket down here, thought maybe somebody was killed."

"Nobody yet," Mrs. Wright said. "Sorry to disappoint you." Percy Larkin looked at the two women and then at his brother. "You know what she reminds me of, Bysshe?"

"Which one?"

"The little one. Mrs. Left-Wright."

"What?"

"A fox terrier. A little white-haired fox terrier always yapping."

Mrs. Wright opened her mouth to screech at them but Mrs. Starbuck beat her to it. "You two get on out of here right now!" she yelled. "Go on! Shoo! Get out!" She flapped her arms as if they were two chickens that had wandered into her house. "You don't come onto my property and insult my friend, not while I'm around. Git!"

But they didn't move. Mrs. Wright would have reached down to pick up two rocks and thrown them straight at those empty faces if she hadn't known how simple-minded they were. There was no sense getting mad when simple-minded people said insulting things they couldn't even understand themselves.

"A fox terrier," Bysshe Larkin said. "A fox terrier beside a Great Dane."

"Get the hell off this place, we got a job to do!" Mrs. Starbuck said. "Go home and learn some manners from your sister, you empty-headed so-and-sos."

Mr. Porter left the back of the truck, from which he had watched everything that had gone on, and stood right between those two. He put a hand on the elbow of each brother and spoke so softly Mrs. Wright had to strain to hear. "These ladies are all upset about the job ahead of them," he said. "If you want to help, how about going back to close those gates so the calf won't run out onto the road when it's free? If you come back tomorrow Mrs. Starbuck will let you see if it's hurt or not."

The Larkin boys looked at the women, and then at each other. They started their motors and rode three circles around the four of them before they took off up the hill.

"Empty as wind," Mrs. Wright said after them, "flighty as birds."

"I hope them two are sterilized," Mrs. Starbuck said. "I wouldn't want to see any more Larkins around."

"You can't sterilize people if they don't want it," Mrs. Wright said. "And they're just the kind, them and all the people with no intellect, who would refuse to have it done. You and me are paying to keep them on the road, spreading their low-IQ seeds."

"They didn't come in here to spread seeds," Mr. Porter said. "They were just curious."

Mrs. Wright looked at him. How tolerant could you be? "I'm surprised to see a man with a teenage daughter so free and easy about them," she said.

"Don't be crude, Millicent," Mrs. Starbuck said. "You'll make Charlene blush."

"Well," Mrs. Wright said. "As soon as we see how many stitches John Porter is going to need in that hand we can get busy and haul your calf out."

Mr. Porter levelled his cool green eyes to hers and held out both his hands. "There's not a thing wrong with it," he said, and showed her they were exactly the same, not a bump or a scrape.

"Then get back under that truck with the rope and hitch it good and tight. This calf may disappear from sight if we don't get a move on around here."

And it *had* slipped a little. It looked to Mrs. Wright as if it had dropped a few inches farther into the well, probably from kicking and banging with its back feet. It puffed and snorted from the effort of hanging there, its white eyes running wild, waiting for help.

"It'll be bloated," Mrs. Starbuck said. "We may have to puncture it."

"Don't be silly," Mrs. Wright said. "They get bloated when they're on their backs. This one's just scared, and probably scraped up a little. Bull or heifer?"

"Bull. It's marked for fall slaughter."

Mr. Porter got into Mrs. Wright's pickup and started the motor. He drove ahead slowly until all the slack in the rope had been taken up, then he eased ahead while the two women and the girl watched the rope tighten around the calf's chest.

"Wumph," was the noise the calf made, and Mrs. Starbuck screamed. "Stop! For Christ's sake stop the truck. You'll break him in half."

Mr. Porter stopped the truck and came back to see what was wrong. Mrs. Starbuck was down on the ground with her arms around the calf's head. She looked as if she were trying to pull it out of the well all by her herself. "You can't do it that way," she said. "It has to go up. Up. Pulling it *along* like that will only break its bones."

Mrs. Wright would like to have kicked her out of the way, a big heavy woman like her down there acting so immature. "I'm sorry, Edna Starbuck, that my pickup doesn't fly so I could pull your stupid calf up the way you want."

"Don't you stupid-calf me. You come over here to help and end up running the whole show, bossing everybody. Maybe there's something wrong with your eyes, Millicent, but most people could see that if you drag a calf along the ground out of a well something's going to snap."

"I think it already has," Mrs. Wright said. "I think your mind has snapped. If you could just see yourself right now, you look like a know-nothing bohunk straight off the boat. Screaming and hollering like a fishwife. Get up on your feet."

"All we need is a pulley. To hang up in one of those trees. We could run the rope through it."

Mrs. Wright hardly ever raised her voice. When she did she suffered for it a long time after. She thought of what Percy Larkin said about her being a little fox terrier, yapping, but she pushed the image aside. "Get up," she said. "Get up. Get up. Get up. John Porter, you drive that truck ahead. We're getting that calf free."

Mr. Porter looked from Mrs. Wright to Mrs. Starbuck and then backed off. "We better all just cool down and do some thinking," he said. "We're not getting anywhere this way."

"Then *I* will," Mrs. Wright said. She marched over to the truck, got in, and put it into low gear. If Mr. Wright were here he'd just shake his head at the way they were carrying on. If I acted like that, he'd say, where would we all be? If a lawyer acted like that, what a mess we'd have.

Mrs. Starbuck shrieked. As Mrs. Wright let the clutch pedal out and felt the truck begin to move she glanced out the back window and saw her lifting Mr. Porter's axe. She swung with both hands well over her head and brought it down on the rope. The truck leapt ahead and stalled.

Mrs. Wright was tempted to start the truck up again and drive home, just drive straight out of here with rope dragging behind like a tail and leave the stupid woman to solve her own problem. But it wasn't in her to leave a job undone. She got back down to the ground and turned to give Mrs. Starbuck a piece of her mind.

Mrs. Starbuck was facing her with the axe held up once more over her head. She's going to kill me, Mrs. Wright thought. She's going to throw that axe and it will land right in the middle of my chest and kill me. She dragged me over here to help her with her calf and now she will slaughter me in cold blood.

Mrs. Wright had never before seen such hatred as there was in the woman's eyes. In that stunned second they were staring at each other Mrs. Wright had a vision of her husband visiting Mrs. Starbuck in jail and offering to be her attorney.

Then Mrs. Starbuck brought the axe down square on the calf's forehead, raised it and brought it down again. The head dropped forward between its forelegs, chin on the ground, and shuddered. Pink froth bubbled from its mouth. Mrs. Wright couldn't help but think of the way Edna Starbuck, halfway across the field, had stopped with her head down as if to say I just can't go on, just like that calf.

Mrs. Starbuck raised the axe again. She hissed. She looked at Charlene Porter cowering under a fir tree, and at Mr. Porter with one foot ahead as if he wanted to come closer and take his axe away, and at Mrs. Wright standing at the side of her pickup truck wishing there were some way she could write all this up for the paper and knowing she couldn't. Then she said "Go home" to them, hissed it at them as if they were a herd of balky cattle. "Get out of here. Leave me alone."

Mr. Porter lifted his hat and put it back on again. Then he stepped up and released his axe from Mrs. Starbuck's grip. His daughter put her hand in his and they started walking up past the stumps and blackberry bushes towards home.

Mrs. Wright didn't move. She wasn't budging. She trained her eyes on Mrs. Starbuck's and held them steady. No screeching fishwife was going to beg her for help and then tell her to go. She stared straight into those two round eyes until Mrs. Starbuck looked away and sat down beside her dead calf. She took her baseball cap off and ran it under her nose and wiped her forearm across her eyes.

"Edna Starbuck," Mrs. Wright said, "I think you must be insane." And she swung around to get back inside the cab of the pickup truck.

By the time she had the engine started Mrs. Starbuck was at the window. Her big face, a brighter red now than ever before, shone through a smear of tears. "Don't tell Mr. Wright," she said.

Mrs. Wright stared. She knew there were people who were afraid of her husband but it had never passed through her mind before that Mrs. Starbuck was afraid of *anything*. "He wouldn't be interested," she said. "You can do whatever you want with your own livestock."

Mrs. Wright wanted to go home. What was she doing over here anyway, with all the work *she* had to do at home? "Step back," she said, and when Mrs. Starbuck had taken her hands off the truck she started up the hill away from the well, away from that calf, and rode the bumps and hollows with impatience. At the barn she was careful to close the gate behind her. She didn't even want to think how much trouble there'd be if Mrs. Starbuck's cattle got off her farm and out onto the road, stopping traffic and eating up other people's lawns.

II

Charlene was already sitting on the verandah chair and watching the gable of Mrs. Starbuck's house when her father came up out of the bush and headed across the orchard towards her. She leaned ahead, elbows on her knees, and rested her chin in the palms of both hands so she wouldn't be tempted to glance his way. Here, though the verandah roof hid her from the sun, she felt as if the warm heavy air she breathed had just been exhaled by someone else.

Out in the front yard hot air wrinkled upward from the short green orchard grass, making the apple trees and plum trees seem to waver a little, as if they'd been dipped in water. Along the path that led to the picket gate and the gravel road, the oyster shells were a white so harsh that it hurt her eyes to look. A big lazy cat, somebody's stray, stretched and settled to sleep at the base of a honeysuckle bush.

Charlene sighed at her father's approach. She had run ahead and left him on the trail up from the back of Mrs. Starbuck's farm. Well, let him walk alone if he couldn't be bothered to do any more than he had to help Mrs. Starbuck. She was in no mood for new disappointments.

Ordinarily Charlene would have stood up to anyone and defended Mrs. Starbuck, would have said her behaviour back at the well just showed she was upset about something and didn't realize what she was doing. Charlene liked to see the best in everything if she could. And anyway, she guessed Mrs. Starbuck had earned the benefit of a thousand doubts. But after yesterday, when she discovered not quite by accident what that woman had kept locked up in her attic for who knows *how* long, she didn't feel quite so sure.

Because she knew now; the secret was out: and oh, how she wanted to tell someone about it! Her father; anyone. Back there she had been aching to walk right up to Mrs. Starbuck and say "I knew. I saw him!" Maybe then she might have been given some kind of explanation.

She did not want to believe it. Not any more than she wanted to believe what her eyes had let her see Mrs. Starbuck do to that poor calf. Because after all, Mrs. Starbuck had lived next door and been the only grown-up woman in her life, her closest friend, for two years now. And besides, hadn't her father taught her to think of people, *all* people no matter what they did, as made in the image of God? For nearly twenty-four hours she had been trying her hardest to insist that Mrs. Starbuck, despite all the evidence that seemed to be piling up against her, was still the same perfect woman she'd known all along, totally incapable of such ugly behaviour. But it wasn't working; she'd been betrayed.

When she was concentrating like this, thinking hard, her blue eyes looked as if they were rocketing through the air, ninety miles an hour, drilling two straight holes through space to another world. It was what her father called her furious face, put on like a mask whenever she didn't want to look at him.

And yet she saw. Though her eyes and her mind were on that fake-brick triangle beyond the fence-line alders, she saw him approach. He was not a big man, not heavy and tall like some, but he walked as if he were unaware of this fact, put each foot in turn out too far in front—as if he had all the leg in the world to use—then had to withdraw it and set it down closer than he wanted. As a result, he came across that orchard in quick jerky movements like a machine. He reached up and yanked the peak of his cap down almost to his eyes and ran his free hand over his beard.

To show he was angry.

"I thought I knew that woman," he said, when he'd reached the step in front of her, "but I guess you never really know anybody else."

And disappointed too, just as disappointed as she was, though he still didn't know the half of it.

She could remember only one time when he had got mad—furious mad—and that was when her mother had gone off to live in the Queen Charlotte Islands with a used-car salesman. Charlene was only five years old then, so a good nine years had gone zipping by with no more than just the odd hint of that old fury. It took a lot to get him worked up.

Her mother had been pretty: small with black black hair and blue eyes snapping. A turned-up little nose that belonged on a girl, not a woman. And Charlene (how she hated that name! She wanted to be a Miranda or Lorene at least) was probably not going to be the littlest bit pretty, though maybe people who were content with large blue eyes wouldn't notice. Her hair, bleached almost white already by this year's sun, floated in soft fine curls around her head.

"Nothing but temper," Mr. Porter grumbled. "Just plain bad temper, like a kid throwing a tantrum and *bang* there goes a yearling bull."

"Not temper. That was something else, I don't know what."

Another yank on the front of that cap, and he started up the steps. "Spoilt-rotten temper. I saw a man once, beat his son almost to death for throwing a tantrum about something or other."

"And whose temper was worse?"

"What surprises me," he said, using his handkerchief to wipe the back of his neck free of sweat, "is how she thinks so much of those cattle and then can turn around and knock one on the head." He turned in the doorway and stood with the outsides of his wrists pressed hard against the jambs, his favourite trick. "If they're so much better than my Holsteins how can she do a thing like that?"

Charlene didn't know anything about cows. A Holstein looked the same as a Hereford to her, except for its colour. She knew her father raised his for the milk and Mrs. Starbuck raised hers for the meat, but she didn't really care. What was a cow when there were people who were so much more important and interesting?

Her father took one step ahead onto the verandah and let his arms rise, by themselves, until they were level with his shoulders. He looked at her as if he expected applause.

"That doesn't prove anything," she said. "That doesn't prove a thing, except make you look like you're planning to ascend."

Mr. Porter looked out, first at one horizontal arm, then at the other. "You could be right," he said, and let them drop to his thighs. "A pure case of expectations fulfilled."

"A kid's game," she said, and looked away.

But did not miss his look. She'd hurt him, and driven him inside to eat his lunch alone.

He'd recover. He always did. He didn't even know about the mess she'd unearthed, but when he did it wouldn't frighten him a bit, he'd have an answer for that too. Sometimes it was discouraging to see how he could so easily handle just about any situation you could hand him. But right now Charlene was ashamed to tell him she didn't know what to do with the discovery she'd made yesterday.

Because yesterday afternoon she had gone calling on Mrs. Starbuck. To pod peas again, perhaps, or just to talk. Or maybe just to be there and listen to the summer sounds in company.

But there was no sign of Mrs. Starbuck at the house. The door was open to the flies and no one answered her call. Back at the barn, she thought. Because her funny old car was home, like a fat brown chicken sunning itself in dust. Back in the fields maybe, admiring her cows. While flies and neighbours can step right in and take over.

And did. Just one step in at first, to see if Mrs. Starbuck's boots were inside the door, to listen for footsteps in the bedroom or upstairs. Then a second step to be sure. She wasn't being nosy yet. Mrs. Starbuck had always made her feel at home.

But had never taken her upstairs. The steps were worn in the centres, covered with rubber treads. And upstairs (just her head above the floor at first, as if expecting someone there) was a huge sewing room, a treadle machine in the very centre, surrounded by heaps of cloth and paper patterns, boxes of clothes.

Clothes for who? she wondered, and moved on to discover a small shirt and pants. Boy's clothes. Some new, some old and patched, some not even finished yet.

This far into forbidden territory already (listening hard for sounds of Mrs. Starbuck's return below and ready with an excuse: "I was sure I heard your voice upstairs but it must've been wind") she tried a door and opened it and looked into the other half of the upstairs floor, unfinished, a storage room for old books and magazines, a broken table, an old-fashioned mirror.

Nothing else. Not a thing else except a hole in the ceiling and the slightest sound, no louder than a page being turned, a leaf being stirred. She walked on the ceiling joists across the room to the ladder, set the ladder upright, and climbed up until her head was above the hole.

"Mrs. Starbuck, what are you doing way up here?" she said, but saw nothing. A black triangular room under the rafters. She had seen cages this shape for brood hens, to hatch their eggs.

Then she saw something human huddled up against the farthest wall.

She crept forward on her hands and knees, heart pounding, knees itching from the sharp pieces of ceiling insulation between the joists. About half way across the space she stopped and concentrated all her energy into her eyes, trying to see clearly through the half light and pick out features in the face that looked back. It was a boy. "Well for heaven's sake, why did you want to scare me like that?" A boy in shirt and jeans, hunched against the wall. "What are you doing up here anyway?"

But he didn't answer. When she lifted her hand to move forward a bit more he made some kind of hissing sound at her and pulled his feet right up under himself, hid his face from her sight. Then she put her hand down, unseeing, into a dish of cold food.

And fled. Scrambled back to the hole and rushed down the ladder, hoping to make it outside before she was sick.

Which was another one of her failures. Being sick, she told people, who could never understand anyway, was against her religion. She could remember her father being sick only twice in her life and both times he was able to snap out of it in a very short while. She had learned all the principles, knew how, but it always seemed harder for her. And failure was worse when there was someone like her father around.

Charlene and her father were the only members of their religion in Cut Off. There was no church in the nearest town, either, but this didn't matter too much as the weekly lesson was published and they could study it at home. "And maybe it's better this way," Mr. Porter said. "We can try practising it every day instead of saving it up for an hour-long session on Sundays." He taught her all she needed to know, a definition of man: God is Truth and Love, and man his perfect reflection. His perfect idea. Each lesson was different but eventually came around to the one essential point, that every human being is a spiritually perfect idea, incapable of sickness or inhumanity or fear.

For a long time as a little girl she didn't know that not everyone thought this way. She believed it and practised it and saw its results but had no idea that while she was trying to see the people around her as perfect despite their actions they were seeing her, in return, as anything but. "A smart-alec brat" was what a mother of a friend called her. Because she had said, when she wasn't allowed to visit the friend who had a cold, "I won't catch it, maybe he'll catch my health." The mother had turned almost purple at that. And an old man, once, hacking away with his allergy, had called her a snot for having the nerve to say "If you'd only stop *believing* you're sick."

So she learned to be careful. She refused to pretend there was anything reasonable in the way other people took sickness and fear and disasters for granted and even expected them, but she kept her mouth shut about it. She watched others sometimes as if they were all mad, the way a child who had learned to solve problems based on the assumption that two plus two equals four might feel on discovering that everyone else was building whole cities based on the belief that two plus two equals five. But she knew better than to shout warnings.

In school, though, it wasn't always easy to be inconspicuous. Whenever the school nurse visited and lined everyone up for polio vaccine or inoculations she was the only one left sitting in her desk.

"I suppose you think *you* can't catch polio or smallpox?" one teacher had said.

"Not think," she answered, "know. If I only thought I couldn't catch them probably I would."

The teacher sniffed, as if to say, "We'll see about that," and went on marking some papers she had laid out on her desk.

"It was arrogant of you to answer like that," her father told her, later. "That teacher'll think you're a smart-alec."

"But I told the truth," she said. "Does speaking truth mean they have to force you into loneliness?"

"Some people think truth is only what they can see or touch. She didn't even know what you were talking about."

She had told Mrs. Starbuck something of her isolation, but what could she expect? Mrs. Starbuck could add two and two and get five like everybody else. She told Charlene a girl her age had no business being so serious. She said, "You should be thinking of little-girl things, never mind worrying about religion and things like that."

And now, it looked almost as if Mrs. Starbuck was throwing a challenge at her. As if saying *"Now* am I so perfect, Miss Smart?" As if trying to make it impossible for Charlene to think of her as anything else but a violent mad woman and a lawbreaker.

But some calmer part of herself insisted that she was thinking nonsense. Jumping to conclusions. Maybe the boy was just some runaway who'd chosen that attic to hide in. Maybe Mrs. Starbuck didn't even know he was there. He could be hiding from mean foster parents or the police. He could be sick or dying. But there was that dish of food. And all those boy clothes around the sewing machine. And more than once in the past year Charlene had heard sounds up in that attic which she'd passed off as bird sounds or a rat. Like it or not, she had to believe that Mrs. Starbuck was guilty.

And didn't even know yet that her secret was out.

Nor did her father know, who stood beside her again, eating a sandwich. He bit off a corner, winked at her, and narrowed his eyes to show what she was missing. When he'd swallowed he took a good look all around the front yard and said, "Yessir, she was mad."

"Just leave her alone," Charlene said. "She had reason."

"Oh not her. I mean Mrs. Wright."

She looked up and saw laughter sitting in his eyes. "Oh *her*."

"I thought the top of her head was going to go *zing* straight up in the air. It'll probably take her a week to get over it. I wouldn't be surprised if she actually expected Mrs. Starbuck to throw that axe at her."

Charlene swallowed a giggle. "And those Larkins!"

"Well," he said.

"Calling Mrs. Wright a fox terrier." She put her hand over her mouth but the giggle leaked out.

"They're just grown-up kids," he said. "There's no harm in them."

"Spreading their low-IQ seeds!" she cried. The giggle was out, had escaped, was shaking her whole body.

Her father pulled a face, an attempt to look as small and cranky as Mrs. Wright. "I'm surprised," he said, as stern as could be, "to see a man with a teenage daughter so free and easy about such scum!"

She tried to bark like Mrs. Starbuck: "Don't be crude, Millicent!" but she collapsed instead in a fit of giggles and had to put her face right down. Oh, why did people have to take anything seriously?

But her father was still Mrs. Wright. "Some day, Mr. Porter," he invented, "your daughter may just end up married to one of those morons if you insist on being so tolerant."

"Oh no, not that," she laughed, "I'd rather die."

Because she nearly had, anyhow, the one time she had let them close, had nearly died of fright. "Those three," she said. "ought to be locked up somewhere."

"Now now," he said, a warning, a hand on her arm.

And she understood what he meant. Yes, even those three, with their warped sense of humour and limited intelligence, were people too and just as true as she.

Try telling her that the day last year when she went into their back yard for eggs (mud and feathers right to the floor) and the two men rode motorcycles around and around her getting so close to her toes she cried out at last for Shelley. Try telling her they were perfect reflections of God too like everybody else when they tried to get her on their bikes. ("Too scared, eh C.P.? Too scared to sit a motorbike.")

"Not scared, just sensible. I got this funny ambition, I want to grow up alive."

And Shelley too, on the front step combing her long black hair and singing, "She's only fourteen," as if it were a crime or an affliction that couldn't be helped.

"There's fourteen and fourteen," she said.

"And you're the scaredy kind," Shelley said. "If I ride one will you the other?"

So she had sat on Bysshe's seat, arms clamped around his chest, a voice inside saying "He might not have much brains but he's kept himself alive on this thing, maybe I have a chance," and rode that black machine four times around the yard (chickens scattering at every turn). And was just breathing easy that it would soon be over when he turned left instead of right and went out onto the road, spraying gravel like chicken feed in every direction, and speeded up.

"Go back," she cried, and would have pounded his back if she could have pried her hand loose. "Stop and let me off, I've had enough."

But enough or not there was more. Twenty miles more up Cut Off Road at sixty miles an hour at least, then onto gravel and dust for fifteen more of logging road; down into the ditch and up again to avoid the watchman's gate (her screaming now and considering her chances if she just let go and fell), around two small lakes as flat and smooth as corners chipped from mirrors, and up a dozen switchbacks through newly logged-off mountainside (him rising as natural as a huge black bird up those slopes) until they skidded to a stop by a river and waited while their own dust caught up and swirled around them and thinned out.

"Now there's just one thing I want to do," she said, when her feet were on the ground, "to show how much I appreciate the ride." She tightened her fist, pulled back her arm, and hit him as hard as she could in the middle of his chest.

But he laughed. "You're no fighter," he said, and took off. Glided down the slope as if all of this, all this mountainside and sky belonged just to him.

"Caliban!" she yelled after him, but he didn't hear, and anyway he wouldn't have known what she meant.

She was left, spitting dust and curses, at the top of that hill. When his brown cloud had settled, she looked down on the road ahead like a dropped rope leading round-about back to home. She was left with nothing but a noisy whiskey-jack for company and thirty-five miles to walk.

I bet they think I'm scared of a big old brown bear jumping out of the bush to eat me, she thought, and (glancing behind to be sure) started walking. I bet they think I'm terrified to know I couldn't possibly get home before dark. I bet they're sitting down there in their mucky yard laughing at me, sure I'm listening for sounds of footsteps behind or cracking branches in brush.

She sang two verses of a hymn her father had taught her but got too interested in the wild blackberries at the side of the road to go on. She was knee-deep in vines, face smeared with red juice, when Mrs. Starbuck's old paint-peeling car came chugging up the hill and stopped. "Weren't you even going to try getting home?" Mrs. Starbuck said.

"I forgot," she said. "I knew someone would come. I just wish I had a bucket with me though, these berries are too good to leave."

Mrs. Starbuck got out and pried off a hub cap. "Here's all the bucket I got, so pick. We'll make jam together and I get half."

They picked three hub caps full before Mrs. Starbuck's back started to ache. Charlene set them out on the back seat, went back to fill a plastic bag she'd found, then got into the car and slammed the door. "Too bad I don't have time to pick another hub cap full for Bysshe," she said.

Mrs. Starbuck started her motor. "Them three," she said. "They'll kill somebody yet. No sense at all."

"Oh they've got sense all right," she said. "They just don't know it was meant to be used. What brought you up this way?"

"Not sightseeing exactly. You should've heard the story I had to tell that watchman. I ended up doubting it myself. That Bysshe rode into my yard and right up onto the verandah and said 'Guess who's just starting down the side of Handlebar Hill?' I told him I hoped it was doom, heading for him, but he laughed and said no it was Charlene Porter who was too scared to ride back."

"That's a lie. He left me."

"I figured it was. I thought, well I can't afford to see Cut Off from the air so why not a bird's-eye view from the hills? Here I am, and look at that sight."

They both looked down at the land below, a thick green rug with roads like worm trails winding through, farm fields like shaved-off squares. The strait, blue-white from here, looked full and thick and slow. "Let's get," Charlene said. "Those blackberries are soft and this sun'll drip juice all over your back seat."

The next day she walked over to help make jam but Mrs. Starbuck already had the berries on her stove. "They haven't boiled yet," she said, "you can help me scald out the bottles."

She washed the jam bottles in the sink with hot water and soap, then set them on a rack and let Charlene pour boiling water from the kettle over them.

"Bysshe, you're in this bottle, stop screaming. Percy, here you are, here's your turn, take it like a man. Shelley, don't cry, it'll only last a minute. No sense swimming, it takes the skin off anyway."

"I'm surprised at you," Mrs. Starbuck said. "A person brought up the way you are shouldn't talk like that. Leave me to do the mean things."

"There's nothing mean about you," she said. "I've never seen you mean."

Mrs. Starbuck chuckled. "Oh, I learned a few things from my husband. He was an expert."

"How come you never had any kids?"

Mrs. Starbuck turned away quickly. "Here. Look here. These berries are started to boil. You take this wooden spoon and stir a while."

All that morning they worked together (like mother and daughter, she thought) until every one of those berries, mashed down and sweetened with sugar, was safely stuffed inside a jar and capped with wax.

Mrs. Starbuck closed her eyes to breathe in the smell. And in the silence Charlene heard a sound in the attic. A bird has got in, she thought, for it was nothing louder than a small body hitting once against a board. It could even have been something knocked over by a mouse or rat. "There's something alive up there," she cried. "Hey you, come down! Mrs. Starbuck, you've got bats in your attic!"

Mrs. Starbuck sat down heavily, dropped her body into a chair with a wumph that knocked her own breath out. "Look at me," she said. "A fat cow in these clothes. You'd be ashamed of me for a mother. Anybody'd be ashamed of me."

"Not me!"

Oh no, she'd take her out and parade her around and say "my mother" every second sentence. "I think you're perfect," she said. Mrs. Starbuck was about as far as you could get from that pretty little blue-eyed mother she remembered but she'd do. She'd do just fine. "I'd just love it, Mrs. Starbuck."

"Well I've had one husband already, all I could bear in this life. And your father's still married to that other one, up there." She pointed vaguely north. "So right now's as close as we'll ever be to related, like it or not."

"It'll do," she cried, but listen: "There it is again. You do have bats up there!"

Mrs. Starbuck slapped her heavy thighs. "I may have bats in my belfry but there's not one in my attic. Not a thing alive up there. Let's go pick some peas."

"There's only one thing I don't like about your father," Mrs. Starbuck said when they were outside. "The way he's taught you all that religion stuff since you were too young to know what it means."

Charlene laughed. "I've never believed anything I couldn't turn around and prove," she said. "Christ didn't come to start up a church or make himself into a hero. He came to show what we could all do for ourselves if we'd just recognize what we are."

"Just the same, I think a person should wait until he's grown up before picking a religion, when you're old enough to know what you're doing."

Charlene stood up from picking and faced the sun. "How old were you when you made your choice?"

"Me?" she said. "Me, I still don't know what's what. Forty-eight years old and maybe never will."

And now, watching her father head down the lane towards the chicken sheds, Charlene too wondered if she knew what was what. But pushed that thought aside as quickly as it appeared, because she did know this: it was sometimes hard to hold on to what you know is real when everything is trying hard to hide it from you. She'd been betrayed, not by truth but by a friend. The real Mrs. Starbuck was hiding behind a new and ugly mask, the mask of a cheat and a criminal.

And yet, behind the betrayal there was a sense of excitement. This was something that happened only in newspapers, to people in far-off places, to twisted and warped and violent people, or silent and sneaky people. But not to them! Not to Mrs. Starbuck and to her and to, yes, to Mrs. Wright. They were not people who were written up in the back pages of the big-city newspaper beside stories of two-headed calves and freak drownings and axe-murder trials. They were three women (she included herself, now, after this) who lived in Cut Off and passed from day to day through ordinary, growing lives. Happy, mostly happy, and knowing each other so well.

Until Mrs. Starbuck became a monster.

She tried to straighten out her thinking, put it in line with what she'd been taught. Her father would be disappointed if he knew what thoughts she'd been allowing in. She tried to see behind that new monster surface, to insist on the perfection beneath. If she refused to see anything in Mrs. Starbuck but the truth of her God-qualities, she knew, all this mess would somehow straighten out and things could go back to normal. Her father could do it, and so could she.

But she couldn't seem to stick to it. Because there was the boy, too, to think of. Shut up in that room like an old coat that's out of style, not even able to see the sun shining out there or the dust rising along the road. Worse off than an animal. How could she push that picture from her mind as if it didn't exist?

Maybe Mrs. Starbuck let him out when no one else was around. Maybe she kept him there only when there was company. But if that was so, why was he there yesterday? Why wasn't he running all over the house, playing? There wasn't a toy in sight.

And maybe she'd been wrong all along. There was still the possibility that Mrs. Starbuck didn't even know about the boy, that he'd hidden up there just yesterday morning and could be gone by now. She'd been told often enough at school that she needed to learn to control her imagination a little, not let herself get carried away so easily.

When her father had gone behind a chicken house, she started walking down the road, felt hot dusty rocks burn the soles of her feet. She would go over and face the ugly business and get it over with. There was no sense trying to solve a problem until you knew what it was. Grasshoppers clicked in the long grass. And somewhere in the trees a cicada's song whirred, high and thin as the hum of telephone wires. Sing your heart out, she thought. Seventeen years you've waited underground for this day so sing!

But again Mrs. Starbuck wasn't at the house. Still back at the well, maybe, still sad about the calf and ashamed to come home. She knocked and called, heard only silence; then ran upstairs, all the way up to the top of that ladder and crawled into the attic space. Nearly choking on the beat of her own heart.

And "Come on boy," she heard herself say. "We're getting you out of this place." Because he was still there, still real.

She moved close enough to see his face, which was round and pale as the top pastry of an uncooked pie, nearly as featureless. No sunlight had come anywhere near. "You're hardly half my size, we can manage. You're free. This is your lucky day."

The child (she guessed ten years old) pushed right back into the corner, whimpering, and curled up into a ball. "Just hold onto me," she said. "I'll get you out of here."

He put his head down and wrapped his arms around it so he couldn't see her.

And she, she was St. Joan. She was Miranda when her father released the spell. "I don't know how long you been up here but it's too long," she said. "Get ready to see the world."

She saw that there was no way she could get him out of this attic without his co-operation. Even if she managed to drag him over to the hole, he would have to go down the ladder by himself. "Look, I'm going to show you what you're missing," she said. A thick piece of cardboard was nailed up against one end wall, covering a small window she had noticed from outside. She would rip it off. "I'll let some light in here and you can look out and see how pretty it is. Hear the grasshoppers. Smell the roses. See everything so pretty in the sun."

She tore the cardboard away from the wall and, yes, there was a window. A small square hole without glass, facing Mrs. Starbuck's flower gardens and up the driveway to the road.

"Just look at that," she said. "You've never seen anything so pretty, I bet."

But the child was still curled up, face hidden. She laid hands on him for the first time, grabbed both arms and dragged him closer to the hole in the wall. "Look!" she said. "Just look at that! Don't you want to go out there and be free?" She put fingers in his hair and yanked the face up so he couldn't avoid the view. "There. That's the world you're missing. A beautiful place, and the middle of summer too!"

The boy opened his eyes, jerked back, and screamed. The pastry face split, fell apart, became one huge gaping mouth that screamed so loud she had to cover her ears.

And fled, ran down ladder and staircase, ran out of the house, ran with that scream still loud behind her down the lane to the barn (past Mrs. Starbuck at the gate, holding it open, mouth ready to say "What's the matter with you, Charlene?") and didn't stop until she was in her own house, under the heavy comforter that lay on the top of her bed.

"Look," her father said, "you could be mistaken, see. It could all be just a mistake. The world hasn't fallen apart." He smiled, to show her he meant it. Creases ran out from his eyes all the way to his ears.

But, "It has!" she said. "I tried to set him free."

Her father ran a hand around his jaw, squinted his eyes even harder than before, sucked a hole in his teeth. "You took too much on yourself. You didn't stop to think or wait to find out what it was all about. It's thought that solves problems, not just action."

Charlene pulled the blanket even tighter around her neck. She wished she could slip right down inside and disappear altogether. "All I wanted was to show him how pretty the world is."

"And scared him," he told her. "Maybe to you it's a pretty day but to him it's blinding and horrible. You ought to known that, how our senses are only beliefs we're educated to."

She nodded. Her father sat on the edge of the bed and put one finger into the curls by her ear. In another room a radio droned on, a bored male voice reading news. "We'll work on it," her father said. "Mrs. Starbuck will be needing our help so we'd better start giving it some thought."

But she didn't care about his words. She knew only that there was no disappointment in his eyes and she was grateful for that.

III

That evening Mrs. Starbuck lay on her sagging bed, flat on her back, and cursed her luck. There was no use in doing anything else, as far as she could see, because no matter what she tried it was bound to turn out wrong.

She kept her eyes closed against the dying light, waiting for dark. Her fingers counted off the keys in her hand, one at a time, slipping them around the key ring to drop, clinking, against the others: ignition key, trunk key, house key, ignition key, trunk key, house key.

Once, she had known how to hope, too, like everybody else, how to dream and plan and scheme. Now, though, she could plan all she wanted, work all she could, hope all she dared, but she knew that it took only one nosy girl to wreck everything. What was the use? Mrs. Starbuck's face on the white pillow looked as if it had gathered in all the day's burning sun and reflected it now, red as a fiery peony, deep almost as blood.

And up in the attic, two floors above her in the crotch of the roof, the child was whimpering. Her child. Her son.

Mrs. Starbuck groaned. Now, now she was in trouble. Up to her bloody eyeballs in it. This time that girl had really poked her big nose in where it wasn't wanted. Why hadn't she just taken her father's axe and walked up to Mrs. Starbuck and bashed in her brains? That would have been a lot easier, and maybe even what she deserved after this morning. Or why didn't she just push her down the well or burn her to death in this old house? It would have been more merciful. Because Mrs. Starbuck was sure that if she had been given just a few more days she might have got around at last to doing something about getting herself out of this mess.

Still, right after supper she had got into her big old paint-peeling sedan and driven over to Mrs. Wright's to try saving what was left. And the first thing she had to do was apologize to the little scrunch for the way she had acted back there at the well. She knew Mrs. Wright wouldn't do a thing for anyone who didn't have good manners.

"Really, Edna," Mrs. Wright said. "No amount of apologizing can erase the way you talked to me." She kept her face turned slightly to the side, to let Mrs. Starbuck know how hurt she was. "I thought we were friends."

"We *are* friends," Mrs. Starbuck said. She sat in one of Mrs. Wright's living-room chairs and felt, as she always did in this house, that she might be getting grease from her clothes on the green embossed upholstery. "I was under strain. Stress and strain. A person might say anything."

"Not anything. Not anything you didn't mean." Mrs. Wright brought a mug of coffee, and put it on a cork mat on the stereo set beside Mrs. Starbuck. "And besides, it was your actions not your speech that need explaining. That poor calf." When Mrs. Wright sat on the chesterfield with her own mug of coffee her feet didn't quite reach the floor.

Mrs. Starbuck picked up her coffee but it was too hot to drink. "Emotions," she said. "I just got carried away under all that stress and strain."

Mrs. Wright sneered. "Emotions," she echoed. "You better just learn to control them. I like to have all mine right here where I want them, so I can turn them on or off whenever I please."

"I guess I just have more than others," Mrs. Starbuck said, and took a gulp of coffee that scalded the whole inside of her mouth.

"If I was you I'd be seeing a doctor, not sitting around apologizing. That kind of behaviour is irrational."

Mrs. Starbuck knew that Mrs. Wright used that word because she thought she wouldn't understand it. Mrs. Wright sometimes liked to use the English language as if it were something foreign that only she had learned. Maybe she had got a late start in school and was constantly being surprised at what knowledge she'd picked up. Mrs. Starbuck didn't mind. If someone wanted to put on airs in front of her she didn't care, as long as she wasn't expected to do the same.

The second thing she had driven over for was to talk to Mr. Wright. She'd never spoken to any other lawyer in her life and was afraid even of him. She didn't know what she was going to say but it was obvious that if she was going to do something about bringing that child back down out of the attic she would need to know some answers to a few questions about the law. It was her own child and what she did about him was her own business, she felt, but she also knew that the rest of the world wouldn't feel the same way. People would start asking questions. Judges, doctors, police. Officials would start nosing around. Before she knew it the child welfare people would be laying charges and making all sorts of ugly noises about what she'd done.

But Mr. Wright wasn't home. "Golfing," Mrs. Wright said.

"What time does he get home?" Mrs. Starbuck asked.

"Oh late. It's business, really, you know. They're playing a game but at the same time they're talking business."

Mrs. Starbuck got up to leave. "I would've thought he'd want to stay home once in a while and help you around the place, pull a few weeds."

"Oh Mr. Wright isn't interested in farming," Mrs. Wright said. "If he was, I'd still be over there where you're living and you'd be somewhere else."

And now, back in the house Mrs. Wright had lived in for so many years and would still like to live in if it weren't for her husband (Mrs. Starbuck hadn't missed those looks that said "This place is going downhill without me.") Mrs. Starbuck lay on her bed, eyes closed, slipping keys around and around on the aluminum ring. Outside, she knew, the sun was ready to drop, like a child's hot penny, into its slot behind the blue scarred mountain. When it was darker, when the shadows had blended into one another, then she would open her eyes.

Mrs. Starbuck was scared. She could hear, faintly, the child's whimpering two floors above her. She could hear the sharp clinking of the keys as they fell against each other in her hand. She could hear her own breathing, shallow and quick, like the breathing of an old old man. She had been a widow for a year now, and she didn't see how she could go on living alone for very much longer. Not with *them* all starting to gang up on her: police, doctors, lawyers, neighbours.

Not that Mr. Starbuck had ever been much help or comfort. He was a mean little bastard who would just as soon hit her as put his arm around her, but just the same he was another adult around the place to share some of the responsibility. That was something.

She hadn't realized until he was dead that she had been sharing the responsibility for this child with him for years. She thought up until then that just because she pleaded with him to let the child down and because she was as kind as she could be to the boy, that it was all his fault and none of her own. But when he died and she went upstairs to say it's all right now, you can come down, the child had snarled at her and refused and would have bitten if she'd forced him. Then she knew whose fault it was.

The boy's name was Searle Starbuck. She'd hated the name but her husband insisted on calling him after a grandfather or something Back East.

"You mean Cyril," she said.

"No. Searle. S-e-a-r-l-e."

"That's no kind of name."

"That's *his* name. Searle Starbuck, named after Searle Starbuck, potato farmer and politician."

So they put Searle Starbuck on the birth certificate and for fourteen years she called him Richard, though never aloud. Richard Starbuck sounded like a famous movie star or an inventor. It was a strong masculine name and she could see him as a handsome middle-aged man making a speech somewhere, accepting an award, tilting his head to applause.

But he had never made a speech, and never would. Nor would he ever hear the sound of applause. Searle Edwin Starbuck had been born partly deaf and had never learned to speak. When he was three years old and still hadn't said anything beyond gurgling baby sounds and animal grunts, Mr. Starbuck decided he was retarded. "Just keep him out of my sight," he said. "I don't want no mental case in my family."

"Being slow is not the same as being mental," she said.

"Just the same, I have no son until he can say my name. When he can stand up and say 'Roydon Tindall Starbuck, you are my father,' then I'll call him son."

She tried. She tried every way she knew to teach him that sentence but all she got was tears. Even when she discovered it was his hearing and not something in his mouth that was wrong, she still couldn't find a way of getting him to say those words. There were days when he didn't even want to walk, but crawled on the floor like a dog.

She discovered he liked candy. His eyes brightened and he started to slobber whenever he saw the dish so she tried to withhold candies as a bribe.

"No," she said. "Not until you say it."

He groaned and snarled, stamped his foot.

"No sir, not a single candy until you at least try."

He growled louder and kicked the cupboard door, looking at her as if he could cheerfully kill her.

"No. No candy until you say Daddy. Say Daddy."

The child threw back his head and screamed. He screamed one long steady sound that could have come from a grown man's throat; and didn't stop, though his face was turning blue, until she put a candy into his hand.

"Here, you stupid little bastard. I hope you choke on it."

She was so upset by the way she'd spoken to the boy that she took him to a doctor in town while Mr. Starbuck thought she was having a tooth filled at the dentist. The doctor, an old man with runny eyes, asked if he'd ever had a bad fall.

"Not that I know of. Why?"

"Because it's more than his ears. There might be damage."

"Damage? What kind of damage?"

He put one of his old wrinkled hands on her shoulder and she pulled away. "We won't know for sure until we've given some tests, of course, but there could be brain damage."

She never went back. The doctor was a fool and too old to know anything. And besides, if the boy was retarded or damaged what good did it do to know about it? Mrs. Starbuck was his mother and could do more for him than any tests of old men could do. She would teach him to say "Roydon Tindall Starbuck you are my father" and look after him all her life.

But Mr. Starbuck's relatives arrived from Back East to stay with them for a few days. A phone call from town asking for directions to their place gave them fifteen minutes to do something with the boy.

"Lock him in the tool shed while they're here," Mr. Starbuck said. "You can take food out to him and they won't ever know."

She looked at him as if he'd gone mad. "This is your son you're talking about, not a goat or a sheep."

"Just do it," he said. He had put on his best clothes for the company and was starting to shave. "They don't even know we got a goddam kid. And *he* won't know the difference. I don't want them seeing what we got stuck with. Give him a snort of whiskey to make him sleep. You can slip food out to him when no one's looking. I don't want to be ashamed."

"I won't do it," she said. "If it's so important to you we'll both move out, stay somewheres else until they're gone. I won't lock my baby up."

He swung on her and raised the hand that held the razor. "Do it," he said, and his little red eyes flashed. "Do it."

And when the company had left, thanking her for all she had done to make their holiday enjoyable and congratulating him for choosing such a thoughtful pleasant wife, he announced that the arrangements suited him just fine and the child could stay there for ever as far as he was concerned.

When fall came and the nights started getting colder he let her bring him into the house and put him in a back room. Whenever she protested, he just raised his hand and looked as if he could strangle her without batting an eye.

They had to move, because there were neighbours who remembered seeing the boy. Mrs. Starbuck wept when she walked out of that house, a small cedar-shaked farmhouse surrounded by apple trees, and wondered why she didn't leave her husband, just take the child and find some place of her own to live. Some day she would. But first she would teach him to speak. She would bring him out into the kitchen where he was hunched over his supper at the table like someone driving a motorcycle and she would tell the boy to say it. "Roydon Starbuck is my father," he would say, and she would say—just as her husband was grinning from ear to ear with pleasure—"But not any more" and pick the child up and take him away from there. It was a day worth waiting for.

And while she waited, they moved seven times. Mr. Starbuck would get it into his head that a neighbour or the paper boy or a travelling sales-man had heard the boy or seen his face at the window, and they would pack up all their furniture and rent another place. Always they moved in at night, drove in with the headlights of the old car turned off so that no one could see there were three of them. When they found Mrs. Wright's farm two years ago, though, they had liked it so much that Mr. Starbuck bought it. "We're here to stay," he said, because it seemed ideal. Porter's farm, the nearest place, was a quarter-mile away. Mrs. Wright's new house was way out on the highway. And best of all, it had an attic with only one small window they could cover up and a ladder they could take down and hide somewhere on the second floor.

Mrs. Starbuck, now, saw her whole life as nightmare. That was the problem, she thought. She had lived in a nightmare and didn't even have enough damn sense to see what it was. She believed it was real and ac-cepted it as normal. No one else would have put up with a man like Mr. Starbuck. No one else would have got used to having her own child a pris-oner in the attic.

She imagined Mrs. Wright married to Mr. Starbuck. That little terrier would have chewed him to pieces. In a ladylike way, of course, Mrs. Wright did everything in a proper way. But she wouldn't have let him boss her around that way, threaten her, and lock the child up. She imagined Mr. Starbuck telling little Mrs. Wright "Lock him in the tool shed" and nearly laughed out loud. She didn't laugh though, because she realized it was Mrs. Wright and not her husband that looked silly and unnatural in her mental picture. Mrs. Wright would say "Roydon, you're being irrational." She would say, "I can tolerate a lot, Roydon dear, you know I'm very broad-minded, but one thing I will not tolerate is irrationality. It just doesn't make sense to lock a child up. I believe you are insane."

Maybe I'm stupid, Mrs. Starbuck thought. Perhaps all her life she had been a stupid woman and never known it. She knew she wasn't as smart as Mrs. Wright; no lawyer could stand to be married to her for long; but she had got as far as grade nine in school with fairly good marks before her parents sent her out to work. The teacher had written on one of her report cards *Edna earns good enough grades but she lacks initiative.*

That sounded like a Mrs. Wright word. Initiative. It was true too. Would a person with one bloody ounce of initiative have taken a whole year before doing something about that boy? A whole year, logging and burning and planting fifteen new acres just to keep out of the house, before getting around to facing what had to be done?

A sudden image of herself, this morning, standing over that trapped calf with Mr. Porter's axe raised to smash in its brains, scared up the fear again that lay waiting in her chest. What had happened to her? What kind of person was she turning into? She loved her cattle; they surrounded her like a living wall and she loved them singly and together. What had she let herself become when her feelings could go so badly out of control that she was capable of a thing like that?

Lying on that bed, she wished her husband were here just long enough to help her out. Come back, she thought. You were a miserable rotten little man. I was glad when they phoned and told me you had died in that hospital but you could *act.* You could make decisions and act on them. No one would ever find Roydon Starbuck lying on a bed waiting for something to happen, just waiting.

He was rotten, she thought. But right now she wouldn't even mind if he came back and went upstairs and cut that boy's throat and took him away. It would be a solution and no one would know.

Mrs. Starbuck put her hand over her mouth at the thought. She opened her eyes. The room was nearly dark, dark furniture had blended into its own shadow so she couldn't distinguish one from the other. They had always moved at night.

She ran both hands down her body. Mr. Starbuck's plaid shirt, worn thin from a year's washings, was stretched tight across her chest. His pants were still strong and smelled of grease. She had had to take the seams apart and sew in an extra ten inches down either side to fit them around her hips and thighs.

Suddenly Mrs. Starbuck sat up. My God, had she worn these things over to Mrs. Wright's? No wonder the woman thought she was mad. Had she gone into that house and sat down and drunk coffee looking like this? Her face burned. Thank goodness Mr. Wright hadn't been home. He would have been sure she was crazy.

They had always moved at night. She could feel it now, the gentle rocking of the car under her, the cool night breeze across her face as they drove slowly and quietly down a new driveway. She could hear the night calls of unseen birds and the squeak of a bottom step welcoming them home. She could taste the salt taste of tears as she picked up the sleeping boy from the back seat and carried him inside, following the flashlight beam of her husband who led them silently to his newest prison.

Richard Starbuck, famous actor, famous inventor.

Mrs. Starbuck got off the bed and removed her clothes. Then, in the dark, she took a dress from the closet and slipped it on over her head. She was going for help. She gave the telephone only a glance as she passed; she hated it and used it only for long-distance calls that couldn't be avoided.

She didn't realize she was barefoot until she was in the car but had no intention of going back for shoes. While the movement was in her she was going to use it before it died out. She backed the car around and drove up the driveway to the gate. Just being behind the wheel of this old car could make her feel better. It was a battered old sedan as plain and bulky as herself, and responded as if it could read her thoughts. How many times, she wondered, had it helped them out of trouble?

At the fork in the road she hesitated. Since Charlene Porter was the one who had discovered the boy in the first place maybe she should go there first. Charlene liked her. They were steady people. Their religion or whatever it was had got them through a lot of rough spots. But they would want to pray or something, probably, and that was one thing Mrs. Starbuck was not prepared to do.

Besides, hadn't the girl herself, that Charlene, told her once that prayer doesn't change the truth? She said it just puts your thinking more in line with it or something like that. Mrs. Starbuck didn't want to be put in line with what seemed to her right now to be the truth.

Going to the Larkins' place passed through her thoughts. She saw herself knocking on their door and going into the shack and asking for someone to help (How? How? How help?) But she saw their faces, three blank stupid faces showing her only their contempt. Shelley would show pity too, of course, but like the boys she would feel disgust at the sight of a woman as solid as Mrs. Starbuck going to pieces. They expected her to be a rock, it must seem to them that anyone with more intelligence than their own should be able to solve any problems the world was capable of serving up.

Probably they wouldn't even feel *that* much. She could see them watching her like a cluster of vacant indifferent cows, three stupid Holsteins with no more feeling for her or anyone else than Mr. Porter's bull. There was no point in looking for any kind of aid in that direction.

And that left only the Wrights.

"Edna Starbuck, you're barefoot," Mrs. Wright said. "Have you been drinking? And this is your third visit today."

Mrs. Starbuck went up the steps and into Mrs. Wright's house. It was cool inside, and very light. She had to squint to see and couldn't seem to find a place to sit down.

"For heaven's sake, woman, what's the matter with you?" Mrs. Wright said. "Can I get you something?" She pushed papers into a neat pile on the table. "I was just writing up my column. You look as if you've stepped right out of a coffin."

"Your husband. Is Mr. Wright home yet?"

"Good heavens no. They stay after the game for a few drinks in the clubhouse. Edna, if you could only see yourself."

Mrs. Starbuck sat down on something. "Then I'll wait," she said. "He's got to come some time."

Mrs. Wright looked as if she were going to explode. Her rooster-leg arms were folded tightly across her little chest. Her lips were pressed together. "I've never been one for judging others," she said. "But when I do I always judge only by what I see. I believe that's only fair. And today I think I've seen a lot more than I should've."

"It's nothing to do with you," Mrs. Starbuck said, waving one hand as if that were enough to make Mrs. Wright disappear. "This is business."

"Business?"

"Yes. Business. Lawyer business."

Mrs. Wright whirled around twice, as if she were looking for something to hit Mrs. Starbuck with. "You don't know any lawyer business. You've never even talked to a lawyer before. What kind of business?"

Mrs. Starbuck was tired. She felt as if a terrible weight were sitting on her head, pushing her down. She expected to collapse like a telescope, head inside her shoulders, chest inside her hips. "This will be strictly between me and him," she said.

"What you should be looking up at this time of night is not a lawyer at all but a psychiatrist." Mrs. Wright stepped back after those words and watched Mrs. Starbuck's face, waiting to see if this time she had gone too far.

Mrs. Starbuck shook her head. "Maybe I've been crazy all my life," she said. "Maybe I've been asleep and just dreaming my life. But right now I think I am saner and more clear-sighted even than you are." She paused for a moment, then added, "If that's possible."

Mrs. Wright pushed her face in very close and spoke softly. "In that case, Mrs. Starbuck, Mrs. Level-headed and Clear-sighted Starbuck, you just may understand what I'm going to say. Mr. Wright does not come home on Friday nights. After he's played his golf he does I-don't-know-what and gets home just in time for breakfast."

Mrs. Starbuck's eyes opened wide and watched Mrs. Wright step back. She stood up. "Oh my God," she said. She got out of the house as fast as she could and dropped her heavy body onto the front seat of the car.

Mrs. Wright called from the bottom step. "Wait. Can't you tell me? Can't I help?"

But Mrs. Starbuck backed out onto the highway and drove halfway home before she remembered to change out of low gear. The car, which she was sure had caught some of the panic she felt, trembled and sputtered and coughed. When she stopped in front of her own house she put her forehead down on the steering wheel and waited. She didn't know what she was waiting for but she listened hard, breathing silently, as if she expected a bolt of lightning to zig-zag down the sky and strike the whole lot of them at once.

Strike Mrs. Wright, she thought. Wipe that white-haired little scrunch right off the earth and do everyone a favour. Nobody'd miss her. And Charlene too, wipe that mind of hers so clean she can't remember a thing, or recall betrayal. Then come over here and get us both, that boy, that shell of a boy, then me.

When she looked up she was surprised to see that her headlights were still on, that they cut a piece out of the night, a long rectangular room between her and a wall of trees, silver-leafed and still. A cat slunk through the grass, paused to turn headlights of his own back on her, then moved on out of sight. She strained her eyes to see into the space behind the trees but there was nothing. It was as if any light that passed through gaps in the leaves uncaught had abandoned the effort and died out without reaching any goal. This wall, this blank unfeeling wall of trees, was wrapped like a stockade fence around them all: the Porters, the Wrights, herself.

Mrs. Starbuck sighed. There was to be no lightning then and sitting here accomplished nothing. She found herself wishing again for the mean little man who had always packed them all off in the middle of the night to some place where they would be safe again for a while. At least he could act, move, while she felt as if she could sit here until she starved to death or died of fright.

At last, though, she stirred. She got out of the car and walked to the house, her bare feet slapping on the narrow concrete walk, then went inside and climbed the stairs to the second floor. She turned on every light switch she passed. At the top of the stairs she stopped to catch her breath, her heavy body aching from the effort, both hands on her knees and head bent right over as if she'd lost something on the floor.

Then she moved forward with a deliberateness that surprised herself. She couldn't have stopped. She opened the door to the storage room, went in, and slid her hand up and down the wall until it bumped into the light switch and turned it on. Then she set up the ladder and climbed it, puffing, both feet on each rung, and pushed her head up through the door in the ceiling.

The boy was asleep and too heavy for her to carry this time so she shook him awake. "We're moving again," she whispered to him over and over until she was sure it connected somewhere inside that head with other memories and made sense. "We're moving again, going some place nicer this time."

She went ahead of him into each room to turn out the light, then came back and guided him forward. "This time it will be different," she promised him. "This time it will be nicer." And she helped him down the steps as if they were both blind, both unsure, both frightened. Telling herself: it will soon be all over, we'll be able to relax, the nightmare will end.

When he was in the car she slammed the door and went around to her own side to get in. "I still don't have any shoes on," she said, swallowing a giggle. And remembered too, that she hadn't packed a suitcase for either of them. "I'll come back and move the rest," she said.

Again the headlights hit the wall of trees. "We'll find another place, nicer than this," she said. "A little farmhouse somewhere, surrounded by apple trees, a little house covered with cedar shakes."

She started the engine and backed the car around. She patted the dashboard gently: Help me once more, she told it, just one more time. Then said, "This time we'll never have to move again," and put her hand on the boy's knee. His head rested against the window on his side. He looked as if he had gone back to sleep.

I won't turn the headlights out, she thought. This time I won't sneak away. She drove slowly up her driveway, feeling the car vibrate beneath her like a purring cat. Don't stop, she thought, don't stop for anything until you've got us somewhere safe. "And something else, Richard," she said, trying his name aloud for the first time in fourteen years. "There won't be any prison in this next house, no locked doors. You'll live with me the way a son should."

For a moment she thought that somehow the door on his side of the car had fallen open and she slammed on the brakes. But he wasn't falling, he was leaping free of the car, squealing; he landed on one foot, rolled, then leapt to both feet again and started running, ahead of her, down the road.

She didn't get out to catch him, she drove behind, her front bumper inches from his legs. He's never run before, she thought, he's never even done much walking. Sooner or later he will tire or fall or forget how to move his legs, or realize he doesn't know how to run. Then I'll stop and pick him up and take him away. Just take it easy, she whispered to the car. And felt something of herself drain down through her fingers and into the wheel.

His figure in the light ahead of the car was like a puppet dangling, his legs and arms all uncoordinated and loose. And yet he kept on, slowly, and did not duck off to the side to escape or fall to his knees to be caught. He fled before her as human as a shadow, down the darkened tunnel of road beneath the trees.

But as Mrs. Starbuck was approaching the bridge another pair of head-lights came around the corner and bore down on her, coming too fast.

"You'll hit my son!" she screamed, and jammed one foot down on the brake pedal. Without taking the time to pull on the handbrake or turn off the engine or even change out of gear she pushed open the door and leapt out (commanding "Wait here" as if to a servant or child), then ran ahead to catch the boy before those other headlights could hit him. In front of her own still moving car her hand touched him, just brushed him, a split-sec-ond before she stumbled and fell to her knees. The other car squealed, sprayed gravel, stopped only a few feet away from her.

The bumper of her own car, like a chrome-plated hand, caught in the back of her dress and dragged her forward in the gravel. She fought, thrashed her hands about and kicked her feet, but it was as if she were fighting a monster she couldn't see, as if all the world was on her back. Pieces of gravel got into her mouth, stones scratched her legs, dust clogged her eyes. A tooth broke and the flesh on one arm peeled back like a wet sleeve. Then, almost gently, the car nudged her over the bank and pushed her ahead of it down the slope like an insistent policeman to the creek, gaining speed, and then rolled ahead to rest one tire in the middle of her back. The other front tire sat in the water and lost air through a hole punc-tured by a sharp piece of stone.

Mrs. Wright got out of her pickup and ran to the edge of the bridge, the edge of the world. "What is it? What is it?" she screamed at the dark. But no answer came from all that empty space, and below there was nothing to see but slow water, moving like thick brown syrup through the circle of light thrown by the one unbroken headlight. Then, somewhere, there was the sound of trees rustling and something—perhaps a deer leaping free— moved through the night away from her, so close she could hear breathing.

She went back to the pickup and got a flashlight from the glove compartment, then picked her way carefully down the bank to the edge of the creek and shone the light on Mrs. Starbuck's face.

One of Mrs. Starbuck's eyes was under water; the other, a dull plastic ball, stared swollen and incredulous up at Mrs. Wright as if Mrs. Starbuck in the last failing moment had seen something she badly needed to tell about. But from her open mouth only dark fluid bubbled out and was carried away by the moving water. Mrs. Wright snapped off the flashlight and let the dark fall around her again like a collapsing tent.

"I can't believe it," she told Charlene later, when she had used the Porters' phone to call the police. She sat down at the kitchen table as if the knowledge was too heavy for such a small person to carry standing up. "And yet I saw she wasn't right. I could see there was something wrong with her. That's why I was headed over to her place tonight, to see what I could do."

Charlene watched the little woman's tight scaly fingers bend and straighten. "Wasn't anything wrong with her," she said. "She just didn't know what was what."

They looked at each other for a moment, like two women who did know what was what, and then their eyes slid away and towards the window that faced the road. As if both hoped to find Mrs. Starbuck out there in that dark, coming towards them, shouting that it was all right now, that it had all been a mistake.

"But the boy!" Charlene cried, suddenly remembering.

Mrs. Wright eyes jumped. "What boy? What are you talking about?"

Charlene put her hand over her mouth. "You didn't even know about him?" she said. "She never told you?"

"About who?" Mrs. Wright folded her little arms and sat back. "All I know is what I see. How am I supposed to know anything else?"

And, staring into that window which in the night was only an inferior sort of mirror, she contemplated the two pale reflections of their startled faces.

II

The Trench Dwellers

Macken this, Macken that. Gerry Mack had had enough. Why should he waste his life riding ferries to weddings and family reunions? There were already too many things you were forced to do in this world whether you liked them or not. "And I've hated those family gatherings for as long as I can remember," he said. "Why else would I move away?"

The problem was that Gerry's Aunt Nora Macken really did believe family was important. She used to tell how the Mackens first settled on the north slope of the valley more than fifty years ago when Black Alex, her father, brought the whole dozen of his children onto the Island in his touring car and started hacking a farm out of what had for centuries been pure timber land. And would tell, too, that by now there was hardly a household left in all the valley that wasn't related to them in one way or another. What Aunt Nora called The Immediate Family had grown to include more than four hundred people, three-quarters of whom were named Smith or O'Brien or Laitenen though she called them all the Mackens.

There wasn't any real substitute for having a lot of relatives, she said. And the people who knew her best, this tall big-footed old maid living out on that useless farm, said that yes, she was right, there was no substitute for family.

And because Nora Macken lived on those three hundred acres of farmland which had gone back already in two generations to second-growth timber, she thought it her duty every time there was a wedding or a funeral to call a reunion of The Immediate Family the day after the ceremony. More than three hundred relatives gathered. The older people, her own generation, spent the day in the house telling each other stories about Black Alex, reassuring one another that he really was as mean and miserable as they remembered, but that it couldn't be denied he was a bit of a character, too, all the same.

The young adults drank beer outside in the grassy yard or on the verandah and talked about their jobs and their houses, and each of them tried to find out how much money the others were earning. The children chased each other between the dead orchard trees and climbed the rickety ladders to the barn mow and fought over the sticky slices of cake Nora Macken put outside on a folding card table in the sun.

As for someone like Gerry Mack, her nephew, who was the only member of The Immediate Family ever to move off Vancouver Island, these events were more than he could bear.

When Gerry was twenty years old he very nearly married Karen O'Brien, a pretty blonde he'd gone all the way through school with. They went to movies together on Saturday nights and sometimes to dances, and afterwards they parked up the gravel road to the city dump to kiss each other until their mouths were raw. But Karen was already a member of The Immediate Family and had half a dozen brothers eager to increase the population. Gerry balked at marriage. He was the son of one of Nora's older brothers and had wished since the time he was six years old that he'd been an orphan.

Soon after dumping Karen O'Brien he met a stoop-shouldered secretary named April Klamp, who was plain-looking and very dull and wore clothes that looked as if they were bought for someone else, perhaps her mother. But she was an only child and had no relatives at all, only a pair of doddering parents who didn't care very much what happened to her. Gerry asked her to marry him a week after their first meeting and of course she accepted. No one before had even given her so much as a second look.

Some members of The Immediate Family had a few words to say about it. It seemed odd, they said, that a young man as vibrant as Gerry couldn't find himself a wife who was more of a match. Aunt Nora, too, thought it was unusual, but she'd given Gerry up long ago as not a real Macken at heart. And besides, she said, it could have been worse. He could have married a churchgoer (something no Macken had ever done) or worse still, remained a bachelor (something three of her brothers had done and become cranky old grouches as a result). "Just watch him," she said. "He'll cut off his nose to spite his face."

Gerry didn't particularly care what any of them thought. Before his wedding he took two letters off his name and became Gerry Mack. He got no argument from April, of course. She was quick to agree that having too much family was worse than having none at all. She didn't even mind that he insisted on getting married seventy miles down-island by a minister she'd never met so that it would be impossible to have a reception afterwards. And when he told her they would live on the mainland she merely nodded and said it was about time one of the Mackens showed a little spunk. Personally, she said, she'd always hated living on an island. She agreed with everything that Gerry Mack said and never took her eyes off his face while he spoke. It was clear to everyone that when Gerry married her what he got was not a separate person to live with but an extension of himself. Aunt Nora said he could have gone out and bought a wooden leg if that was all he wanted.

Though she added, "At least they won't ever get into a fight. An extra limb doesn't talk back."

Their intention was to move far inland, but Gerry hadn't driven a hundred miles up the Fraser Valley before he realized he couldn't stand to be away from the coast. They turned back and settled in a little town on the edge of the strait, facing across to the Island, directly across to the valley where he had grown up. They bought a house fifty feet from the beach, with huge plate-glass windows facing west, and began saving their money to buy a small boat of their own so they could fish in the evenings.

Because he was a young man with a good rich voice and many opinions, Gerry had no trouble getting a job as an open-line moderator for the new radio station. He spent the first week voicing as many outlandish ideas as he could think of and being as rude as he dared to people who phoned in, so it didn't take long for him to draw most listeners away from the competing station. Within a month he had a large and faithful following on both sides of the strait. People didn't say they listened to CLCB, they said they listened to Gerry Mack's station.

What pleased him most was knowing that whether they liked it or not, most of The Immediate Family would be listening to him every day. He could imagine them in their houses, cringing whenever he was rude to callers, and hoping no one else realized where he'd come from, and saying Thank goodness he'd had the sense to change his name. He made a habit of saying "So long, Nora" every day as a sign-off but didn't tell anyone what it meant. People in the mainland town guessed that Nora must be his wife's middle name or else the name of a grandmother who'd died when he was a little boy. None of them ever guessed, of course, that Aunt Nora Macken over on the Island sat by her radio every morning for the whole time he was on and went red in the face when he signed off, and told herself maybe he was the only real Macken in the lot after all, though she could spank him for his cheek.

And that, he thought, will show you that here's one Macken who has no need for family.

Though he did not know then, of course, that even the most weak-minded and agreeable wife could suddenly find a backbone and will in herself when she became pregnant. He was sitting in the living room with his feet up on the walnut coffee table looking for good controversial topics in the newspaper when she handed him the wedding invitation that had arrived in the mail that morning. "I think we should go," she said.

"The hell you say," he said, and read through the silver script. "We hardly know them. Who's this Peter O'Brien to us?"

"A cousin," she said. "But that doesn't matter. I think we should be there for the reunion the next day."

Gerry put down the newspaper and looked at his wife. She was rubbing a hand over her round swollen belly. "What for?" he said. "I've been to a million of them. They're all the same. I thought we moved over here to get away from all that."

She sat down beside him on the sofa and put her head against his shoulder. "It's been a year since we've even put a foot on the Island. Let's go just for the fun."

He looked down into her plain mousey hair, her white scalp. She had never asked for a thing before. "We'll go," he said, "but only on the condition that we leave the minute I can't stand any more."

They took the two-hour ferry ride across the strait, and though he sat with a book in his lap and tried to read, he found it hard to concentrate and spent a lot of time watching the Island get closer and bigger and more distinct. He hated sitting idle, he was a man who liked to be doing things, and right now he would have preferred to be at work in the radio station or digging in his garden.

Aunt Nora outdid herself. "Lord," she said. "This must be the best reunion ever. There are three hundred and fifty people here, at least, and listen to that racket! When the Mackens get together there's no such thing as a lull in the conversation, there's never a moment when tongues have ceased."

"They do seem to have the gift of the gab," April said.

"A Macken," Aunt Nora said, smiling, "is a sociable person. A Macken enjoys company and conversation."

Macken this Macken that, Gerry thought.

His cousin George Smith put a bottle of beer in his hand and steered him across the yard to lean up against someone's car. He said he couldn't understand why Gerry put up with all the bullshit he had to listen to on his show. He wanted to know why Gerry didn't just threaten to quit his job if people wouldn't smarten up.

Gerry noticed that the whole back yard and orchard were filled with parked cars, and that against nearly every car there was at least one pair leaning and drinking beer and talking. Only the old ones were inside. April was standing straighter than he'd ever seen her, laughing with a bunch of women gathered beside a new Buick. "It doesn't matter a damn to me what they say," he told George Smith. "It's just part of my job to listen. Sometimes I tell them to go take a flying leap, but what the hell? Who cares?"

George told him he'd cleared over fifteen hundred dollars last month, working in the pulp and paper mill, most of it from overtime. He said he couldn't understand why most of the rest of them worked in the logging camp or in stores in town where there was hardly any overtime at all. It was overtime, he said, that made it possible for him to buy this here little baby they were leaning on. He pushed down on the front fender of the sports car and rocked it gently and with great fondness. Then he asked Gerry if a person working for a radio station got paid a salary or a wage, and what kind of car was he driving anyways? Gerry pointed vaguely across the yard and said as far as he was concerned it was just a way of getting places. But George told him if he got enough overtime within the next few months he intended to buy himself a truck and camper so he could take more weekends off to go fishing up in the lakes. "Everybody's got one," he said. "One time I went up to Gooseneck Lake with Jim and Harriet and there were sixteen truck-and-campers there already. Nine of them were Mackens. Even old Uncle Morris was there, driving a brand-new Chev, and he only makes the minimum wage at *his* job. I told him, I said How could you afford a thing like that? and he said It pays to have a son in the car-selling business. I said I bet you'll be paying for that thing for the rest of your life."

"And he said?" Gerry said.

"Nothing," George said. "He just told me I was jealous. Ha!"

April came across the yard and led Gerry away towards a large group of people sitting in lawn chairs in a circle and doing a lot of laughing. But Aunt Nora, tall Aunt Nora with all her dyed-black hair piled up on top of her head, intercepted them and took them inside so that Uncle Morgan, who had been sick in the hospital the whole time they'd been engaged, could meet April. "It won't do," she said, "to have strangers in the same family." She pushed them right into her cluttered little living room and made someone get up so April could have a comfortable chair. Gerry leaned against the door frame and wondered if old Black Alex realized when he was alive that the dozen kids he'd hauled onto the Island in his touring car would eventually become these aging wrinkled people.

And of course it was Black Alex they were talking about. Uncle Morris said, "I mind the time he said to me Get off that roof boy or I'll stuff you down the chimney!" He laughed so hard at that he had to haul out a hand-kerchief to wipe the tears off his big red face.

Aunt Nora, too, shrieked. "Oh, that was his favourite! He was always threatening to stuff one of us down the chimney." Though she was care-ful to explain to April that never in his life did he do any such thing to any of them, that in fact the worst he ever did was apply the toe of his boot to their backsides. "He was a noisy man," she said, "but some of us learned how to handle him."

Then she drew everybody's attention to April and said, "As you can eas-ily see, there's one more little Macken waiting to be born. Boy or girl, we wish it luck."

"D'you know?" Uncle Morgan said. "Not one person in the family has ever named a child after Dad."

"No wonder!" Aunt Nora cried. "There could only be one Alex Macken. No one else would dare try to match him."

"Or want to," Aunt Katherine said. "Suppose they got his temper too, along with his name."

"One thing for sure," Aunt Nora said. "He'll have plenty of cousins to play with. He'll never run out of playmates or friends." Then, remember-ing, she added, "Of course, as long as they keep him isolated over there on the mainland I suppose he'll miss out on everything."

"It's terrible having no one to play with," April said. "Especially if you're too shy to go out making friends on your own. Just ask me, I know. At least with cousins you don't have to start from scratch. Nobody needs to be scared of a relative."

"Right!" Aunt Nora said, and looked right at Gerry. "Though there are some people who think loneliness is a prize to be sought after."

Gerry Mack knew, of course, that something had happened to the wife he thought was a sure bet to remain constant. It came as something of a sur-prise. After all, who expected an adult's foot to suddenly turn into a hand or start growing off in a new direction? He brooded about it all the way home on the ferry and wouldn't speak to her even while she got ready for bed. He sat in his living room until he was sure she'd gone to sleep, then he tiptoed in to the bedroom and undressed without turning on the light.

The next day he held off the phone calls that came into the station and kept the air waves to himself. From his little sound-booth he could look out across the strait. "From over here," he told his listeners, "from here on the mainland, Vancouver Island is just a pale blue chain of mountains stretched right across your whole range of vision. A jagged-backed wall between us and the open sea. Go have a look. Stop what you're doing for a minute and go to your window." He waited for a while, and thought, not of the housewives who were moving to the ocean side of their houses, but of the islanders who were over there listening and wondering what he was up to.

"There it is," he said. "Twenty miles away. I bet you hardly ever notice it there, like a fence that borders the back yard." He drank a mouthful of the coffee he kept with him throughout the show. "Now those of you who've been across on the ferry know that as you get closer those mountains begin to take on shapes and change from blue to green and show big chunks of logged-off sections and zig-zag logging roads like knife-scars up their sides. And closer still, of course, you see that along the edge of the Island, stretched out along the shelf of flatter land, is a chain of farms and fishing villages and towns and tourist resorts and bays full of log booms and peninsulas dotted with summer cabins. All of it, ladies and gentlemen, facing over to us as if those people too think these mountains are nothing but a wall at their backs, holding off the Pacific."

He gulped coffee again and glanced at his watch. He thought of the mainlanders looking across. He thought of the islanders wondering what the hell he was talking about. Then he said, "But the funny thing is this: to those people over there on that island, this mainland they spend most of their lives facing is nothing but a blue chain of jagged mountains stretched across their vision like a wall separating them from the rest of North America. That continent behind us doesn't even exist to some of them. To them we look just the same as they do to us."

Then, just before opening the telephone lines to callers, he said, "What we live in is a trench. Do you suppose trench-dwellers think any different from the rest of the world?"

His line was busy for the rest of the morning. Most wanted to talk about why they liked living in a place like this, some asked him couldn't he think of a more pleasant comparison to make, and a few tried to change the subject to the recent tax increase. One long-distance call came in from the

Island, an old man who told him he was jabbering nonsense and ought to be locked up, some place where all he could see would be bars and padded walls. "If you want to live in a trench," he said, "I'll dig you one. Six feet long by six feet deep." Gerry Mack hung up on his cackling laughter and vowed he would never cross that strait again.

But April told him that didn't mean *she* couldn't go across just whenever she felt like it.

So that when the next wedding invitation arrived he was ready for her announcement. Even if he didn't want to go, she said, she was heading across and taking Jimmy with her. He couldn't deprive her for ever of the pleasure of showing off her son to his family. And Jimmy, too, had a right to meet his cousins. She was pregnant again, and there was a new hard glint in her eye. Gerry Mack, when she talked like that to him, felt very old and wondered what life would have been like if he'd married Karen O'Brien. If that's what happened to women, he thought, you might as well marry your own sister.

When she came back she told him the reunion of course was a huge success and everybody asked where he was. She'd stayed right at Aunt Nora's, she said, and it was amazing how much room there was in that old farmhouse when everyone else had gone home. She'd felt right at home there. Jimmy had had a wonderful time, had made friends with dozens of cousins, and could hardly wait for the next time they went over. And oh yes, Aunt Nora sent him a message.

"What is it?" he said, weary.

"She says there's a wonderful new man on *their* radio station. She says she doesn't know of a single Macken who still listens to you. This new fellow plays softer music and isn't nearly so rude to his callers. She says people do appreciate good manners after all and she can't think of one good reason for you not to be at the next wedding."

"At the rate they're marrying," he said, "The Immediate Family will soon swallow up the whole Island."

"The Mackens believe in marriage," she said. "And in sticking together."

Mackens this Mackens that, Gerry Mack thought.

"Nora told me her father used to say being a Macken was like being part of a club. Or a religion."

"Do you know why they call him Black Alex?"

"Why?"

"When he was alive people used to call him Nigger Alex because his hair was so black and you never saw him without dirt on his hands and face. People over there never saw a real black man in those days. But the 'children' decided after his death that Black Alex was politer and what people would've called him if they'd only stopped to think."

"Well at least they called him something," she said. "It shows he was liked. It shows people noticed him. I never heard anyone call you anything but Gerry, an insipid name if I ever heard one. Pretty soon those people over there will forget you even exist."

"That's fine with me," Gerry Mack said, and went outside to sprinkle powder on his rose leaves.

But she followed him. "Sometimes I don't think it's family you're trying to get away from at all. I think it's humanity itself."

"Don't be ridiculous," he said. "If that was what I wanted I'd have become a hermit."

"What else are we?" She was on the verge of tears. "You don't let Jimmy play with anyone else's kids, none of them are good enough for you. And we've hardly any friends ourselves."

"Don't harp," he said. "Don't nag at me."

It passed through his mind to tell her she had no business going against his wishes when it came to bringing up the boy. But he was a strange kid anyway, and Gerry had always been uncomfortable with children. It was easier to let her do what she wanted with him.

When April went across to George Smith's wedding (his second) and took Jimmy and the baby with her, he knew she would not be coming back. He wasn't surprised when she didn't get off the Sunday evening ferry. He didn't even bother watching the ferries coming in during the next week. The only surprise was the sight of Aunt Nora getting out of a taxi the following weekend and throwing herself into the leather armchair in Gerry's living room.

"My God," she said. "It looks as if you could walk across in fifteen minutes but that damn ferry takes for ever."

"Where's April?" he said.

The wedding, she told him, was lovely. Because it was George's second the girl didn't try to make it into too much of a thing, but just as many people turned out for it as for his first. "He's got a real dandy this time," she said. "He's not going to want to spend so much time at his precious pulp mill when he's got this one waiting at home. She's got outdoor teeth of course, but still she is pretty!"

Gerry said George's first wife hadn't been much to look at, but then George was no prize himself.

Then, suddenly, Aunt Nora said, "I think she'll be asking you for a legal separation."

"Who?" he said, stupidly.

"I told her she could live with me. There's too much room in that old house for one person. I'll enjoy the company. I remember Dad saying if a Macken couldn't count on one of his own relatives in times of trouble, who could he count on? That little boy of yours is going to look just like him." She stood up and took off her coat and laid it over the back of her chair. Then she took a cigarette out of her purse and lit it and sat down again.

"If you want to come back with me and try to patch it up, that's all right."

"Patch what up?" he said. "We haven't even had a fight."

But she acted as if she hadn't heard. "I'll tell you something, Gerry, you've got spunk. Maybe you're the only real Macken in the whole kaboodle."

"Ha."

"And if you and April patch it up, if you want to live on the farm, that's all right with me too."

"Why should I want to live there?"

"It's the family homestead," she said, as if it was something he might have forgotten. "It's where your grandfather started out. Where the family began."

Gerry grunted and went to the refrigerator to get himself a bottle of beer.

"Well, somebody will have to take it over some day," she said. "You can see what's happened to the farm with just an old maid living on it. He never should have left it to me in the first place. Except, of course, it's the best place for holding family get-togethers and I know if it was left to anyone else they'd never get done."

"Look," he said. "You got her and my two kids. Three for one. That sounds like a pretty good trade to me."

"I just can't believe you don't care about those children," Aunt Nora said. "Those two little boys. No Macken has ever abandoned his own children. It doesn't seem natural."

"Natural," Gerry Mack said, and tilted up his beer.

But when she caught the morning ferry home he did not go with her. In fact, he was to make only one more visit to the Island, and that would not be until two years later when he attended his son's funeral. Aunt Nora phoned him in the middle of the day to say the boy had drowned in a swimming accident. The Immediate Family was at the funeral, four hundred or so of them, standing all over the graveyard where Mackens were buried. He'd sat beside April in the chapel but when they got to the graveside she seemed to be surrounded by relatives and he was left alone, on the far side of the ugly hole where they were putting his son. Aunts and cousins were weeping openly, but April in their midst stared straight ahead with her jaw set like stone. She appeared then to have lost all of the slump that was once in her back. Even her mousey brown hair seemed to have taken on more life. When their eyes met she nodded in a way that might have been saying "Thank you" or might have been only a dismissal, or could perhaps have been simply acknowledging that she had noticed his, a stranger's, presence.

Aunt Nora, afterwards, cornered him in her little living room. She seemed smaller now, slightly stooped, getting old. There were deep lines in her face. "Now," she said. "Now do you see where your place is? Now do you see where you belong?"

He turned, tried to find someone to rescue him.

"This whole farm, Gerry, it's yours. Just move here, ·stay here where you belong."

And it was April who rescued him after all. She came into the room swiftly, her eyes darting with the quick concern of a hostess making sure everything was going well. "Oh Nora!" she said. "Uncle Morris was asking for you. I promised I'd take you to him."

When the old woman stood up to leave, April let her gaze flicker momentarily over him. Her complexion against the black dress looked nearly ivory. Beautiful skin. She would be a beautiful woman yet. "George Smith was wondering where you were," she said. "I told him I thought you'd already gone home."

For several years after that Aunt Nora visited the mainland every summer to report to Gerry on his wife and remaining son and to tell him all about the weddings and reunions he'd missed. April, she told him, had taken over the last reunion completely, did all the planning and most of the work. And some people on the Island were listening to him again she said, now that he was only reading the news, once a day.

But she stopped coming altogether years later when he sold the seaside house and moved in with a woman far up a gravel road behind town, in a junky unpainted house beside a swamp. She had nearly a dozen children from various fathers, some Scandinavian, two Indian, and one Chinese, and her name was Netty Conroy. Which meant, Aunt Nora Macken was soon able to discover after a little investigation, that she was related to more than half the people who lived in that mainland town, not to mention most who lived in the countryside around it. It was a strange thing, she told The Immediate Family, but she still felt closer to Gerry Mack than to any of the rest of them. Perhaps it was because she, too, had had a tendency to cut off her nose to spite her face. Everyone laughed at the notion because of course, they said, Aunt Nora had always had everything just the way she wanted it in this world.

Every Day of His Life

"If that Big Glad Littlestone ever gets married," some people said, "there won't be a church aisle on the Island wide enough for her to walk down."

"Poor girl," the more sensitive said of her. "The size of a logging truck and almost as loud. Thirty-six years old already and still no sign of a father for that boy of hers."

But Big Glad didn't waste time on people's opinions. Because here it was June again, which was her lucky month. It seemed to her that in all the years she had lived in this old house (measured by the life of that heavy lilac bush, covering half the yard) there had never been a June that felt so lucky. In the woods, all tangled up beneath the fallen hemlock slash, and hidden in the copper grass behind her place, the wild blackberries were ripening early and every day she found a brand-new patch to pick and fill her pail to make her wine. And the honeysuckle flowers all over the side of her house had never smelled so sweet.

But the early evening was the best time, the luckiest time. Every day that month, as soon as she had finished washing up her supper dishes and got Roger started at his piano practice, she came out onto the porch, stood breathing deep with her hands on her hips to take in all the scents the sun had stirred up during the afternoon, then walked out into her yard to water the tomato plants. And every day, too, she wore the same clothes: those little red sneakers, that same white bulging T-shirt, those striped knee-length shorts. And, of course, that was the way Mr. Swingler first saw her, in those clothes, in that garden, bending over her precious tomato plants, a sprinkling can in one hand.

What *she* saw first was a little round head that rode the top of the picket fence to the gate, then stopped and turned and looked at her, unblinking, perhaps trying to believe she was real. For a long time she stared right back. Then the gate swung open and a small bow-legged body carried that head down her path.

"Hey mister," she said. "Get your feet off of my gardeshias."

The little man hopped one step to the side and looked down at the flowers he had crushed. "Them ain't gardeshias, missus, they're geraniums."

"It's Miss," she said and stepped back, for she was spraying water on her own foot. "Miss Littlestone. And I don't know one flower from the other. When the logging camp closed down and they hauled all the other houses away I just went from yard to yard and pulled up what I liked."

The man lowered his eyes again but they popped back up to stare at her. She waited for him to speak but he just went on chewing and staring. Those eyes looked like two painted rubber balls controlled from behind by elastic strings.

Well, she couldn't stare back all day. She went up on the front verandah and picked a large red apple out of a box. "Have an apple," she said, and held it out for him.

"No thank you," he said. "The name's Swingler. This time of year I wouldn't say thank you to no man for an apple dried up and wrinkled as a old prune."

"Not store-bought ones," she said, and took a bite to prove it. "These are store-bought ones I got last Saturday in town. Must be grown in California or somewhere down there."

"No thank you," he said again, though she had half eaten it by now. For some time she stood there on that verandah, eating the apple, trying not to stare back at those rubber-ball eyes, and trying even harder to think of something to say. Her teeth started working around the core and she spat three seeds over the railing.

"That," she said at last, with a slight nod towards the mountain off behind her house, "is the prettiest sight on this island." She said this as if the mountain were fenced right into her own back yard and her name tacked on it.

The little man turned and put both hands on his hips to study the mountain, head cocked. "Not bad," he said.

"Not bad?" she said. "You won't see prettier."

"But you don't own it," he said. "Nobody owns a mountain."

This sounded like criticism to Big Glad, a reflection on her character. In a voice hard enough to show that no one walks uninvited into her yard and insults her, she said, "Where are you headed for anyway?"

"Paper mill," he said, eyes still on that mountain. "Looking for a job."

"Then you're a little off course, mister." She threw the core across the fence right from where she stood. "Took the wrong turn twelve miles back. Paper mill is on the coast; you're headed straight into mountains. Are you walking?"

"Don't see no taxi parked, do you?"

He said this without expression, certainly without sarcasm, yet it was too much for her. She drew back against the wall and folded her arms. "Well, I'm the only one lives in here, me and my son, and I got a car all right but I ain't driving you all the way back to the highway. You got a long walk ahead of you."

For answer he swung to look at her again and said, "Lady, you got the daintiest feet I ever seen."

Now Big Glad knew this was the luckiest month ever. She crossed her ankles and stood with the toe of one red sneaker pointed like a ballet dancer. "Thank you, kind sir," she said, and did a mock curtsey. Then she did a complete turn, on one foot, for him to see every side.

"Don't mention it, I'm sure," he said and jammed a cigarette into his mouth.

That he had a mouth she hadn't noticed before. Now she realized that there was more to his face, to his body, than two painted rubber-ball eyes. The top half of his head came forward—forehead, eyes, nose—as if something behind were pushing on it. The bottom half, his mouth, his chin, slid away from her, sucked back as if he had swallowed his own teeth and half his jaw. In fact, she thought, if he'd just turn his head he'd probably have no chin at all.

Because he wore a pair of loose overalls and a plaid shirt so big the sleeves had to be rolled up to meet his wrists, she couldn't tell what his body was really like. She guessed his age at fifty-five.

"Forty-seven," he said. He lighted the cigarette and ground the match into the gravel of her path. "Born forty-seven years ago on my old man's farm down near Victoria, lived every place on this island you could name since then. Never been in here before, though."

"Me, I was born in this old shack. There's been a new coat of paint on those shakes every year of my life. Only time I ever leave the place is to go to town, or when I go off for a month or two to cook in a logging camp up the coast."

Mr. Swingler looked around the clearing, at the bare spots in the grass, the piles of old brick and overgrown lilac. "How come they all moved?" he said. "Why didn't they stay right here like you?"

"Oh, as soon as the camp shut down they fell all over themselves to buy the same house they'd been crabbing about for years while they rented them. Then they hauled them out to the highway so they could watch the traffic go by. Front lawns the size of aprons. And for Saturday-night entertainment they sit at the front window and hope for an accident."

"Why didn't you move too?"

"Mister Swingler, that is a silly question. I like it here, it's much better with all them people gone. Sounds of trucks and cars and brakes squealing can't measure up to a squirrel's chattering or a deer in the underbrush."

Mr. Swingler did not say anything to that; he looked right past her. His chewing stopped. "What's that?" he said, and the chewing started again.

"Where?"

"Behind you. In the doorway."

Big Glad looked and there was Roger standing with his nose pressed flat against the screen door. "That's my boy," she said to the man, and, "Get your face away from that filthy screen," to the boy. Then she said to Mr. Swingler, who had moved up to stand at the foot of the verandah steps below her, "He's got plenty of talent, everyone says. Just ten years old, too."

Mr. Swingler glowered at the boy as if talent was the one thing this world could do without. He scratched behind one ear for a full minute. "Talent's all right," he said. "But you got to have guts as well."

At this the child's face faded into the shadow of the room behind. Big Glad moved in front of the door as if to protect her son. The boards creaked beneath her.

"Roger's all right," she said.

"Sure," he said. His gaze tried to penetrate the screen.

"They all say he'll go far."

"Sure," Mr. Swingler said. He walked over to one side of the lawn. He came back with both hands in his pockets. "Where's the best place for looking at that mountain?" he said, while inside the house the boy started finger exercises on the piano.

Big Glad came down off the verandah and took another look at the mountain. Maybe he had seen something she'd missed. "What do you mean?" she said. "That looks good from anyplace."

He took the time to look at her as if she were a simple child. Then, lowering his eyes, he shrugged and turned his back to her. "I'm going to paint it."

"Well, why didn't you *say* you were an artist? The best view anywhere is right from the top of my roof. But where do you keep your paints and stuff?"

Mr. Swingler looked at the steep gable roof like an engineer estimating its strength. Satisfied with what he saw (Lord, he'd need to be, she'd had it all re-done just three years ago, before Momma died), he nodded, said, "Show me where your ladder is and get me a few pieces of paper and your kid's water colours," and turned again to the view.

Big Glad had her thoughts on *that* kind of talk but this time she kept them to herself. Instead she asked, "Don't you carry nothing with you? Artists are supposed to carry a knapsack at least, but you just rely on people having kids with water colours?"

"A toothbrush," he said and without even turning to face her pulled a blue worn brush from one pocket. "And a razor." And he pulled that out too, from the other pocket, and held them both up high in case there was something wrong with her eyes. Then he faced her. "Now if you'll just show me where you keep your ladder."

She did. She pointed to where it was lying in the long grass down one side of the house. Then, because she had never met an artist before—an eccentric one at that—she hurried into the house, excited, to get him his paper and paints.

He went up the roof first, holding the pad of paper and Roger's Donald Duck paint set, and sat on the peak. She followed him on her hands and knees, carrying a glass of water and a pencil, cursing the tiny stones that cut into her skin and broke her fingernails. Then, puffing (Oh Lord, if Momma were alive she'd have another heart attack just at the thought of her daring), she sat beside him on the ridge facing the mountain and tried to make herself comfortable. "My goodness," she said, "this *is* nice up here. A little hard on the rear end, though."

Mr. Swingler braced himself by putting his feet wide apart. "You'll have to be quiet," he said.

She held her breath to please him and saw that he held the pad of paper on his lap, ready for action. The tin of paints was on the roof between his feet, one end propped up on a rock to keep it level. She heaved a great sigh and offered her face up to the sun as if here she was, ready for whatever was ahead. Let it happen, she thought, and planted her feet wide apart for balance, like him.

When she looked down again he had sketched in the scene with his pencil and was putting a light blue wash over the whole paper. She sniffed hard, said, "Just smell that lilac," and folded her arms under her great breasts.

But Mr. Swingler wasn't smelling flowers. Without even slowing the motion of his brush on that paper he said. "Can't you get that racket to stop?"

"What racket?"

"That kid of yours. That piano racket right below us."

She hadn't even noticed. Roger practised so much his noise had become part of the natural background for her. She had always thought there was nothing like music to calm the nerves. But apparently Mr. Swingler didn't agree, so she stomped one foot hard three times on the roof and listened to make sure the message was understood.

It was. The sounds from the piano became so soft they might have been coming with the sun from across the woods.

"That was Rachmaninoff," she said.

For a long time, for perhaps five minutes, she remained silent and watched him work. When the sun had dried the wash (he held the paper up as if to catch the rays that came at them horizontally across the tops of the firs), he began to work at filling in the colours of the lower slopes of that mountain. She couldn't see how a paint brush would be able to put in all those black snags that stood like rigid hairs down the burned-off side, but that was his problem.

"What we need is a drink," she said.

He didn't say anything to that, so she repeated. "What we need in this sun is a nice cold drink of my homemade dandelion wine."

This time she took his silence for agreement and backed on her hands and knees down the slope of the roof. At the edge she hovered for a moment, swinging her foot around over the eavestrough in search of the ladder. Then she went down and told Roger to play softly from now on if he didn't want a cuff on the ear, because Mr. Swingler was an artist and artists need real quiet if they're going to get inspired.

From a cupboard she took down two of her best glasses (Momma had never let her use them, preferring to do without rather than take a chance on breaking one) and put them on a tray to carry them into the back bedroom, which had become her storage room. There was no furniture in the room except the shelves she hammered together the same day she threw out Momma's bed at last (smelling of medicine and anger and death) and these shelves were filled with her homemade liquor. The one papered wall was lined with bottles of blackberry wine and down along the window wall there were twenty-five gallons of sake. The other two walls displayed her specialty—dandelion wine.

She stepped over the empty bottles on the floor and took down a half-gallon of dandelion wine to fill the glasses. With the bottle held tight against her breasts she listened for a minute to the music and hummed a few bars.

What was going to happen to her she wasn't sure, but whatever it was she was ready. Her heart pounded so hard she found it difficult to breathe. She hummed three more bars of the music to quiet herself and said, "Glad old girl, you got a real artist sitting up on your roof right now, good as trapped, and all you have to do is play it right to have him begging." She drank both glasses fast and filled them again. She put the bottle back on the shelf, picked up the tray, then changed her mind and put the bottle on the tray too, beside those full glasses. With the tray held out in front of her like an offering she marched out past the piano (saying "Play on, Roger, play on" to her son, who would play all night if that was what she wanted) and through the living room, right outside to the foot of the ladder.

"Coming up," she said, and waited with one foot on the bottom rung for him to come to her aid.

But she might have waited all day and night too for all the response she got. So she balanced that tray in one hand and went up the ladder slowly and carefully. When she had the tray balanced with one end on the top rung and the other on the eavestrough she called out again, this time a little louder: "Even a genius can take time out to be a gentleman. Give me a hand."

He did, too. He came down front ways, a way she'd never dare, just as calm as he might if the roof were flat, and bent to pick up the tray. For perhaps a full minute she stared into his eyes and he stared back. They were brown eyes, those rubber balls, and each one had its own road map stamped in red on the white parts.

Maybe that's the sign of a traveller, she thought. Like spaced teeth. Well, traveller or not, he'd just walked down a one-way dead-end street. And unless he were a lot smarter than she thought, his travelling days were over.

He picked up the tray and she followed him on her hands and knees up that slope to the peak. Roger was starting in on something by Grieg. She didn't know the name of it and never did like it much. She stomped her foot again and it softened a little.

She sipped from her glass and let the wine slide down her throat slowly and quietly. No matter what she drank she always drank it like a lady. "My, that is good," she said. "I think this is the best batch I ever made." And she sipped again, pursing her lips while she thought it over, then nodded as she swallowed, as if to say Yes she was right the first time. She rolled her eyes to the sky when the warmth started to spread itself inside her. "You ought to have a wife," she said.

"I *had* one," he said, as if what she had asked about was a case of measles.

"What'd you do? Walk off and leave her high and dry?"

Mr. Swingler pushed one hand back through his hair and dug all his fingers into his scalp for a good scratch. "No, not that," he said, and flicked the dandruff out from his fingernails one at a time. "She stepped out onto the road to flag down a bus and was too slow at stepping back. That bus flung her through the air and left her draped over a barbed-wire fence like an empty gunny sack."

Big Glad raised her eyes to the mountain to compare it with his. He wasn't granting it enough power. She coughed daintily into her hand to show she was discreet, then said, "She buried near here?" as if she didn't really care but if he wanted to tell her she'd be willing to listen.

"She's not buried anywhere. She wanted one of these here cremations."

Big Glad never quite approved of cremations; there was something a little bit primitive about the whole idea. She cleared her throat again. "Well, even ashes have to have something done with them."

He swung his head to look at her, perhaps to see if she could take it. "I swallowed them," he said, and picked up his brush again to go on with his work.

Big Glad gulped at that, and swallowed too, and made a face. "Then you must be crazy," she said, and took another, longer drink from her glass.

"I read it in a history book," he said, and with one more stroke the peak of that mountain stood up, hard and true against the sky. "Some old queen did it way back when. Mixed the ashes in a glass of wine and drank the whole lot down."

She wondered when he ever stayed in one spot long enough to read a book but said nothing about that. Instead she asked, "Why?"

He lifted his head at that as if here was one question he had never expected. He thought for a while. "Why? It seemed kind of romantic to me to keep my wife inside of me."

"Did you ever think of what happened to what didn't stay inside you?"

Evidently he hadn't considered that and wasn't going to now. He went on with his painting.

Still, she wished she had thought of that. It made her mad that she had never thought of anything as smart as that. Not that she had ever had anyone to do it to. Her father had fallen down a well thirty-two years ago. And Momma died so mean a person would have choked on her ashes. There had never been anyone she'd cared that much about. She wondered if anyone would ever drink her ashes.

And speaking of queer people, she had known a few too in her time. "That reminds me of my mechanic," she said, "the one who works on my car."

"That car," he said.

"What's the matter *that* car?"

"I've been here more than an hour, most of the time sitting right up here on this roof, and I still haven't seen that car you keep on talking about."

"A car is not something you set up on a post like a flag for all to see. If you'll just lower your eyes a little you'll see a gradge with door *closed* and *locked*. And if you'll just squint a little you might be able to pick out the orange colour of it through the window."

He looked, lowered his gaze and squinted against the sun, peered at the little roof-sagging building she meant. "Orange," he said, and picked up his brush again. He painted a tint of orange on the sky behind the mountain.

"That's not the colour of the sky," she said. "You're putting things there that you can't see."

"That's what I want to see," he said. "That's what the picture needed."

Big Glad refilled both the glasses from the bottle, though his was not empty. "I guess a man could set up here every day of his life painting that mountain and never paint it the same way twice."

"I guess," he said.

"I guess a place like this one here of mine is just exactly the right kind of place for an artist. He could paint his whole life long."

"Lady," he said, "you're right," and plopped that picture right into her lap so she had to close her knees fast to keep it from slipping right through.

It took a full minute for his words to sink in. When she realized what he meant she gulped another mouthful of her drink and said, "You mean you *like* it here?"

He turned to her and carefully lifted his painting from her lap. "I knew as soon as I came in sight of your house that this would be the kind of place I'd like to live in the rest of my life. Just look at that mountain! I never painted so good."

But Big Glad wasn't wasting breath on pictures. "Mister Swingler," she said. "Are you telling me that you want to move in, to live downstairs with me and Roger, to be a part of this family?"

He stopped admiring his own work long enough to look at her.

"Well, I think that's what I been saying."

Big Glad sighed and sat back and folded her arms. "No man has ever slept under my roof without taking out a marriage licence first."

Mr. Swingler did some deep thinking about this. His eyes swung up to take in that mountain again, and then down to the sagging garage below. "I guess that makes sense," he said.

"It's only fair to my boy."

At the mention of her son they both listened to the sounds of Rachmaninoff again, sifting soft as sunlight up through the rafters of the house. Mr. Swingler said, "Now if there is nothing else, you get down off this roof and make yourself decent so we can go to town and celebrate."

Big Glad hadn't worn her hat since Momma's funeral. It was a flat-brimmed straw thing, with a cluster of plastic berries at the front. She set it on top of her head and looked in her bedroom mirror, pinching her cheeks to bring back a little colour to them. Then she slipped off her shorts and pulled on a black wool skirt. Again she admired herself in the mirror. Somehow she didn't feel like a bride yet, but that was because it had all happened so fast. Who would have thought this morning that before dark she would have been proposed to?

She tiptoed past Roger (let him find out when they had that piece of paper to show) and went out onto the verandah. Because Mr. Swingler hadn't come down off the roof yet, probably putting some finishing touches on that picture of his, she sat down on the top step to wait and soon she began to shake through her whole body. She put her head down to try and stop the trembling.

When Mr. Swingler came around the corner of the house and saw her he said, "What's the matter with you?"

"We can't," she said.

He put his painted mountain on her verandah railing. "What do you mean can't? What else you been working on ever since I arrived?"

Big Glad was afraid to look up. All she could see was a wood bug working its way across the step. "But we hardly know each other."

Mr. Swingler laughed. "Lady," he said. "You made up your mind to catch me the minute I walked inside your gate. I could've been a murderer for all you cared."

She looked up at him. She hadn't thought of that. "You could still be a murderer. Or a thief or escaped convict. I don't know a single thing about you."

He winked at her and slid closer, one arm laid out like a broken wing on her railing. "If we get the licence we'll have three days to wait before we can make use of it. I guess by that time you'll know me pretty well."

"And if I die," she said, and swallowed. "And if I die, will you drink my ashes?"

He looked hard at her and thought a moment. Then he said, "Miss Littlestone, after the first time there's nothing to it."

At that Big Glad began to cry. She bowed down her hat, put her face in her hands, and sobbed. After a while she felt better, because after all she was a bride and brides do sometimes cry, and looked at Mr. Swingler, who was holding out one hand like a porter waiting for a tip. "*Now* what do you want?" she said.

He moved closer and bent down over her so that she could see those road maps of his again. "If you'll just give me the keys to the garage," he said, "we'll be on our way."

The Religion of
the Country

When Brian Halligan's mother telephoned from halfway around the world in West Cork to tell him his poor old father had died, Halligan, who never failed to make the proper expected gesture, offered to fly over immediately for the funeral. "What rush is there?" her voice screeched at him. "Haven't I waited fifteen years for a visit out of you? Little good you can do the old fellow now." So Halligan told her he would be there by the end of the month: he needed that much time, he said, to find someone he'd trust with the bookstore while he was away, and he wanted to get as much use as possible out of his season's theatre ticket before it became out of date.

Since moving to Vancouver Island, Halligan had made it his habit to cross the strait as often as possible for plays and operas and poetry readings at the university. It was his way, he would explain down his long thin nose at you, of resisting the logger and coalminer mentality of the island. He was terrified of being converted to vulgarianism. But the few people of the town who had noticed his existence at all dismissed his high-class habits as simply a poor foreigner's attempts to feel superior. Not even his carefully preserved English accent bothered anyone.

Because of the accent it was a surprise to learn that Halligan had been born in Ireland. "Of Ascendancy stock, of course," he said. His parents had moved with him to England when he was only two years old. "'Tis no country for Protestants any more," his mother had flung over her shoulder as they left, but within a year she'd become so homesick for her little village of Ballyvourney and for the black-and-white cows that grazed all over the rocky hills around her house that she abandoned both her husband and her son to return and live by herself. The old man stayed on in London with Brian where he built up a fairly good drapery business, but as soon as the son had finished university and sailed for Canada, he retired to his wife's cottage and spent the rest of his life (according to the mother's letters) tending a single cow named Deirdre-of-the-Sorrows and talking the ear off Jack Sugrue in Mills Bar. It appeared to Brian Halligan that his parents had abandoned their past and joined the peasants.

Halligan's bookstore was on a short street that opened at one end onto a view of the business core of town, so he was able when business was slack —which was most of the time—to lean his long frame in the open doorway and watch a good deal of what went on. Every weekday Matt Bickham, a fat little college instructor who had become Halligan's only friend, dropped by after class to stand and help contemplate the scene. "It's a silly town," Halligan complained. "They waste their lives accumulating things, grabbing and hoarding, fighting over bits of land and stabbing each other in the back to get ahead. And if they have any spare time you'd never catch them reading a book, they're off somewhere in the mountains shooting animals or killing fish." Matt Bickham, who didn't have an English accent and so could afford to look at the underside of a question, said that the town was only a hundred years removed from the frontier. "In a frontier it's the business of the people to build houses and kill animals. No frontiersman had the time to sit around reading a book of poems. That'll come later." Halligan, sniffing, said that if it came much later he would have starved to death waiting, because right now he was barely meeting expenses in the bookstore.

"Besides," he said, "how can a college teacher like you make apologies for ignorance?"

Bickham was a man who rubbed both hands up and down on his round chest while he thought up his answers. He appeared to be watching a series of pages turning in his mind's eye. There were times, though, when after all his thinking he chose not to answer at all, especially when he could see that Halligan had got up on what he called his "high English horse" about one matter or other. He preferred, rather, to change the subject completely.

"My sister's in town again. The wife said to ask you around for some supper."

Halligan, of course, despised his friend's sister. He was a man who believed himself to have a high opinion of women, and could not forgive her for failing to measure up to his notions. She owned a small hotel in a west-coast logging settlement, no place for any lady, and to make matters worse she liked to talk about her weekend hiking expeditions and elk-hunting trips into the mountains. He listened to her talk, always, with a pinch-nosed disdain, which she never seemed to notice or, if she did, chose to ignore. He did not, however, allow her presence to keep him away from a meal cooked by Teresa Bickham, who was a beautiful woman with some experience in a French cooking school. Class was class and had to be appreciated wherever it was found.

Throughout his twenties Brian Halligan had expected that any day he would turn a corner and bump into the perfect woman, who would immediately fall in love with him and become his wife. He knew that despite what people called his affected distant air he was nearly handsome, that in the carefully chosen clothes he always wore he looked like a man of quality. He knew too that he was a man of intelligence and that the only reason he was not a financial success was that he refused to embrace the values of the people he lived amongst. Several girls, some of them pretty, interested him for a while: he took them to the local movie theatre, or walking on the trails through the wooded park, or driving up the Island highway to dance in one of the touristy seaside villages. But there weren't any who could be invited to accompany him across the strait to an opera. A redheaded secretary named Kitty Kenary had very nearly caused him to fall in love, but she had an infuriating habit of stopping in the middle of her sentences to snort in her nose. By the time he'd reached his thirtieth birthday he was convinced he'd be a bachelor all his life, poor and alone.

He was thirty-six and still poor, and still very much alone, when his father died and his mother demanded his presence in the mountains west of Cork. Two months after his thirty-seventh birthday, with the help of a bank loan, he drove a rented car up the Lee Valley to Macroom and then farther up the winding road to the mountain village where his mother's house nested like a squat white hen between the roadside garden wall and a high rock-strewn hill patchy with heather and stunted furze. The air was thick with the sweet turf smoke from her chimney.

"Burning peat?" he said. "In this century?"

Which showed how much he didn't know of things, she told him. She hammered dark brown bricks of turf down into the firebox of what looked to Halligan like an ordinary wood stove standing under the chimney hole at the end of the room which had once been an open fireplace. Then she sat at the wooden table in her apron and rubber boots while they had a "sup of tay" together. She looked, he thought, like someone who had tried with all her might to copy the people he'd seen in the tourist booklets, just so she could fit in.

"But I do not fit in at all," she complained. "They won't let you fit in."

"Except for those few months, you've lived here all your life."

"I have, yes. And I could live here another hundred years and not change a thing."

Halligan went to the front window, set deep in the thick stone wall, and peered out at the countryside. Across the road, beyond a fringe of trees, a hill rose up like a perfect dome, criss-crossed with green hedges and crowned with a heap of stones. "It's a wonder to me that you've stayed, then, if that's the case."

"I wouldn't know how to live anywhere else," she said, and rattled an open tin of cookies across the table towards him. "A fish out of water is what I'd be in any corner they put me. There's some that's not meant to fit in."

"Nonsense," he said. "It's that church. They've chased everybody else out but themselves. They've probably forgotten that it's possible to *be* anything else."

"Hush hush hush hush hush," she said, checking each of the windows for hidden villagers. "You'll not speak of my neighbours like that."

"But your family's been Irish for three hundred years! There isn't a thing about you that seems English to me." Not even her speech. She'd gone peasant right down to her thickened tongue.

She raised one eyebrow, as if to say "That's all you know about it" and poured more tea into her own thick mug. She had become an old lump of a woman, he saw, wrinkled and dry. The skin under her eyes sagged in a series of overlapping folds; her upper lip was covered with coarse black hairs. Her teeth had been pulled out and replaced with a new set which was too big, with white unnatural gums and black stains on the fake enamel. For most of that first day she sat at the table, drinking tea and talking about his father. Sometimes she stopped in the middle of a sentence to gaze out of the window for a while, and looked astonished to find him still sitting there across from her when she shook off whatever memory had carried her away.

"'Tis sure by now you're a true Canadian, over there on your island. You'll be finding the old land here a poor poor place beside."

It was a fine beautiful island he lived on, he told her. Especially when the dogwood trees were blooming or the pink arbutus bark was being shed. But you wouldn't find a castle in your backyard there.

"And what is a castle now but a pile of stones and a handful of history? 'Tis not much value to the cows."

She would not leave the house with him to walk through the village or to show him the valley, which he had not seen since a brief visit in his university years. She was no tourist, she said. It would be as pointless as poking around in the familiarity of her own skin.

He walked alone in a soft almost imperceptible rain past the houses and the few little shops in the village. Past the tall-spired church with its lawns and flowers and past the dull grey fenced-in National School. The few people he saw nodded shyly at him and glided by as silently as cats. The famous friendly Irish, he thought, buttoning up his heavy coat. They looked as if they expected him to bite. Or thought he'd come to spy.

He remembered St. Gobnait's shrine. On his last visit he'd crept up to it silently, hoping to witness some pilgrim stand up from praying, throw crutches or wheelchair into the hedges, and walk away. It had been a disappointment, of course; most of Halligan's expectations disappointed him sooner or later. Nevertheless the little shrine had fascinated him and he found himself, now, almost without conscious decision, leaving the highway and following the little road that crossed the narrow stone bridge and led up the slope beneath the thick leafy trees. Smelling the harsh throat-burning odour of urine, he went on up past a farm where cows, standing ankle-deep in muck, stared at him through their clouds of circling flies.

The shrine looked pretty much as he remembered it. On the high side of the road a tall graceful statue of a woman stood amongst shrubs and flowers by the doorway to the little excavated stone hut. Four white cups, half filled with rain water, sat on the stones at the holy well from which, he'd been told, pilgrims drank before kneeling to pray. The base of the statue was cluttered with things: a dried-up wedding bouquet, a miniature plastic doll in a cradle, a pen, a rosary, a half-dozen plastic statuettes and crucifixes. Halligan smiled, and thought of the fun that would be made if such a thing could be found at home. Plastic babies and wedding bouquets!

A little man appeared, suddenly, from within the walls of the stone hut. He stepped out, leaning on a walking stick, his tiny red face cracked by a wide gap-toothed grin. "Once a year," he said. "On my birthday. I stop by here to have a word with the man above. This is my eighty-first." He put his right hand out, pointed a finger. "I should be in the next world, long ago, but I'm not in any hurry at all to get there." He shook his head, held up a finger as if to add: Aha, that was a good one! Didn't I tell you so! His grey tweed cap was torn, his wide loose pants were spattered with mud and cow manure.

At a loss for words Halligan looked up at the sky. White clouds were moving past quickly, and bits of blue were opening up. "It's going to be a nice day after all," he said.

Again the sudden finger, the cocked head. "Oh, it's a fine day altogether."

"Plenty of magpies around here."

"There 'tis, yes."

"And pigeons."

The little man told him that St. Gobnait came down here in the seventh century to found a nunnery right there, right across the road there in that graveyard, in those old falling-down stone walls. He said that was the saint's grave, that mound with the big slabs of slate on top, and that build-ing beside the grave was a Protestant church.

"Yes, 'tis," he said, as if this too were a great joke on Halligan. "But 'tis all boarded up now. There's only one family of them left in the valley."

When Halligan told him he'd come here from British Columbia to visit his mother in the village, he said nearly everyone in the valley had a son in America, that he himself had two over there (besides eight in various parts of Ireland), one in Chicago, and the other in New York. "But it's a lovely boy ye are, to be coming home like this. Those two bostoons of mine have not been seen in this land since they caught the ship that took them away." The finger went up again, and the eyes twinkled, as if this too was a joke on Halligan he hadn't been able to foresee.

When he told his mother about the little man at the shrine she nodded, smiled, said Yes that would be old Michael Donegan, a fine gentleman. And yes, she had been up to the shrine herself once, years ago, but it had all been overgrown with weeds. And it had been embarrassing to see some-one down on his knees right out in plain view of cows and farmers and any tourist who felt like driving by. These people, she said, just take it for granted that everyone else is the same as they are.

"Will you come home with me now?" he said. "Will you come live with me?"

She shook her head, slowly and, he thought, sadly. "'Twill be lonely here without the man. But I'll have my friends here, all the same, and the familiar places."

Relieved in a way that surprised even himself, he became more gen-uinely concerned. "Isn't there a cousin?" he said. "Don't I remember some mention of a cousin, somewhere in the country?"

She looked square at him. There was no way he was about to spoil the enjoyment of her misery. "Cousin Polly *turned*," she said. "A convert. Of course she was always a wee bit crazy in her head, and it was a way of being cared for. The nuns have got her in a home in Cork where she won't be coming to any harm."

"It's likely a good thing you're not coming home with me," he said. "It would only upset you to see the way those people race through life trying to grab all they can. It's a land of greed and ignorance."

"Find another place so," she said. "No one is forcing you to stay there."

Yet he did stay. He showed up at the bookstore the day after his plane landed, re-arranged some of the books which had got out of place on the shelves, filled in an order for a hundred new paperbacks. He loved the shop. He loved the books: the feel of their covers, the patterns of their words. He wished he could force the whole population of the island to read every one of them. Perhaps then they would discover what they'd been missing. Maybe some of them would even begin to buy books and help put a little money in his pocket.

But he worried. He worried about his mother's loneliness. He felt guilty if he got busy in the store or involved in a conversation and forgot about her for a while. It was almost as if he believed that everything that added something to his life was taking something away from hers. Yet he couldn't help knowing that while he was concerned about the old woman's loneliness he was actually worrying about his own.

Bickham's sister told him, "For a mother who deserted you so young she's sure managed to turn you into a momma's boy."

"You've got too much time to sit around feeling sorry for yourself," Bickham said. "What you need to do is get busy with things, get involved."

The sister's idea of getting involved was to take him on an overnight hiking trip down the lifesaving trail on the west coast. He went, more or less just to please his friend, and came home scratched, bruised, and totally exhausted. He spent the next two days in bed recovering, his head spinning with the roar of the open Pacific, the smell of pines and hemlock and sitka spruce, the sight of gigantic cliffs and the foaming spray of the waves that crashed against the rocks below.

And then, at the age of thirty-seven, after all those years of despising the sister with her coarse bush manners across Matt Bickham's dining-room table, he found himself growing fascinated by her against his will. There had been plenty of time, following her down that long trail, to get used to the width of her backside and the masculine harshness of her laugh. Her face, with its weather-beaten skin and pinched beak nose, had not become less homely from familiarity but at least there was a good deal of life in the bulging eyes that mocked him from under their little hood-like lids.

"The trouble with you bloody Englishmen, even today," she said, "is you expect to come out here like colonizers and let the natives do all the dirty work while you sit around enjoying what you call 'culture.'"

She laughed at his reddening face and added: "Foreign culture."

One evening Halligan invited the Bickhams and the sister, whose name was Babe, to dinner at his apartment. He rented the second floor of a square white pioneer house that stood on a hill looking down over the town. It had been built a hundred years ago by a carpenter just arrived from England and was filled with furniture and paintings brought over on the boat by the present owner's grandmother. Halligan had searched the town for some place with a little class and decided that this houseful of Victorian clutter was as close as he was going to get. At least there were chandeliers and some antimacassars and plenty of old books.

No cook, Halligan had learned how to prepare only the things it was necessary to keep him alive. For his company he ordered a meal over the telephone, to be delivered in a truck, ready to be put on the table. All he had to do was put out the cutlery and china and chill the wine. It was necessary first, of course, to haul all the books off the chairs and up off the middle of the kitchen floor and stack them over in a corner. Unlike many booksellers he was not content just to be surrounded with books at work or to read from the shelves at the shop, but bought copies for himself to read and thumb through and keep at home. As a result, the shelves behind the glass doors had been filled for years; the books had spread out all over the room.

When he opened the door, however, only Babe was there, standing at the top of the staircase in plaid pants and a calf-hide cape. She raised one eyebrow. "Matt felt sick at the last minute so Terry suggested I come alone." When she tossed her head he saw there was a huge gold ring hanging from one ear. Suddenly, she laughed, the way Halligan imagined loggers laughed at the dirty jokes they told each other in the bush.

"I don't know how you keep that hotel of yours in business, you spend half your time down here."

"I may be the soul of the place," she said, and stepped inside, "but when I'm away the flesh still seems to hold together and continue without me." Beneath the cape, which she flung off in one swirling motion, she was wearing a blouse cut so low she looked ready to fall out of it.

Halligan was completely useless in unforeseen circumstances. "But I ordered enough food for four people."

She whisked two plates and a handful of cutlery up off the table and winked. "Then I'll just have to stay long enough for us to eat twice."

Which she did. They ate slowly all that they could of the fried chicken, washing it down with a bottle of Australian wine, then put the rest in his little refrigerator until five o'clock in the morning when they took it out again and called it breakfast. Between the two meals she taunted him for his stand-offish attitudes and he criticized her for being so raucous and unladylike; she laughed loudly at his notions about educating the local population, and he listened scornfully to her stories about the loggers and fishermen who visited her hotel; she told him a son had no obligations towards a mother who'd abandoned him as a baby, and he said knowing it was one thing but feeling it was another; she sneered at his attempt to remain an Englishman though he was obviously planted firmly on this island, and he told her at least he had some clearly defined roots, which was more than could be said for her. Before long she had shown him that what she had instead of roots was a quick mind, a body she knew exactly how to handle, and a determination to make the most of both. And he had shown her that he was perfectly willing to be seduced out of his attitudes for the sake of her continuing company. When she left she'd agreed to put him up in her hotel for a week and take him fishing in the mountain lakes that lay close by, and he'd agreed that on their honeymoon he'd take her to Ireland to meet his mother and visit a few castles.

"A married man can't be content to stay a bloody pauper," she said. "Especially if he plans to travel. You better smarten up that business of yours, make some money. Start buying things, furniture, get yourself a car, start looking at property."

When she had gone he went out too, and walked in the pale pre-dawn light down the hill into town. All was silent, grey. The trees in the pioneer graveyard were as motionless as the headstones below. He walked on the painted concrete sidewalks past block after block of stores, reading the advertisements in their darkened windows. He kicked a piece of loose newspaper away from the door of his own shop. When he came out at last onto the high grassy park above the harbour and sat on a bench near the painted totems, a breeze had begun somewhere out over the strait and plucked small waves out of the surface of the water, and the sun was just appearing over the peaks of the mainland mountains. Halligan wondered what on earth was happening to him.

He sat there for more than an hour, until a drunk stumbled up the steps from the sea-edge path and offered him a drink from his bottle. "Don't forget," the man said, and burped. "Don't forget today's the, is the day of the loggers' sports. Don't forget to be there." Halligan, starting away, promised that he wouldn't forget, though he told himself he would kill himself first. There was a matinee performance of *Rigoletto* across the strait that afternoon, and if he hadn't been so tired he would be catching the ferry across, certainly not watching axe-throwers and men with chain saws.

But he slept through most of that day, and when he awoke it was too late to catch the ferry. Babe telephoned and invited him to the dance that followed the loggers' sports. "It'll be a real eye-opener for you," she said. He didn't want his eyes opened that way, he said, and took her instead to the cocktail lounge of the Coal-Tyee Hotel. They met some of her friends there and within an hour had moved upstairs to the beer parlour where fifty or sixty people from the Island's west coast were celebrating.

Their honeymoon was a short one, financed by Babe's savings account. They flew from Vancouver to Toronto, ran through the airport and caught another plane to Shannon. With a rented car picked up at the airport they drove south through the patchwork hills, stopped long enough for Babe to climb up the spiral stairs of Blarney Castle and stare in horror at the people who nearly broke their backs in order to kiss a piece of stone slimy from other people's lips, drove slowly through the wide curved shopping street in Cork, and then headed west into the country. She made him stop and tramp with her across farmers' fields to inspect every crumbling castle and prehistoric standing stone and tiny shrine along the way. She raved about the difference it would make to her hotel to have one of those in her back yard and complained that all she had to offer was a lot of thick bush and a lake full of deadheads. When they pulled up in front of his mother's cottage she leapt out of the car and took three photographs, saying she wished she could cut this piece of village out and take it back home with her just the way it was.

Halligan's mother found Babe's loud enthusiasm upsetting, and asked him to make up excuses to get her out of the house. As long as her daughter-in-law was inside she tended to stare off into space and answer only his simplest questions, but when Babe was off in the car exploring the countryside or talking to people in the village or tracking down some historic spot mentioned in the tourist brochures, the old woman told her son that life had got much worse even than she'd feared.

"'Tis a trial just to be getting out of the bed in the mornings," she said, "and wondering what is the point of it at all when there is only yourself to talk to."

"Come now," Halligan said, "I don't believe that none of your neighbours ever drop in to visit."

The old woman's eyes shifted away. "Oh, they're in and out of the house all day long like a lot of magpies. But there isn't a one of them that's a relative. What is a woman without a family?"

She had indeed deteriorated, Halligan saw to his horror. The skin of her face had dried and shrivelled, her messy hair was so thin he could see patches of scalp, her whiskers were like silver needles hanging above her lip. The little kitchen, which on his last visit was whitewashed and spotless, now looked as if she had decided to leave dirt and food and pieces of clothing just wherever they happened to lie until she should die and escape them all.

She stood at the stove, one thick hand pressed against her back. "I took to visiting my cousin Polly but she died. Tim Murphy drove me down to the city once a week in his lorry so I could visit with her. Addled-headed as she was, at least she was related. But they sent word up last week that she'd dropped dead in chapel. Poor old thing. And now what have I left?"

Suddenly Halligan felt angry. "What you have left is the rest of your life to do with as you please. You can sit around feeling sorry for yourself if you want, but you'll have nobody to blame but yourself."

She turned and let him see that her eyes were full of tears, tipped up her chin at him accusingly. There is no end to the cruelty you can expect to suffer at the hands of a heartless son, she seemed to be saying, and if Babe hadn't clomped up the front walk at just that moment he would have found himself making all kinds of impossible promises. It was not easy for a man like Halligan to meet those watery eyes or ignore that chin.

"I found an old geezer who's offered to take me out hunting," Babe announced, and threw herself into the nearest chair. "He called it shooting. What could you shoot around here?"

"Rabbits," the old lady snapped.

And Halligan, too, found himself snapping at her. "They have no cougars here," he said. "Or elk."

Babe Halligan looked from one to the other as if trying to figure out what kind of nonsense she'd walked in on. Then she pulled off her rain-drenched sweater and started brushing her hair. "You'd think that bloody sky would eventually rain itself out, but it goes on and on. Doesn't it ever stop here? One old fellow down the road told me he's been turning the hay in his field every day for three weeks now and can't get it dry enough to put in haystacks."

The old woman took the discarded sweater and hung it on the back of a chair close to the stove. She heaved a sigh and opened the oven door. "The sisters are after writing me to come down to the city and collect Polly's things. I thought, if there's ever a time that car is idle, we could drive in together." It was clear from the way she said it that she expected either her son or his bride to say it was a terrible idea and suggest she have the things mailed or burned.

But Babe thought it would be great fun and insisted that they go right away. She grabbed the wet sweater off the chair back and put it on. "There's no sense sitting around in this gloomy place listening to the rain. Let's go."

The old woman looked at her daughter-in-law with gratitude but frowned immediately afterwards, as if suddenly disapproving of such recklessness. She pulled on two cardigans and a coat and was the first one out the door. "It's easy to find," she said. "And didn't Sister Angela tell me she'd have the things near the front door?"

She sat in the middle of the back seat and talked steadily the whole way down out of the hills and along the road beside the river. She told them Cousin Polly had advised her to go to America if ever Brian married so that she could mind her grandchildren, but she'd told Polly she didn't believe Brian would ever find himself a wife. She told them William

Penn's father had lived in that castle near the bridge and hadn't he gone on to become a famous man in America? Babe said that not all of America was the one country, but the old woman went on to tell that Michael Donegan's son in Chicago had got killed in a factory explosion and the insurance company had sent him a lot of money. He marched around like gentry now, and had a taxi come all the way out from Macroom whenever he wanted to do a bit of shopping. "If that's what having money will do to a person I'll thank you not to take me home with you, as I understand that everyone there is as rich as Michael Donegan."

Halligan drove inside the iron gates of the home and parked near the great oak door but he refused to go in. Places like that spooked him, he said. And nuns made him nervous. He'd just sit and wait, thank you, just don't be too long. It was probably even damper inside an old stone building than it was out here in the rain, and anyway he didn't suppose Cousin Polly had owned so many things the two of them couldn't carry them.

"Occhh, Babe," his mother said, heaving herself up out of the back seat. "It's afraid of religion he is. Scared one of the sisters'll baptise him when he's not looking." She chuckled loudly and made a face at him through his window.

Just as he dreaded, when they came back out a half-hour later two nuns came with them. Babe had one of them by the elbow and was talking loudly, making big gestures with the paper bag she held in her hand. The old woman hurried ahead, dumped an armload of things in the trunk, and then hurried back to bring them around to his side of the car.

"Sister Angela," she said. "And Sister Mary Rose." As if he had begged to be introduced.

The taller one bent and put a hand in through the window for him to shake. There was a pink flush spot high up on each cheek. "Ooh," she said, straightening. "And don't you see the resemblance, Sister Mary Rose? 'Tis Polly all over again."

The other, an older woman, squinted. "'Tis, 'tis," she said. "The image of her! The very image."

Halligan's mother blushed, grinned with pleasure. "The eyes, I suppose. He has the eyes sure."

"Oh the eyes, the mouth," Sister Angela exclaimed, and put one hand on the old woman's shoulder. "You'll not be missing Polly so very much, dear, with that one's face to keep her near."

"She was very happy here," the older nun said, bending down to speak through the window. As if Halligan, having the silly old bat's eyes, would be the one most interested. "'Tis a saint she was, to be sure. Never a harsh word. Always a smile. Dear, dear Polly."

"She is heaven's gain," Sister Angela said, putting out a restraining hand lest the other get carried away. "Come, Sister Mary Rose, let us not keep these people. They have a long journey ahead of them."

When Halligan had turned the car around, Sister Angela held up a hand to stop him, then came close and dipped her head to the window. "Monday?" she said, and the old woman leaning forward in the back seat whispered "Monday" back.

Once they'd left the cobbled courtyard Halligan drove, silently, up the river as far as the city park. Then he turned in his seat and looked at his mother. "Monday what?"

"Leave her alone," Babe said.

"What did that woman mean by whispering 'Monday' past my ear?"

The old woman pointed her chin again, but this time there were no tears. She opened her door. "I always enjoys walking through the roses," she said. And grunting, heaved herself out.

"Don't nag at her," Babe said, glaring.

They got out of the car and headed in through the park gate after his mother, but she had already got inside the circular labyrinth paths of the rose garden. From the outside he stood and hollered at her: "Now what have you gone and done, old woman?"

A row of men sitting with their backs against the grey museum wall looked up, alarmed.

"Now what have you done? Come out of there and tell what you've got up your sleeve now."

The old woman had worked her way across nearer to the other side of the garden and Halligan rushed around the outside edge to be closer. She bent down to the roses, inhaling, smiling.

"You can't do that kind of thing just for your convenience," he said. "You have to have better reasons than that."

"After my little visits with Polly, Tim Murphy always drove me down here to this park. But this is the first time I haven't felt like an outsider, even here."

"It's your country," Babe said. "It's your home. There's no reason to feel like an outsider."

Halligan felt himself nearly choking. "Never mind that!" he shouted. "Just tell me what it is you and those nuns have cooked up between you."

Babe sat back on a bench and stretched her legs out in front of her. "She's going to start taking instruction."

"What?"

"Shh. Keep your voice down. People are looking."

"Let them look! What the hell kind of thing is that to do?"

Halligan's mother came out from behind the roses and sat on the bench beside Babe. "Don't shout," she said. "I'm an old woman, and it makes me nervous to have all that noise around me."

"A fine thing," Babe said. "Scaring an old woman."

"A fine thing, too, when a woman too old to know her own mind gets sucked in like that."

"Tch, tch, Brian my son. Don't I know my own mind the same as the next one? Don't go blaming the sisters. 'Tis no idea of theirs at all."

"Sold out is what you did. Sold out for the sake of belonging."

The old woman gathered her coat together and fumbled with her thick fingers at the button. "And what is it I've sold? What have I lost?"

Halligan was still muttering to himself about the feeble-mindedness of old women when they flew out of Shannon a few days later.

When his mother was received into the Church, Babe, who had just sold her hotel, suggested that they use some of the money to fly to Ireland, but Halligan preferred to stay home and pretend it wasn't happening. And anyway, he said, he was busy helping Matt build a Chamber of Commerce float for the First of July parade. When a coloured snapshot arrived in the mail Babe said she'd never seen a bride so radiant. "She just looks as if she'd washed all her loneliness and confusion off in the morning's bath."

"If she had a bath," Halligan growled.

With the money from the hotel they bought the shop next to the bookstore and expanded into a book-and-record shop with an emphasis on the faster-selling rock albums. They also put a down payment on a house high up the hill overlooking the whole town, and Babe decided that thirty-three was not too old to get pregnant. Halligan, to help pay for the house, began to sell real estate in the evenings for a friend whose firm was expanding. The day he made his first big sale, a thirty-acre farm, a letter arrived from his mother saying how happy she was to hear she was about to be a grandmother at last. She'd put a tiny plastic crucifix in the envelope, for the baby when it came. Halligan cursed and threw the thing in the garbage pail. Babe, who had swollen up all over as if she were about to burst and rarely left the easy-boy chair in the living room, laughed at him and asked him what was the matter, was he scared there was black magic in the plastic?

Halligan's mother lived for another four years, and though she wrote one cheerful letter to them every month up until the time of her death, she never once visited them in Canada. Halligan didn't invite her. "She made her choice," he said. "Let her be happy with *them*, she doesn't need us."

When the news of her death was cabled to them by the parish priest he didn't bother to attend the funeral. "I wouldn't understand a word of it," he said, "a whole lot of nonsense." And besides, he had discovered an old man who just might be ready to sell a hundred-acre piece of waterfront property which was ideal for subdividing, and if he took time to go gallivanting around the world someone else might get there first to grab it. Land development was a cut-throat business, he said, and there was no room in it for sentiment.

By the River

But listen, she thinks, it's nearly time.

And flutters, leaf-like, at the thought. The train will rumble down the valley, stop at the little shack to discharge Styan, and move on. This will happen in half an hour and she has a mile still to walk.

Crystal Styan walking through the woods, through bush, is not pretty. She knows that she is not even a little pretty, though her face is small enough, and pale, and her eyes are not too narrow. She wears a yellow wool sweater and a long cotton skirt and boots. Her hair, tied back so the branches will not catch in it, hangs straight and almost colourless down her back. Some day, she expects, there will be a baby to play with her hair and hide in it like someone behind a waterfall.

She has left the log cabin, which sits on the edge of the river in a stand of birch, and now she follows the river bank upstream. A mile ahead, far around the bend out of sight, the railroad tracks pass along the rim of their land and a small station is built there just for them, for her and Jim Styan.

It is their only way in to town, which is ten miles away and not much of a town anyway when you get there. A few stores, a tilted old hotel, a movie theatre.

Likely, Styan would have been to a movie last night. He would have stayed the night in the hotel, but first (after he had seen the lawyer and bought the few things she'd asked him for) he would pay his money and sit in the back row of the theatre and laugh loudly all the way through the movie. He always laughs at everything, even if it isn't funny, because those figures on the screen make him think of people he has known; and the thought of them exposed like this for just anyone to see embarrasses him a little and makes him want to create a lot of noise so people will know he isn't a bit like that himself.

She smiles. The first time they went to a movie together she slouched as far down in the seat as she could so no one could see she was there or had anything to do with Jim Styan.

The river flows past her almost silently. It has moved only a hundred miles from its source and has another thousand miles to go before it reaches the ocean, but already it is wide enough and fast. Right here she has more than once seen a moose wade out and then swim across to the other side and disappear into the cedar swamps. She knows something, has heard somewhere that farther downstream, miles and miles behind her, an Indian band once thought this river a hungry monster that liked to gobble up their people. They say that Coyote their god-hero dived in and subdued the monster and made it promise never to swallow people again. She once thought she'd like to study that kind of thing at a university or somewhere, if Jim Styan hadn't told her grade ten was good enough for anyone and a life on the road was more exciting.

What road? she wonders. There isn't a road within ten miles. They sold the rickety old blue pickup the same day they moved onto this place. The railroad was going to be all they'd need. There wasn't any place they cared to go that the train, even this old-fashioned milk-run outfit, couldn't take them easily and cheaply enough.

But listen, she thinks, it's nearly time.

The trail she is following swings inland to climb a small bluff and for a while she is engulfed by trees. Cedar and fir are dark and thick and damp. The green new growth on the scrub bushes has nearly filled in the narrow trail. She holds her skirt up a little so it won't be caught or ripped, then runs and nearly slides down the hill again to the river's bank. She can see in every direction for miles and there isn't a thing in sight which has anything to do with man.

"Who needs them?" Styan said, long ago.

It was with that kind of question—questions that implied an answer so obvious only a fool would think to doubt—that he talked her first out of the classroom and then right off the island of her birth and finally up here into the mountains with the river and the moose and the railroad. It was as if he had transported her in his falling-apart pickup not only across the province about as far as it was possible to go, but also backwards in time, perhaps as far as her grandmother's youth or even farther. She washes their coarse clothing in the river and depends on the whims of the seasons for her food.

"Look!" he shouted when they stood first in the clearing above the cabin. "It's as if we're the very first ones. You and me."

They swam in the cold river that day and even then she thought of Coyote and the monster, but he took her inside the cabin and they made love on the fir-bough bed that was to be theirs for the next five years. "We don't need any of them," he sang. He flopped over on his back and shouted up into the rafters. "We'll farm it! We'll make it go. We'll make our own world!" Naked, he was as thin and pale as a celery stalk.

When they moved in he let his moustache grow long and droopy like someone in an old, brown photograph. He wore overalls which were far too big for him and started walking around as if there were a movie camera somewhere in the trees and he was being paid to act like a hillbilly instead of the city-bred boy he really was. He stuck a limp felt hat on the top of his head like someone's uncle Hiram and bought chickens.

"It's a start," he said.

"Six chickens?" She counted again to be sure. "We don't even have a shed for them."

He stood with his feet wide apart and looked at her as if she were stupid. "They'll lay their eggs in the grass."

"That should be fun," she said. "A hundred and sixty acres is a good-size pen."

"It's a start. Next spring we'll buy a cow. Who needs more?"

Yes who? They survived their first winter here, though the chickens weren't so lucky. The hens got lice and started pecking at each other. By the time Styan got around to riding in to town for something to kill the lice a few had pecked right through the skin and exposed the innards. When he came back from town they had all frozen to death in the yard.

At home, back on her father's farm in the blue mountains of the island, nothing had ever frozen to death. Her father had cared for things. She had never seen anything go so wrong there, or anyone have to suffer.

She walks carefully now, for the trail is on the very edge of the river bank and is spongy and broken away in places. The water, clear and shallow here, back-eddies into little bays where cattail and bracken grow and where water-skeeters walk on their own reflection. A beer bottle glitters where someone, perhaps a guide on the river, has thrown it—wedged between stones as if it has been here as long as they have. She keeps her face turned to the river, away from the acres and acres of forest which are theirs.

Listen, it's nearly time, she thinks. And knows that soon, from far up the river valley, she will be able to hear the throbbing of the train, coming near.

She imagines his face at the window. He is the only passenger in the coach and sits backwards, watching the land slip by, grinning in expectation or memory or both. He tells a joke to old Bill Cobb the conductor but even in his laughter does not turn his eyes from outside the train. One spot on his forehead is white where it presses against the glass. His fingers run over and over the long drooping ends of his moustache. He is wearing his hat.

Hurry, hurry, she thinks. To the train, to her feet, to him.

She wants to tell him about the skunk she spotted yesterday. She wants to tell him about the stove, which smokes too much and needs some kind of clean-out. She wants to tell him about her dream; how she dreamed he was trying to go into the river and how she pulled and hauled on his feet but he wouldn't come out. He will laugh and laugh at her when she tells him, and his laughter will make it all right and not so frightening, so that maybe she will be able to laugh at it too.

She has rounded the curve in the river and glances back, way back, at the cabin. It is dark and solid, not far from the bank. Behind the poplars the cleared fields are yellowing with the coming of fall but now in all that place there isn't a thing alive, unless she wants to count trees and insects. No people. No animals. It is scarcely different from her very first look at it. In five years their dream of livestock has been shelved again and again.

Once there was a cow. A sway-backed old Jersey.

"This time I've done it right," he said. "Just look at this prize."

And stepped down off the train to show off his cow, a wide-eyed beauty that looked at her through a window of the passenger coach.

"Maybe so, but you'll need a miracle, too, to get that thing down out of there."

A minor detail to him, who scooped her up and swung her around and kissed her hard, all in front of the old conductor and the engineer who didn't even bother to turn away. "Farmers at last!" he shouted. "You can't have a farm without a cow. You can't have a baby without a cow."

She put her head inside the coach, looked square into the big brown eyes, glanced at the sawed-off horns. "Found you somewhere, I guess," she said to the cow. "Turned out of someone's herd for being too old or senile or dried up."

"An auction sale," he said, and slapped one hand on the window glass. "I was the only one there who was desperate. But I punched her bag and pulled her tits; she'll do. There may even be a calf or two left in her sway-backed old soul."

"Come on, bossy," she said. "This is no place for you."

But the cow had other ideas. It backed into a corner of the coach and shook its lowered head. Its eyes, steady and dull, never left Crystal Styan.

"You're home," Styan said. "Sorry there's no crowd here or a band playing music, but step down anyway and let's get started."

"She's not impressed," she said. "She don't see any barn waiting out there either, not to mention hay or feed of any kind. She's smart enough to know a train coach is at least a roof over her head."

The four of them climbed over the seats to get behind her and pushed her all the way down the aisle. Then, when they had shoved her down the steps, she fell on her knees on the gravel and let out a long unhappy bellow. She looked around, bellowed again, then stood up and high-tailed it down the tracks. Before Styan even thought to go after her she swung right and headed into bush.

Styan disappeared into the bush, too, hollering, and after a while the train moved on to keep its schedule. She went back down the trail and waited in the cabin until nearly dark. When she went outside again she found him on the river bank, his feet in the water, his head resting against a birch trunk.

"What the hell," he said, and shook his head and didn't look at her.

"Maybe she'll come back," she said.

"A bear'll get her before then, or a cougar. There's no hope of that."

She put a hand on his shoulder but he shook it off. He'd dragged her from place to place right up this river from its mouth, looking and looking for his dream, never satisfied until he saw this piece of land. For that dream and for him she had suffered.

She smiles, though, at the memory. Because even then he was able to bounce back, resume the dream, start building new plans. She smiles, too, because she knows there will be a surprise today; there has always been a surprise. When it wasn't a cow it was a bouquet of flowers or something else. She goes through a long list in her mind of what it may be, but knows it will be none of them. Not once in her life has anything been exactly the way she imagined it. Just so much as foreseeing something was a guarantee it wouldn't happen, at least not in the exact same way.

"Hey you, Styan!" she suddenly calls out. "Hey you, Jim Styan. Where are you?" And laughs, because the noise she makes can't possibly make any difference to the world, except for a few wild animals that might be alarmed.

She laughs again, and slaps one hand against her thigh, and shakes her head. Just give her—how many minutes now?—and she won't be alone. These woods will shudder with his laughter, his shouting, his joy. That train, that dinky little train will drop her husband off and then pass on like a stay-stitch thread pulled from a seam.

"Hey you, Styan! What you brought this time? A gold brooch? An old nanny goat?"

The river runs past silently and she imagines that it is only shoulders she is seeing, that monster heads have ducked down to glide by but are watching her from eyes grey as stone. She wants to scream out "Hide, you crummy cheat, my Coyote's coming home!" but is afraid to tempt even something that she does not believe in. And anyway she senses—far off—the beat of the little train coming down the valley from the town.

And when it comes into sight she is there, on the platform in front of the little sagging shed, watching. She stands tilted far out over the tracks to see, but never dares—even when it is so far away—to step down onto the ties for a better look.

The boards beneath her feet are rotting and broken. Long stems of grass have grown up through the cracks and brush against her legs. A squirrel runs down the slope of the shed's roof and yatters at her until she turns and lifts her hand to frighten it into silence.

She talks to herself, sings almost to the engine's beat "Here he comes, here he comes"—and has her smile already as wide as it can be. She smiles into the side of the locomotive sliding past and the freight car sliding past and keeps on smiling even after the coach has stopped in front of her and it is obvious that Jim Styan is not on board.

Unless of course he is hiding under one of the seats, ready to leap up, one more surprise.

But old Bill Cobb the conductor backs down the steps, dragging a gunny sack out after him. "H'lo there, Crystal," he says. "He ain't aboard today either, I'm afraid." He works the gunny sack out onto the middle of the platform. "Herbie Stark sent this, it's potatoes mostly, and cabbages he was going to throw out of his store."

She takes the tiniest peek inside the sack and yes, there are potatoes there and some cabbages with soft brown leaves.

The engineer steps down out of his locomotive and comes along the side of the train rolling a cigarette. "Nice day again," he says with barely a glance at the sky. "You makin' out all right?"

"Hold it," the conductor says, as if he expects the train to move off by itself. "There's more." He climbs back into the passenger car and drags out a cardboard box heaped with groceries. "The church ladies said to drop this off," he says.

"They told me make sure you get every piece of it, but I don't know how you'll ever get it down to the house through all that bush."

"She'll manage," the engineer says. He holds a lighted match under the ragged end of his cigarette until the loose tobacco blazes up. "She's been doing it—how long now?—must be six months."

The conductor pushes the cardboard box over against the sack of potatoes and stands back to wipe the sweat off his face. He glances at the engineer and they both smile a little and turn away. "Well," the engineer says, and heads back down the tracks and up into his locomotive.

The conductor tips his hat, says "Sorry," and climbs back into the empty passenger car. The train releases a long hiss and then moves slowly past her and down the tracks into the deep bush. She stands on the platform and looks after it a long while, as if a giant hand is pulling, slowly, a stay-stitching thread out of a fuzzy green cloth.

Other People's Troubles

In those early years, it seemed that she often dressed in green as pale and just as gentle as the wild mint patch growing not too far from the house. Oh, they would tease her for it; first he (born Barclay Miles but called Duke then for riding the haywagons like some kind of royalty) and then Dora and Mary too—all her children—saying maybe she was blind to any other colour and afraid of wearing red by mistake, which was her only hate, but saying it beyond her reach for safety just in case this once she didn't want to laugh.

The wind too was green, in the metal-flake poplar leaves up against the sky. Those poplars, twenty feet tall now or more, were planted near the house when he was born, and measured out his life in the slow uneven growth of unseen rings. All his life long they were growing, were stretching, were gauging time as strong and just as sure as any clock dong-donging on a mantel shelf.

In that certain year, the poplar's tenth year to the sky, they arrived at the end of a long pale spring and moved on forward into summer, knowing right away that it had to be a hot one. They could sense an orange-sky summer without trouble, for even in June they could walk all the way to the spring without once having to step on the planks, and soon—too soon—the long grass growing down the centre of the driveway started turning copper from the sun. The adults looked out at the farm and then at each other and said, "There's bound to be a fire season this year." Then he, too, looked out at the farm and then at the girls and said, "There's sure to be a damn fire season this year," because they knew even then that when the logging camps closed down and their father stayed home, the farm was far more work than fun.

One day Momma touched his shoulder. "You kids stay out of trouble for an hour or two," she said, because Mrs. Baxter's husband was killed fighting fire and she was going over there.

"Yes," he said. "I guess I know how to behave."

"Then keep an eye on Dora, who doesn't know." Which was true, too, because Dora with her size would just as soon climb a tree right to the highest branch as not, and then holler for help down.

"What can you do for dying?" he said.

"I can try to make it easier by taking cakes over and this pie and by just talkin' a little to her. Which is just about all anybody can do when a woman loses her husband in the woods."

But the woods didn't close that summer. A fire burned all down the side of Whistler Hill and Eddie Baxter died under a falling tree and they did not close. The shallow wells dried up in the valley and cattle drooped and still the logging camps did not close. "They aren't going to close," his father said. "Them big-time managers off to California or Hawaii don't give a damn about safety, and one of these days a spark will fly and the whole mountain will go up in smoke." He had to take his turn once a week staying behind until dark watching for sparks.

How do you watch for sparks is what I want to know. Do you crawl around peering under logs and things smelling for smoke or do you sit up on a stump like a squirrel watching all? Or do you curl up somewhere to read a book until the light is too poor to see by?

Watching sparks was not the only thing his father found to complain about that summer. For reasons known only to himself (kept in, like every-thing else he thought, as if sharing would mean losing too) he objected to the way Momma was called on so often to help people out in their trouble. While she was doing the dishes—he did his best talking when her back was to him, it seemed, perhaps taking strength from the absence of the cool level eyes that could look in too far for comfort—he studied his hands first, dry and hard and cracked, and then said, "For a change you could stay home with your family where you belong and let someone else go." Without even halting the motion of her hands she said, "What can I do? They ask me to come and what can I do about it?" He said, "That's it," and she said, "Yes," and he said, "What is it about you that everybody comes crying to you with their troubles instead of someone else? Why does it always have to be you taking on other people's troubles for them?"

So she shook the soap from both hands and turned to him, saying as she wiped the hands on her apron, "I do what I can. Sometimes it seems there is nothing anyone can do, but they say they prefer to have me there to any-one else, so I go. If you have a strength the others don't have, you just have to share it a little so the weak won't suffer any more than they have to. There's little enough I can do but I do what I can."

What she could do they never learned. What strength she had for others she kept secret from them. There she stood, steady as a fence post and about as tall, and not one person in the house had ever seen just what-ever it was she did when she went out of the house to fix the messed-up lives of other people. So he decided right there, in the half-second it took her to turn around again and plunge her hands down in the hot water, that no secret in the world is strong enough to be kept for ever, and before much longer went by he would relieve her mind of the weight of all that private knowing.

And just as if she knew his thoughts and was every bit as anxious as he was to share that knowing, she gave him his chance not more than two days later, came up to him while she struggled into her coat on the hottest day of July and said, "You got nothing better to do than stirring up mud wasps with your feet?"

He pulled his bare feet away from the tap and drew them under him on the bottom step. "Not much," he said.

"It would be too much I suppose to expect an almost-ten-year-old boy to get the idea all by himself that he could be out hoeing or maybe carrying wood."

"Never thought of it," he said, "but if that's what you want." He drew his feet out again and almost stood up.

"Never mind," she said. "I guess I should know by now that the only things boys think of by themselves is food and trouble and usually they're the same thing. Come with me."

"Where we going?"

"Never mind that too, just wash up and come on. What have I got this coat on for, in this weather?" She took her coat off (new that Christmas and green as grass like everything else) and threw it over a chair, then dived into her bread drawer and took out two loaves of bread she had baked yesterday. "That's all I've got in the house," she said, and then he had to run to catch up before she got to the garage.

He settled himself back in the car seat and prepared himself. He imagined her walking into a house of sorrow where women wept softly and then making them coffee and cooing words of sympathy. He imagined black dresses and flowers and whispering. But no amount of imagining in the front seat of a car would have prepared him for what did happen.

Because she did not walk in. She stopped the car in front of Sandy Melville's house and left him sitting there while she went up the hard dirt path to the door and put the loaves of bread there on the step. Then she came back, slammed the door hard, and sat waiting.

Quickly the door of the little house opened. Emma Melville, with half her face the colour of a ripe plum, her body wrapped up in a long housecoat patterned like a tree, peered down at the bread, then up at the car, frowning, until she recognized the car or Momma sitting there behind the wheel as if she just never quite got away in time, and beckoned them in.

He would rather stay in the car, he said (meaning it now) but no, she pushed him ahead of her down that path just as if she needed him this time and couldn't go alone. She pushed him right in that front door, past a huge wood stove with a reservoir at one end and a line of washing above, past a flowered chesterfield strewn with magazines, and shoved him into a red-and-white wicker chair. He picked up a magazine with a naked woman on the cover and opened it.

"Sit down," Momma said.

Emma Melville stood in the middle of the room with the two loaves of bread in her hands. She looked as if bread was the one thing in this world she did not know what to do with.

"Sit down," Momma said again. "You look like you could do with a cup of coffee."

Emma Melville stood looking for a minute longer. She opened her mouth to say something, but closed it, then opened it again and said, "You set down, Lenore Miles. You ain't here to sip coffee with no one. You set down and start listening, I have a lot to tell."

The two women sat down at the table and stared at each other across the loaves of bread. Momma said, "Then start telling."

Emma squirmed. "What I got to say may not be right for young ears over there."

"Oh never mind that. He's got his nose in a book and won't hear a thing," Momma said, who should have known better than that, seeing not one page turned yet.

"That bastard," Emma said.

Momma stiffened.

"Yes. You mean Sandy."

"Yes, yes Sandy. Yes, that shifty-eyed bugger. Yes, him. Lookit here."

He looked too and saw the large purple swelling on the side of her face. There was no missing that, even without an invitation.

"And this!" Her hand opened the housedress and pointed to something he could not see.

"That's something," Momma said.

"Well, that's all the thanks I get for going into town last night and dragging him out of the beer parlour before he got too drunk and started smashing up expensive furniture like the last time. This is my thanks, not that I expected any. He let me haul him out past all those laughing people and drive him all the way home and then, *then*, when we're all alone, he says *Couldn't you at least take your hair out of pincurls, Emma, before you came huntin for me?* And then he laughed, and right in the middle of a laugh he stopped and knocked me down like a stone to the floor and kicked me, *kicked me*, Lenore, the way you kick a dog."

"Did you yell?"

"Did I yell. I cursed and screamed, and then you know what he did?"

Momma said, "I don't know as I want to."

Just try not telling, he thought, his eyes on the plum swelling. Just you try stopping now with these four ears pricked up to listen. He wondered what she had pointed to inside her housecoat.

"My God, Lenore, he dragged me into the bedroom."

He did not intend to laugh. His body just jerked upright in the chair and before he knew enough to stop it he had laughed right out loud like an idiot, one sharp crooked sound he couldn't swallow. They both swung their heads around fast, glowering, Momma saying "You hush" with her voice and "Blast your hide" with her eyes, and then swung back again as if not a sound had come from him and all that mattered in the world could be found right there on the table with those loaves of bread.

Momma sighed and heaved her shoulders. "What now?" she said.

"Now he's gone. He walked out of this house and said he'll never come back."

Momma said, "He's done it before. He'll be back."

And what Emma Melville didn't like she ignored. "He said never. He said nothing could drag him back. He said he'd rather sleep in people's barns than come back here."

He had heard crying before, but nothing in ten years of listening to just about every kind of sound a farm or family had to offer had quite prepared him for what he had to listen to now: first, deep and heavy breathing uncontrolled, then hoarse rasping sounds building steadily until he might have been listening to a cow coughing from a thistle stuck in her throat. Suddenly the room smelled no longer of the bread they had brought in but of some staler odour, onions, maybe, that stayed around soaked up in the woodwork or wallpaper to fight and beat out anything new that might enter. In the wicker chair he was aware of that and the sound too, and, no longer pretending to be reading the magazine, he watched the heaving body of the woman with horror and fascination and then looked over to his mother, green and solid across the table, thinking, even before she noticed his staring, *Now, let's see you do your stuff*, in a manner he would never have dared to speak aloud. But Momma's eyes caught his, and maybe reading there just what thoughts went on behind, she got out of her chair and said, "You go out to the car, Duke, and wait for me there."

Still wanting to see how she worked her miracles, he said "No" and barely got that one syllable out before she answered, "I said go out in the car and wait. This is not for you to see."

Or anyone else, he admitted. Still, she had brought him all the way over here to see her in action and he did not want to miss it now. He said, "No," again.

"You get, Barclay Miles, or I'll tan your backside. Get out to that car."

He got. He went out that door no one had thought to close (would the whole neighbourhood have to hear her panting and wheezing like a sick cow, and would they all but him hear what she said or did to stop it?) and slammed it hard behind him. In the silent wake of the noise, he considered sitting on the step to hear, but gave that up and went to the car and slammed that door too.

It took twenty minutes on the dashboard clock. He sat there cooled by the shade of a hawthorn tree and, thinking he would never speak to her again as long as he lived, crossed his arms and practised a scowl. But he soon forgot about the scowl and looked up the gravel road before him, at the powder-brown surface itself, at the dust-laden poplars and alders as still as silence on either side, dying. As still as silence, he thought, and how could they stand and be smothered and choked out by dust and never move or struggle? Down the road a boy came, walking, fourteen years old perhaps and staring at the empty sky, stirring up a trail of dust with two bare feet flat and wide as snow shoes. One of the Waddell kids from up the river, with nothing better to do all summer than tramp up and down the roads looking for beer bottles in the ditch. Duke would be darned if he would plod over every crossroad in the valley looking for empty beer bottles for pennies, even if he did live up the river with no father and needed the money for food. He'd starve first, which was about what would happen to him anyway if she didn't get out to the car soon, lunch time being a ridiculous hour to go calling on people.

But the Waddell boy was hardly past the car by the time she and Emma Melville were out on the porch, both laughing and talking as if a nice social call were just coming to an end.

He swung and said, "She okay now?" before she had even hit the starter button.

"She's okay," she said.

"She's not crying any more?"

"She's okay."

He had to shout over the whine of the engine starting. "Why did you bring me?"

They were a half-mile down the road before she worked up an answer to that one. Staring straight ahead as if all she needed to see would be right there in front of her she drove that car grim-faced and a little faster than she should have (having no driver's licence and wanting none) right past the swans on Hanley's pond, past the stand of timber Peter Wilson would not sell to the sawmill for lumber, and right on past the big sawmill itself standing silent and deserted for fear of spraying sparks, before she found the words.

Then she said, "I didn't know she would be in such an ugly mood. It's happened before and I didn't think she would be so ugly this time."

Not everyone can answer straight the first time so he tried again. "Why did you want me to come?"

"You needed to see that," she said, double-clutching to slow down as they were coming to the highway. "There are lots of unpleasant things in this world and I hope you don't ever see half, but that was one you needed to see."

"See what?"

"You needed to see the kind of mean things some men will do to a woman. You wouldn't ever see it at home, but you needed to know and no amount of telling would have been good enough. Maybe some day you will be tempted to do a woman a dirty turn, and you'll remember Emma Melville's black eye and crying."

They were on the highway now, and she drove faster than ever, swinging the car around a farmer and his tractor without even seeing the truck that had to chew up the dust of the shoulder to miss hitting her, and propelling them across a narrow bridge with less than four inches to spare on his side. Sitting in that front seat low enough for the hood itself to seem like a giant shiny field dragging him down the narrow lane formed by the two converging rows of fence posts, he was afraid to turn his head away far enough to look at her, saying instead to the chrome figure at the head of the hood, "That wasn't crying. That was a sick cow choking on a thistle."

"That was crying," she said, and released the accelerator a little. "That was real heart-break crying you heard. Don't forget that."

He knew even then that he would not forget it, whatever it was supposed to mean. She hadn't been wrong about that. He moved closer to her on the seat, and, after making sure no one was coming down the road to see him, put his head on her shoulder. Close up, the green of her dress was a little coarse, not so gentle. He felt the strength of her sifting into him and making him cool. The only thing that worried him was what was he going to tell Dora and Mary when they asked.

What he was going to tell Dora and Mary was one thing he didn't need to worry about. "Daisy calfed down behind the back alders, a pretty little bull," Mary and Dora said. "Not that you'd care, but we had to haul a bucket of water down to poor old Daisy, for the spring's dried up and she looked as parched as a raisin from the heat."

He had two weeks of sun to mull over all that happened that day before they flung something else at him, *they* being fate and twenty pounds of falling cedar limb that dropped its weight down on more than any doctor would ever see. For every day of those two weeks the sun dropped its weight too, sucking the whole world pale by day and retreating at night just long enough to gain new force and momentum for its attack on a new morning. The burnt grass drooped, and the mint, which needed dampness, began to wilt and sag; only the poplars, indifferent or insensitive to heat, flourished as before. Duke spent most of those fourteen days barefoot on the bottom step soaking up the smells the heat lifted (mint and blackberry and the sweet high odour of pine), not enough alive to find himself a spot of shade for comfort.

So that day came, sluggish like them all in a valley that did not know how to live with this much heat, and before he knew it there she was at his shoulder again, saying, "Stirring up mud wasps again, Duke?" as if she couldn't see, and then, "Whose car is that?"

"What car?" he said.

"Coming." She stared at the point where the road slipped behind some trees and out of sight. "I hear it coming."

And it came into sight the colour of fire and just as fast, stopping at the gate and then leaping forward again down the lane chased by its own dust.

When it stopped, two men got out and then turned to help something else set its feet on the ground.

He watched it approach, something not quite human, something between those two men, setting its feet down as if it did not have his father's caulk boots on and as if the wooden walk were broken glass. It wore his father's blue plaid mackinaw too, the one that Duke liked to get close to and smell the grease and sweat. He looked hard, measuring each step with ten heavy heartbeats, and saw that it had a mouth all right, but everything above that was just a big white globe with black holes for eyes. A mummy. Pure white bandages wrapped around and around. A faceless mummy. There was blood on the mackinaw, he saw, a dark stain along the collar. And the hand, too, the hand, smeared red, moving up slowly to touch that white mask.

He yelled, and one of the men said, "Shut up," and the other laughed, opening a large toothless mouth. They kept coming, and he yelled "Momma" three times, and she was there beside him smelling fresh, saying, "Be quiet, Duke," softly.

"Yeah," the toothless man said, "shut that big mouth. Yer old man ain't in any condition to listen to that."

So he stopped, closed his mouth so the yelling was all inside now, and he could hear her whispering, "Oh my God oh my God," and he thought, If that is my father then she will run to him. But she didn't move. She stood there on the step beside him and whispered those words over and over again all the time the toothless man was telling them about the falling limb and the nose laid open and the ear off and the stitches at the doctor's. She did not take one step forward.

It said, "It'll be all right, Lenore. Invite the gentlemen in." From somewhere inside that thing.

With her hand at her mouth, she backed up a step, sobbing, "Oh Albert, oh Albert," twice, and ran back into the house.

Alone now with the two men and his father, he could hear her footsteps thumping up the staircase. She was running for their bedroom. He looked at his father because he knew he had to believe it. He looked and looked, and still it was just a thing between those two men, and no father to anyone in this world. He looked and looked and it did not look back, just stared over his head at the open empty door. Then the man with teeth came up closer and said, "You take your daddy inside and don't make no noise to bother him."

He did not answer that, but walked right past the three of them standing there on the walk as if he could think of a thousand better things to do. Because that was no father to anyone in his world, or she would have run to him. If he just kept walking past those poplars and that mint patch and on into the woods, he would not even have to believe it. Because look how she ran. He thought, let them give me warning, and lay down in the mint beside the verandah to wait.

But waiting was another thing he wasn't ready for. Levelled out like that, with his face close enough to the ground to hear the woodbugs moving, he thought of his sisters, both off to a neighbour's and safe for the time being from whatever it was he was having to face. He thought of Momma running up those stairs and couldn't quite put that together with the image of her walking up to Emma Melville's front door. When he realized (the smell had all been sucked out of the mint) that he did not even know what he was waiting for, he went back to the step and helped his father inside.

"Be patient," his father said, gently.

"Yes sir," he said.

"Thank you," his father said, for his help.

"Maybe she'll be down later," he said. "Sometimes there is nothing anyone can do." But looking up into the black holes in his father's face, he ceased to believe those last words as soon as they were said, as if saying them cancelled any truth there may have been in them once, at some earlier time when life was much simpler that it was now.

III

At the Foot of the Hill,
Birdie's School

There were plenty of reasons to pause.

He had come down out of the hills without rest or incident, though once he had stopped just long enough to eat raw eggs by a stream and cut his finger on a blade of innocent-looking cattail. A nasty wound, but it healed instantly once he'd dismissed it and kept his mind trained like a blue-steel rifle on the coast. Now at the foot of the last and lowest mountain, he sat mounted to look over the town, and picked (one at a time, gently) the pine needles and dead twigs and broken spider threads out of his hair. Hope and the seventeen years, all he'd brought down with him, were light as breath on his mind.

That and the desire, the need, to be quickly corrupted.

Only he wasn't ready to join the McLean gang, which was his one and certain goal. To steal livestock, to pistol-whip Chinese, to shoot Indians right and left, stab policemen, murder strangers, and to be hanged on the gallows at last before his eighteenth birthday. But he needed practice first or how could he expect to be welcome? And anyway, the McLeans were likely to be far away from here, and doing their deeds for all he knew in someone else's lifetime.

Allan McLean Twenty-five years old—the oldest brother—he was tall and bearded and (so it was written) very very mean.

The thing was this: his name was Webster Treherne and the Old Man had kept him alone up there since his second birthday and taught him that time was meaningless and God was All. His mother and (perhaps) his father had retreated before that down the mountain in some other direction with all the twenty others and left the commune shacks to sag and bleach and catch no other voices but theirs. They were a small world but complete: a cluster of leaning sheds in a cedar valley, an old man and a boy; a cow, a dog, a garden, and a few chickens.

Charlie McLean Twenty years old in the pictures, he was the one with the moustache, and with brows as straight as a ruled line, just as mean, it was said, as his brother.

And books. There were plenty of books. There were accounts of history and biographies of great men, collections of poems and tales of love. And every one that he read seemed a warning—that a person so far from crowds was doomed to get lonely sooner or later and go mad. Yet time, a poet told him from the dusty back pages of a fat collection, would take him by his shadow-hand and lead him up out of childhood to the dark swallow-thronged loft of mysteries and manhood. He knew the road of his birth: it was there in the stories of the infamous McLeans, written invisibly between the sentences he read over and over until he was convinced that being bad for a while would be more fun than hanging around for ever on this broken-down farm.

"You don't even know how far out you'll have to walk," the Old Man said.

"It doesn't matter," he said.

"Look, I know you," the Old Man said. "I brought you up. You don't even know if there *is* anything else."

"I do know," he said, "because I can't believe that in all this world there are only two images to reflect the nature of God."

He was just playing with words, though, because he knew for sure that down out of the mountains there were all the people in the books and the people who wrote the books and the twenty-two others who had lived in the commune and left. And at least the McLeans were out there somewhere and the people they were destined to kill (or had killed) and all the other people who were going to get mad enough to hang them (or to have hanged them) and the people who were taking their photographs to put in the books.

Archie McLean At fifteen years he was round and sullen, a nosebiter (some thought that it was being put in jail for biting off an Indian's nose that started their whole long chain of vengeful deeds).

Raising hell. Riding through the countryside screaming "Kill the bastards!" Scaring up fear in people's chests like nervous grouse. You can't ask for much more than that. Except maybe to be there at the last, to wonder if the man you had bribed really had got the job of hangman and cut the ropes the way you promised to pay him for doing, so that when the floor dropped you would only fall through to the ground and then fight your way out.

Alex Hare He was a neighbour, seventeen ("I wish to know what you have against me").

Webster Treherne dismounted, hopped down off the cedar-rail fence, pulled one foot quickly out of the fast-running ditch, and set out down the road towards town. He walked in the pale April sun as if thousands were awaiting his arrival, set his stride to steady and fast, swung his arms as if *they* could help. He walked well out in the centre of the pavement, which was slick as black oil, and soaked up light. His clothes—the deerhide pants, the ancient dark blue suit jacket someone had left behind, the homemade boots—all were older than he was and warm, warm. It seemed more than spring. On either side of the road cola cans gleamed in the roadside clumps of wet grass. A woman stepped out onto the front step of a strange triangular house and yelled for someone to come on inside and watch a television programme. Webster Treherne nearly went over to her fence to find out if she wanted him, too, but thought better of it and did not pause.

Walking, he met a small barefoot boy, straight as a rod under a yoke hung with water buckets, who said, "Where you from, mister?" and "Me, I've been up the river a ways. Spend every blasted day hauling this water." He looked Webster Treherne over from head to foot, then tilted his head towards town. "You'd think someone down in that place would dream up a decent water system. A dime a bucket I get," and then put down his yoke and both wooden buckets to throw a large chunk of coal which hit Webster Treherne on the shoulder and tore his jacket.

Later, a shiny new sports car went by and two yellow-haired girls leaned out the window to make faces at him. One of the girls put fingers into her eyes and nose and mouth and pulled them all out of shape as if she wanted to make him feel sick. He had seen pictures of cars and girls in the books, but the cars had always been clean, and none of the girls had been photographed while pulling ugly faces.

He began to worry. About time and its meaning. About things. About water carriers who threw coal and girls who made faces.

Because here was the town—

(1) A few dozen buildings, some wooden, some brick, but all of them drab and coated with coal dust, facing one another across a dirt road that wound up from the beach. Black slag piles surrounded the town, mountains of coal dust like overturned cones. Out in the harbour a three-masted ship sat heavy and still, waiting for something. On the nearest building: D. L. PETERS GENERAL MERCHANDISE

(2) Blacktop. Blacktop roads. Blacktop lots full of parked cars. And down the harbour a crane loading rolls of newsprint onto a Japanese freighter. Gas stations sat around every intersection as if waiting to pounce, and above them on steel poles their signs revolved like giant eyes watching out for coming business. On a narrow concrete building: G. D. POCK, ROAD SURFACING

It was late afternoon when he walked up the steps of a grey building and knocked on the door.

"I'm Webster Treherne," he said. "Do you have rooms?"

"Rooms?" said the woman who answered the door. "We got plenty of rooms, this is a school." She was a large, sweat-smelling woman who introduced herself as Balk-eyed Birdie. Her left eye, though she tried hard to hold it steady on him, did a loop-the-loop and slid off to one side.

The door was green but inside the front hall everything was a bright red. He felt as if he'd just stepped into someone's mouth. A chandelier hung uvula-like at the far end and swung gently when she slammed the door. A sign on the wall said BIRDIE ATWELL'S FREE SCHOOL and above it a poster told him (black print of a sunset beach) to see Beautiful

British Columbia this year instead of heading east or south.

Besides her sweat he could smell boiled cauliflower.

A school?

"Yes, a school," she said. She pressed her palms together under her chins and pumped her dimpled elbows. "But what would *you* know about that?" She marched ahead of him down the hall, flung a door open the length of her arm and pulled it shut again. "In there. Mr. Muir. Teaches Truth 122."

In the few seconds the door was open Webster Treherne could see three girls and a man, all seated and facing the blackboard as if waiting for some kind of news to write itself in chalk across the board in front of them. On the floor, a fat grey cat turned around and around in a circle nipping at its own tail.

"And here," she said, her face nearly purple with excitement, "is Mr. Mc-Intosh, his room. He teaches a class in love." There were no students in this room, just a man with a moustache who stood up when the door opened, lifted an index finger, said "Aha" as if Webster were just the person he'd been looking for, but Balk-eyed Birdie closed the door in his face.

"And you?" he said. "What do you teach?"

She sucked in her breath, tossed a blood-red apple straight up behind her and stepped back to catch it in the deep soft V of her dress front. "Life," she said, and her bad eye did two loops and slid off to the side for a rest.

He was only seventeen, without much experience in the world, so he said, "That sounds like plenty to me. I've heard lots of people spend a whole lifetime looking for those."

And Balk-eyed Birdie laughed. She had one front tooth capped in gold, one in silver. "Oh we don't teach you how to *find* those things, we teach you how to *lose* them."

"Lady," Webster Treherne said, and jammed out his hand as if straight into fire, "you just found a new pupil. This is the place for me!" He stripped off his clothes and lowered himself into the hot bath she drew for him. When he slumped down low the water came right up under his chin and dead ahead, scratched into the tiles above his feet, were the words *let me play golden* which he read over and over until he fell asleep.

To raise hell. To ride through the countryside yelling "Kill the bas-tards!" To ride on the edge, an apprentice, and watch those four others gallop from murder to murder and on to their deaths as if all of it were not only fun but necessary. Oh Allan McLean, turn, turn your head and acknowledge the boy who rides on the edge! Squint those dark half-Indian eyes at me and say "Come on, kid, the next one's yours."

The trouble was, Webster Treherne was good. The Old Man had seen to that, had told him from the first that the image of a perfect God can't help but be good, was destined by definition to be humane, healthy, and immortal. You couldn't just cancel out that kind of education overnight.

When he had awakened and pulled on his clothes and eaten the thick soup she heated up for him on her old wood stove he went outside for a walk up the main street of town. Going up, he followed the boardwalk past the collieries office, the harness maker and the firehall stables, and went inside a little store whose front verandah sagged under the weight of a huge sign: Hugh Carmichael, Esq., DRUGGIST, LAND DEVELOPER, POST OFFICE. The inside of the building was divided equally amongst its three roles and the proprietor met Webster Treherne in the middle of the room, ready to run to whichever corner was needed.

"Which will it be? Drugs? You got a prescription needs filling?"

"Not that I know of. I never needed any before now."

"Land, then? You're looking for a nice piece of land to build on? I got plenty to show."

"No money," Webster said.

"Then you've come to the Post Office. Mail a letter?"

"Nobody to write to."

Hugh Carmichael, Esq., whirled around twice as if the answer to this nonsense were hiding somewhere behind him, then gave up and rubbed a pudgy hand in his beard. "Would you mind telling me, then, just what it is you came in here for?"

"I'm new in town," Webster said. "Looking around to see where things are."

And he had seen already what he needed to see: that there were three separate cash registers in the room, just waiting to be robbed. A good place to start.

He came out onto the verandah, leaving Hugh Carmichael still scratching around in his beard, and met the small boy again, carrying water, who put down his yoke and threw a big chunk of coal which hit Webster on one cheek and tore away half an inch of flesh. "My aim's improving," the boy said, and picked up his load. "It's just a matter of practice."

Webster slapped the loose flesh back into place and undid the deed. In a universe where all space is taken up with an infinite God of Love there is no room for hatred or harm. An idea cannot be hurt. It had never happened. Going back down towards the school he walked on the concrete sidewalks which were painted in bright colours and inlaid with electric pipes to melt the snow in winter. He nodded to an old lady who came out of an import shop and showed him the fondu pot she'd just bought (on sale, though she admitted to having two better ones at home) and shook hands with a long-haired youth in undershorts who told him he was part of this world, they were *all* part of this world. The sports car went by again, accelerating noisily from a stop light, and the two yellow-haired girls made faces at him. One girl put her thumbs in her ears and flapped her hands. Her tongue flicked in and out like a frog's.

A robbery would be nice. A nice beginning. After all, this was coal, not cattle, country and even the McLeans if they had lived here would probably have got their start by robbing a store. They could hardly expect him to go out and steal cows or horses, after all. What would he be able to do with them if he did?

"It may be interesting for you to go exploring around the town," Balk-eyed Birdie told him, "but Mr. McIntosh has been waiting for you. He wants to get your class started."

"That's all very well," said Webster Treherne, "but when are you going to repaint this ugly hallway?"

They started right away. He went out for the paint while she spread out newspapers on the floor and set up the step ladder.

"White," she said. "What kind of colour is that?"

"The trim can be gold," he said, "or if you want it could be green."

And Mr. McIntosh, who watched them work from the doorway to his classroom, held up one finger and said "Aha." He waited there until they had finished painting the whole hallway, right down to the smallest trim, then scooped Webster into his room and slammed the door. "All right," he said. "It's time we got started."

After his class Balk-eyed Birdie led him upstairs to her own rooms and sat him down at a little table by the dormer window. "Young man," she said, driving a knobby finger into his chest, "I know you from somewhere. I've met you before."

"Not unless you came up the mountain once. And even then I would have been too young for you to recognize."

She shook her head. "It doesn't matter. You're all the same."

The little dormer window looked out across the roofs of other buildings to the harbour. Directly ahead, blocking his view of the strait, was a little island of twisted trees and a few shacks. She told him it was called Gallows Island. "They used to hang people there, right on that point, in the old days."

"Hanged who?"

"Indians. Others."

"What for?"

"Stealing. Shooting. Killing. They hanged the buggers right out there and sometimes just left them a while, in plain view of the whole town."

She made a face at the thought and slapped a basket of fruit onto the table in front of him. Then she sat down across the table and started peeling an orange. "The whole town used to go down to the waterfront to watch that. Everybody. Every single person who could walk and some that couldn't, lined up along the beach watching. There were years when the First of July parade was a comedown by comparison. One time they strung up three all at once, all at one time, three scruffy-looking Yanks who killed one of our police. When they were marched up to the gallows across on the island there the whole crowd on the beach sang right through 'God Save the Queen' and there wasn't a dry eye in sight."

But Webster Treherne was daydreaming again. That island and what she said about it reminded him of the McLean gang, so he told her how his plans were to practise up until he was good enough to be as bad as they were and then go join them.

"Now?" she said.

"Soon."

"Well, suit yourself. There's no telling how long it'll take for you to pass your courses here." She popped the sections of orange into her mouth and then started breaking the peel into little pieces which she stacked up one on top of the other until the whole pile swayed and fell and scattered all over the top of the table. "Some people need more time than others. Those other schools now, all they do is try to fill heads up with things and they can't figure out why it never works. The reason it don't work is they forget you have to knock other stuff out first, to make room. That's what we're here for. To knock stuff out."

Mr. McIntosh knocked stuff out all through the next day. Webster Treherne sat in the classroom listening to a hundred reasons why love wasn't a natural thing for man to feel and how there wasn't anything in this world that deserved it anyway, but all the time one part of his mind was following the McLeans across dusty sagebrush country in hot sun. With them, he pointed guns at terrified ranchers, listened for the sound of an approaching posse. With them he rode into the night, surrounded the pig-scalding farmer by his fire, teased him with the tales of their deeds, then rode off without killing him after all. They had nothing against him; there were too many who really deserved to die. He felt the thudding of the horse's hoofs beneath him, the quick touch of air against his face. He smelled the dust and the horse sweat and the high white smell of fear.

Mr. McIntosh pulled a cluster of grapes out of a paper bag, ripped a handful free and tossed just one at Webster. "If I loved even so much as that one single grape," he said, "I would also have to love God. And then where would I be?" Webster ate the grape and held out his hand for more.

"I didn't come all the way down out of the mountains for fresh fruit," he said. "You'll have to try a little harder than that."

So Mr. McIntosh waited until Webster was asleep on his narrow cot in the back-corner room and hung a hand-painted cardboard sign on the wall beside him. Sometime in the night Webster awoke and lit a match to get a decent look at the big white patch on the wall. It said:

WARNING
If you express even the tiniest bit of love
you will be a part of him. . . . BEWARE

Webster blew out the match and turned away. He decided that tomorrow he would begin, take the first step, move a little closer to his goal.

Asleep, he dreamed of the Old Man, the commune, and a huge black shadow-hand which beckoned him up towards the dark and busy hayloft of the sagging barn.

When he awoke the next morning he had lost all interest in Mr. McIntosh's lessons and went out into the town as soon as Balk-eyed Birdie had given him breakfast. First, though, he helped himself to the gun he found beside the Bible in the drawer by his bed and tied a large red-and-white handkerchief loosely around his neck. Outside, he stopped to watch a miner lead two mules up the street and stop to talk a while with a dressmaker who came out to sweep the boardwalk in front of her shop.

At the door to Hugh Carmichael's triple-duty store he pulled the handkerchief up over the bottom part of his face and took out the gun he'd kept tucked down inside the waistband of his pants.

"I want the money from all three tills," he said.

"At this time of day?" Carmichael said. "There's nothing in them but the little I put in for change."

Webster wondered if he should shoot the proprietor but remembered there were no bullets in the gun. And anyway it was hardly worth while for three near-empty tills.

"What you want to do," Carmichael said, coming closer, his hand buried in his beard, "is go away for now and come back later when there's been a bit of business. This is no time of day for a stick-up."

"Just hand it over. Start with the Post Office."

"And besides, that's the same jacket you had on when you come in here yesterday. Looks like some kind of thing I never seen before, with a rip in the shoulder. I'll recognize your face the next time I see it, you won't get away with this."

But he handed over the money when Webster jabbed the gun in his stomach. Three handfuls of heavy coin. They dropped to the bottom of his pockets and nearly pulled his pants off his hips.

"My wife's sick," Carmichael whined. "Don't do this to me. She's dying."

"I'm sorry to hear that," he said, heading for the door.

"It's the consumption. It's got her for sure." His voice hung onto that last word, dying slowly.

At the doorway Webster turned for a last look at the room. The Mc-

Leans would shoot the fat man, put a bullet right into his ugly face and watch that body collapse to the floor. But he couldn't do that, not even for them. And besides, it had been a successful hold-up; even they wouldn't be ashamed.

"I hope you get it, too!" Mr. Carmichael yelled after him. "I hope you come down with the exact same thing and suffer just the way she's suffering!"

Webster took a taxi well out into the country, then hitchhiked a ride back in with a farmer in a pickup truck. The farmer listened to rock music on his radio all the way in and let Webster off behind Birdie's school.

"What's consumption?"

"Consumption?" Birdie said. Her bad eye shivered like a struck bell.

He hid the money beneath the bed, took off his clothes, and crawled under the blankets. Balk-eyed Birdie came in with Mr. Muir and pulled up a chair to sit where she could look right into his face. "That's Mr. Muir's job," she said.

"What is?"

"To tell about thinks like that."

"Consumption," Mr. Muir said. "Life is very frail."

"TB they call it now," Birdie said.

Webster was only too happy to close his eyes and let Mr. Muir fill in. He listened as symptom after symptom was laid out one after another; each one more gruesome than the last, and felt Balk-eyed Birdie's face close to his—watching his expression for signs of delight or revulsion, whichever. She smelled of sweat and cauliflower.

He opened his eyes and peeked at Mr. Muir, who was talking with so much enthusiasm in his face that he might have been describing a circus. His eyes rolled up to watch the beautiful picture he was painting, his hands darted back and forth, like busy birds.

"And that's not all," he said.

"Not?"

"It's only a beginning," Birdie said, patting his forehead. "Nobody gets that any more. But there's plenty others they *do* get. Hundreds and hundreds. Mr. Muir will tell you about them all and how easy they are to catch and what they feel like."

"Tomorrow," Mr. Muir said. "Be in my classroom right after breakfast. I'll be waiting."

But Webster didn't make it. By the end of the day of the robbery he was coughing. He slept badly and woke up the next morning with a burning forehead and pains in his chest. When Birdie came in she made a face and opened the window. "It stinks in here," she said. Then she took off her clothes and crawled into bed beside him.

"Your chest rattles," she said, and ran a hand down over his groin.

"I can't move," he said. "I feel as if the ceiling has come down to sit on me."

She rubbed her hands in his sweat and dried them in his hair. She rested one huge white breast on his throat and sang a lullaby. She climbed on top of him and lay down but he couldn't breathe so she wrapped her arms and legs around him, gave a few heaves, then rolled right over onto her back and held him prisoner. "You're the best pupil we've had yet," she said.

And cradled in the soft arms of Balk-eyed Birdie, fighting for every breath, rocking gently on her white belly, he saw a quick dark movement out of the corner of his eye. It was the water carrier again, the boy, grinning at him through the open window. "This time I've got you," he cried and threw a great chunk of coal that ripped a foot-long strip of flesh off Webster's back, down almost to the bone.

He rolled onto the sheets and tried to undo the deed. He lay on his back and thought the boy and the coal and the wound right out of existence. They were nothing. But they leapt back; the pain came back into his flesh and he sat up to scream. He tried again and again to think them away but he couldn't remember the reasons. The logic was gone. He couldn't think of a single reason for not believing that pain was as real as he was. He lay on his stomach and wept while Balk-eyed Birdie mopped the blood off his back and poured something into the gash and covered it over with cloths and tape. Then he fell asleep.

The McLeans came in through the open window. First Allan the eldest, then Charlie and Archie (still a kid, two years younger than Webster), and finally Alex Hare, who looked as if he didn't know why he was there. They stood around the bed and looked just exactly the way he had seen them in pictures. Allan, the bearded one, in jacket and waistcoat and bandanna, thumbs hooked into the pockets of his pants. Charlie, too, standing slouched and easy, in looser, dustier clothes. The two younger boys scowled at him as if they couldn't see any reason for not pulling out their guns and shooting Webster Treherne right there in bed without a single word.

"You're a long ways from home," he said.

But Allan McLean just shrugged both shoulders and twisted his mouth a bit to one side. He lifted his head and turned it a little. "Them nooses," he said, "they're ready."

A short dry sound came from Archie McLean's throat. "We promised that Makai something," he said. "He'll cut the rope."

The others snickered and shifted feet. They were proud of this final trick, this ultimate joke on their enemies.

"At least if *we'd* robbed that store today we'd've done it right," Charlie McLean said. "You don't know nothing."

"But you're learning," Allan McLean said, and squeezed Webster's knee. "It's too bad them nooses're ready so damn soon. You might've made out all right."

Archie McLean scowled and Alex Hare spat on the floor. Webster still wasn't sure they weren't going to shoot him or knife him to death. They had never needed much provocation before.

"Let me come with you," he said, his head spinning and the weight of the whole house on his chest. "Let me ride with you just once and find out what it's like. Let me rob storekeepers and shoot Indians, let me scare strangers and threaten women."

"You're nearly a hundred years too late for that," Balk-eyed Birdie sang out. She came into the room and sat on the side of the bed and poured something down his throat. When he looked up again the four men were gone. "You're graduating from this school without even taking all the courses."

"And what have I missed?" he said. "What would your class have taught me?"

"Missed nothing," she said. "You're finding out for yourself. You're going to die." She sat up and folded her hands in her lap like a mother who has just delivered wonderful news. "By the sound of that chest I don't give you long."

"Die?" he said, for no one had ever told him what it meant.

"Die." She nodded as if to unheard dirges. "Die. Expire. Decease. Nobody I've ever heard of got to the stage you're at and recovered. That is the reward you get for learning your lessons well, to get sick and die and then rot in the ground. Just when you've found out what you are, you'll cease to be." She smiled on him as if to say he'd made her proud.

He tried to speak, to tell her he wasn't exactly thrilled with the reward she offered, but his throat was full and it took all his energy just to cough it clear.

"I never seen anyone go through so fast," she said. "You really must've *wanted* it. You've got more than TB."

The phlegm burst clear for a moment and he hurled curses at her. "Do you think *this* is the only reason I came from . . . from . . . ?" But he couldn't even remember where he had come from. She could have convinced him easily that he had been born in this very room just a day or so ago.

"From the mountains, yes. But don't get upset. Mr. Muir will phone a doctor. We'll get you help. They'll send you to a sanitarium or somewhere. There's no hope for you now, but I don't want you kicking the bucket in my place. Do it clean and right, somewhere else, in a hospital."

From the mountains, yes. He had come down out of the hills without rest or incident, though once he had stopped just long enough to eat raw eggs by a stream and cut his finger on a jagged blade of cattail. Down out of the green hills, from the farm, the green and singing farm where grass uncut grew nearly as high as the buildings and an old man's voice rang like stones dropped into streams.

"I can't believe this thing is me," he said, and she swung to frown on him. "You'll never convince me of that. This isn't what I came down here to find."

"It's what you found," she said. "It's what you wanted. A black and smelly grave. How do you like them apples, my friend?"

"Then I've been cheated. This sack of sore bones will never be me, say what you like."

She scowled. "Oh yeah? Then what are you, a fish?"

"Not fish or frog or sack of bones. Something else."

"A sack of horse shit, maybe. A bag of turds."

"An idea. Somewhere else, everywhere. An idea in the Old Man's mind and therefore perfect. You can't destroy *that*."

She cracked a shoe across the side of his head. "Is that the thanks we get?" she yelled. "Is that all the gratitude you can show us?" She stood up and threw things at him, tossed floor mat and lamps and books and pictures and shoes and hair brushes at him until he was nearly buried. She stood in the doorway, her face twisted and red, and screeched. "I don't think you've learned a goddam thing!"

He was sorry that when she came back with the doctor he wouldn't be there, that he would miss seeing them look under the covers and under the bed and in the closet, would miss hearing her curses and her attempts to tell what she didn't understand herself. He was sorry that she probably would never be able to explain the heavy coins or the painted hallway to her staff or to anyone else. But he wished her well and hoped for the sake of her sanity that she wouldn't discover his absence soon enough to go out into the street and somehow by accident discover him hiking in the pale April sunlight up the road that led away from town, up from the harbour past the coal mines, through the farmland and the swamps to the base of the hills. Or hear him sing in his freedom up the long gravel climb through the trees.

After the Season

About fifty miles up the coast past the end of all public roads, in a little bay where the wildest tides throw logs and broken lumber far up the land like spat-out bones, Hallie Crane ran a cafe and a small cabaret for tourists staying at the fishing camp. Although there was a wharf built well out into the bay so fishing boats could tie up without being smashed against rocks, and down in the curve of the shore there was a small gravel beach where the bravest American tourists could run in for a quick swim and rush out again, Hallie's place and most other buildings were perched up on the rock and looked as if a good wind would fling them right out into the strait. The café was so close to the edge it had legs straight down into the water and whenever Hallie wanted to go anywhere, down the slope to Morgan's boat rental or around the bay to the well, she had to walk on a rickety boardwalk that ran right past her door and hung out over the sea. Tourists kept life jackets on their children the whole time they stayed in the camp.

Hallie liked it well enough, at least in the summer. When the last tourists left in September she squinted up her two bright green eyes at them and told them it had been fun just having them around. "Now there'll be nobody here at all for the next eight months except Morgan and me." She had a grown family down-island where the grey ribbon of highway went right under their noses when they sat in their living room, and she could have moved down to stay with them any time she wanted if she was willing to keep off the bottle, but she never did.

She never went back, hadn't seen her own daughter for eight years. They told her when she left not to bother unless she could stay sober, and though she hadn't touched a drink now for two years she still hadn't got around to packing up and catching the boat out for the winter. She could imagine herself landing in on them easily enough, tall and straight and good looking as ever, and hear their shrieks of surprise: "What? You can't be old enough to be this baby's grandmother!" But oh yes, she was, she was fifty-one years old. She could walk like a youngster on her long narrow legs, could tell a joke with all the youth she knew was still inside, could snap her eyes in anger or fun as sharp and quick as she ever could. She touched up her hair now; natural blonde faded out faster than any other colour. But her face, though it had added laugh lines around the eyes and the skin was drier than it used to be, was still striking, still pretty. She could see herself going back, could imagine the fuss they'd make, but every fall when the season ended, a sharp cold fear inside told her to put it off for another year.

During the summer Morgan, who owned the camp and ran it practically single-handed except for Hallie's help, lived down in his rooms behind the boat house and Hallie lived in the back of her café. They treated each other like strangers, like employer and employee, like invisible beings. When he came into the café and sat with his hairy arms folded on the counter, he ordered coffee without looking at her. When she walked down to his place, picked her way along the boardwalk hanging on to the rail, to tell him the plumbing was plugged up or the toaster needed fixing, she walked in and out amongst the boats while she talked, touching them as if feeling whether the paint was good enough to last the season. But when the tourists had gone and Hallie had tidied up the café and the little cabaret room beside it and closed the shutters over the windows, she moved down the hill into Morgan's rooms and stayed there until the first lot of people arrived the next June.

Not suddenly. Not just like that as if they had been thinking about it all summer and could hardly wait. Every year she was a little surprised all over again. Morgan was only thirty-three years old and still romantic, and he insisted on courting her, luring her, as if every October were their first. If she had just packed her suitcase and carried it down the hill and moved in he would have been disappointed, might even have tossed her out, and probably would have pouted all through the winter.

Every October he arrived at her door soon after the others had gone: a grinning, hairy, solid little man. "Dammit," he said, "you're a good-looking woman!" He came up behind and put his arms around her and ran his hands down her breasts and stomach and thighs. "Dammit, you've got it all over them other girls!" She slapped his hands and he went away for a while. But he came back again and again. He told her he was getting so randy for you-know-what that he was scared he'd go crazy and run screaming over the hills behind. He asked her how would she like to be raped. He brought gifts: chunks of smoked fish, handfuls of shells he'd found, magazines left behind in the cabins by tourists. It was usually about a week before Hallie recognized the signals that said it was all right for her to start giving in now. She stopped slapping his hands, stopped threatening to radio out for help, stopped keeping her distance. She packed her suitcase.

This year though, when the last boat had sailed out of sight down the strait, she didn't feel like going through all that drawn-out procedure, she just didn't have the energy. "Cut it out," she said. "I can't see any point in all this fooling around. Can't I just pack up and move down?"

But he insisted. "What do you want to be?" he said. "A whore?" His breath smelled of smoked fish.

"All right, I'll pretend then. I'll pretend I won't do it but we both know I will."

He put his hands on her and told her what a good-looking woman she still was but she slapped the side of his head hard enough to knock him against the wall. "What the hell?" he said, his blue eyes hot with tears.

"You wanted me to pretend, well I'm pretending. Now leave me alone."

He grinned at her. "You don't want me to touch you because you've put on weight."

"Go to hell."

"You're afraid if I touch you I'll find out how fat you've got," he said, leering. "I saw you gorging yourself all summer on them apple pies. Putting on pound after pound."

"I'd like to know how you noticed what I was doing when you never once tore your little piggy eyes off that blonde bitch from Seattle."

"Shoving it in when you thought no one else was looking. Putting on layer after layer of fat. Turning into a big cow."

"I haven't put on a single pound, and," skirting his outstretched hand, "you'll just have to take my word for it."

Two days later they were just getting to the stage where he would threaten to force her when the stranger arrived and interrupted the whole business.

It was the worst October she could remember. Black cloud moved in and sat on them like a heavy lid. Rain came down steadily through night and day. A wind had whipped the sea into such a turmoil and thrown the tide so high up the land that sometimes Hallie expected to wake up in the morning and find herself floating. It was always a small surprise to discover no walls had been ripped off, no windows bashed in, no pieces of roof lifted. She kept a fire roaring in the cast-iron stove and got up several times during the night to shake the grates and add more wood. If she didn't drown, she would probably burn to death.

She was on the boardwalk tossing garbage down for the few gulls that still clung to the coast when she saw the stranger's boat. At first she thought it was nothing but a driftwood log, dipping and leaping with the waves, and when it got closer there appeared to be something alive, a large bird perhaps, perched in the middle and riding. It wasn't until it had entered the bay and came rushing in towards shore that she saw it was a small aluminum boat with a man inside holding on for dear life and not even trying to steer with the handle on the useless little outboard motor. She ran down the boardwalk and across the beach in time to see it thrown ahead onto the gravel, sucked back, then thrown ahead again far enough for the man to leap out, fall to his knees, get up again, grab the rope, and drag the boat up high enough to tie it to a log. He turned two pale runny eyes on her and said, "Thank God I got to civilization."

"You didn't," she said. "There's only me and Morgan and all these empty shacks. Even our radio set-up went on the blink a couple days ago."

He wiped a hand over his wet face, shook himself like a dog, tipped forward to let water run off the back of his neck. "It'll have to do," he said, flicking an ear. "I'm not going back out into that."

Morgan came out of the boat house, walking—as he always did—as if his body besides being solid and heavy was also hot and he had to keep both hands and arms well away in order not to get burned. He looked the little man over like an interesting log the sea had washed in, then looked at Hallie as if to say, "Now what have you done?"

"We better get you somewhere and dry you off," Hallie said.

The little man bent down again and wrung out his straight blond hair, then flung it back with a snap that could have broken his neck, and turned to look out at the water. "I wouldn't want to've spent much longer on that," he said.

"You wouldn't've," Hallie said. "You'd've been *in* it before long, dead as a thrown-back dogfish. Come on, let's get you over to Morgan's place, warm you up."

Morgan stood in their way and scowled at Hallie. Then, suddenly, he smiled as if the scowl had been about something else altogether, and said, "Don't you think your place would be better?"

"Nothing wrong with yours," she said. "It's good and warm."

"Too warm," Morgan said. "And too small. I bet you've got a nice fire on up there in the café, maybe even a cup of coffee."

"Look," the man said, "I don't care where you put me, just so long as I can go somewhere to dry off. I may drown right here on shore if you keep arguing." And he started walking up the slope towards the café.

When they'd stripped him down to dry out his clothes there wasn't very much to him. In his undershorts he looked like a young boy—Hallie had seen bigger bones in a turkey—but his face was the face of a man in his forties. When he handed over his clothes for her to hang up above the stove, looking so small and drenched and lost, she wanted to tickle him under the chin and say, "Cheer up, little man, you haven't fallen off the end of the world!" But there was something about his face, a long narrow pointed face with sunken cheeks and pale fast-moving eyes, that told her if she so much as touched him, treated him like a child, he would snarl and growl and maybe knock her hand away with one of those frail arms.

"Here," she said. "You can put on my robe and we'll dry out your undershorts too."

Morgan eyed him as if he expected to see him turn into a rat and start gnawing the house down. Hallie could see resentment already settling in around his mouth.

"I'm a teacher," he told them when his white jockey shorts were hanging on the line over the stove and he was wrapped up in Hallie's red chenille bath robe. He found a cigar in one of his pockets but it was too wet to light and he threw it in the fire, spitting pieces of damp tobacco off his tongue. "I taught high school geography but I quit my job in June and started exploring up and down this coast."

"You should've tried elementary," Hallie said. "The kids wouldn't've been so big and scary there."

The little man looked at Hallie as if she were the stupidest pupil he'd ever run across. Then he looked up at the bare rafters. "My name is Hamilton Grey," he said. "I have never been afraid of a person, big or small, in my life. Least of all a geography student. What scares me is not people but mankind." And he looked at her again, as if it were all her fault, as if she were the mother of the whole blessed lot. "The stupidity of mankind appals me."

Hallie looked at Morgan and Morgan rolled his eyes. "I don't know anything about smart or stupid," she said. "Nice is good enough for me. If a person's considerate of other people it don't matter how much brains he's got."

He looked up again and snorted. He and the rafters knew she'd just proved his point. "Nice people are spilling oil into the oceans," he said. "Nice people are busy inventing new biological warfare weapons."

He told them he had this theory. Whatever your instincts tell you is right is exactly wrong. He told them instincts were good enough for the individual's survival but all wrong for society. For example, he told them, everybody's instinct says pornography increases sex crimes but the opposite is true, look at Denmark. He told them everybody's instinct says if a kid is bad hit him, but that is the surest way to make him worse. Look at wild land, he said, instinct says tame it, kill all the scary animals, log off the useless trees, turn it into something we can handle. And prisons too, he said. The whole idea of punishment is instinctive but does exactly the opposite to what is good for society.

"Mister Grey," she said. "Is there anything at all good about people in your opinion?"

He looked as if he'd never encountered that question before. He thought for a long time, stroking his pointed jaw. Finally, he said, "Yes, one thing. His potential. Man has one thing—mind—that makes everything possible."

"How long you plan on staying?" Morgan said.

"I didn't plan anything. My motor's conked out."

"I can fix that," Morgan said.

"And I'm not setting out again as long as this storm keeps up."

When Hallie went out into the kitchen Morgan followed her and said, "You let him have your bed and come on down to my place tonight."

She told him he'd better watch his tongue. "There's a spare bed in my back room," she said. "Besides, what would he think of us?"

"He already doesn't think much of us. It wouldn't make any difference."

"He's a school teacher," she said. "It wouldn't be right. I just couldn't do it."

Morgan sat down and tried to pull her onto his knee but she held back. "He doesn't care. It's none of his business."

"My son-in-law is a teacher," she said. "I won't do it."

"In that case," Morgan said, "we will have to get rid of him."

But it wasn't easy. All the next day he worked on the little man's outboard motor. He took it apart, washed every piece in gasoline, put in new spark plugs. He replaced a part in the water pump. By evening it was running as smooth as a new motor but the storm hadn't died down.

"Looks like it's settled in for a long haul," Mr. Grey said, looking out the front windows of the café. "I'm not heading out into that." He brought all his equipment in from the boat—his tent and sleeping bag and cooking utensils and food and books—and dropped them in the middle of Hallie's floor.

"Put them up on the stage out of the way," she said.

So he set up camp on the raised alcove beside the piano that Hallie played whenever there was a crowd that wanted to dance. There was a harvest moon painted on the back wall with SWING YOUR PARTNER printed across it. He set up the tent as if he could foresee rain coming through the roof, laid out his sleeping bag inside, and opened up his camp stove.

"I'll radio for a plane," Morgan said.

"No plane would fly in this," Hallie said. "And besides, the set is broke."

And while he spent the next day trying to get the radio set to work, Hallie tried to find out more about Hamilton Grey. Because it was a long time since she'd talked to any teacher except her son-in-law, a sharp-eyed man who made her nervous, she didn't know how to go about making conversation. She scrubbed floors and cleaned windows and stacked furniture in the dance room and he listened to her questions from behind a book, sitting on the edge of the stage.

"You got somebody somewhere worrying about you right now? Somebody scared you're drowned?"

A page turned. "Mmph."

"No wife? No children, no parents?"

He lowered the book and looked at her. "If I had all that lot hanging around my neck, would I be sailing up and down the strait taking my own sweet time? There isn't a soul to care if I end up at the bottom of the ocean."

"It may not look like it," Hallie said, "but I've got a family. A grown daughter."

There was no indication that he had heard her but she continued. "She's married to a teacher too, like you, only he teaches chemistry and is a lot taller. They live in the same house my husband and I lived in for all twelve years of our marriage, right on the damn highway, only the highway's been widened since then, and every time a car goes by you'd think it was coming right through the living room. I'm surprised they don't move out and build a house of their own, but I guess all the savings they have get used up just living through the summer. They've got two kids."

He turned a page, then turned back to reread the bottom line and turned again.

"I bet you never thought I was a grandmother," Hallie said.

He looked up to see if he'd missed anything, then looked down again.

Hallie shifted chairs around noisily. "If bad manners is something they're teaching at universities now you must've got top marks but I can't say that I'm impressed."

He closed the book but kept a finger between the pages. "What I'm wondering," he said, "is why you haven't gone back to stay with your daughter. How come you're all alone up here with that Tarzan the ape-man when you could be with your family?"

"Scared I guess," she said, quickly, because if she had paused to think about it she would have told him none of his business. "I'd be back on the bottle in a week if I went down there. I'd be so useless—don't know how to talk to kids, not even my own grandchildren, without feeling like a fool—and that long beak-nosed son-in-law watching me like a hawk to see what makes me tick—I'd be throwing back the rye just to get through the day."

After supper Morgan came into her kitchen and said he hadn't been able to get anything on the radio. He sat down at her table, spread out his elbows, and slurped up a cup of coffee. He swore after every mouthful.

"Morgan," she said. "Would you say I'm getting old looking?"

"Naw."

"Well, since he came you haven't said one nice thing to me. If I'm getting old and fat just tell me."

"Hell no," he said, and pulled her down onto his lap. He dug fingers into the flesh of her thigh. "You're still a good-looking woman."

"That Mr. Grey makes me feel old and stupid."

"Oh him," Morgan said, and threw a sneer at the wall that separated the kitchen from the café and dance room. He ran one hand up the inside of her skirt but she put her hand on top of it and held it still.

"You're not doing much to get rid of him," she said. "Maybe he'll be here all winter."

He looked down at the lump his own hand made under her skirt and scowled. "I'll get rid of the bastard," he said, and pushed her off him so he could stand up. "But first I guess I better go in and tell him about the radio."

After Morgan had gone back to his boat house Mr. Grey told her the ape-man had nearly attacked him. His hair was on end, as if he had been running his fingers through it backwards, and his quick pale eyes were darting everywhere. Hallie couldn't help feeling sorry for him; after all he was a teacher and probably not used to people like Morgan, mean and free, without school rules to hold him back.

But just when she was beginning to feel warm inside with the pity she felt, he started to laugh, confusing her. He took out a handkerchief and blew his nose, one hard snort on either side. "You know what he told me?" he said.

"Don't listen to him," she said. "Morgan's liable to make all sorts of threats he won't carry out. There's not much harm in him."

"He said, 'You know what you're buttin' in on?'"

"What?"

"He said I walked in on the middle of a mating ritual, that's what he told me."

"A mating dance of two horny people," Morgan had said. "You landed in here when we'd hardly got started. Hell, every year we go at it all over again like a couple of rutting mountain sheep, only we wait until after the season." He rolled his eyes as if to say, You know what I mean. "Right through the summer while the tourists are here we don't hardly talk to each other. She lives up here in her dance hall serving meals and I live down there in my boat house. A person wouldn't even think we knew each other."

"This is none of my business," Mr. Grey had said.

But Morgan had gone on. "Then every October we look around, see, and there's nobody left here. The tourists are all gone. The loggers, they're back but they're inland a ways. So pretty soon we're sniffing around each other, see, and then we're snarling and clawing each other. Finally we land in bed like a clap of thunder and that's where we spend most of the winter."

"Like a couple of animals!"

"You bet, mister," Morgan had said. "You ever see a mountain sheep going after it? If he wants to he can run sixty miles an hour on his back legs. Think about that coming together!"

Hallie didn't wait for Mr. Grey to tell her anything more that Morgan had said or how he had got around to almost attacking him. She left the room and shut the door behind her, gently so he wouldn't think she was upset. She stood stiffly for a long time in front of the little mirror that hung over the kitchen sink, her head throbbing like an inboard motor, her hand laid out stiff and white against the vibrations of her breast. She was a good-looking woman—the mirror told her that—and not even the dyed hair could make her look cheap. She was one of those women who kept their looks, who stayed smart and slim and attractive even into old age, but that was a different thing from what Morgan had made her sound like. It wasn't a mountain sheep he made her sound like; it was a mink.

She went out onto the boardwalk and sat on a bench that leaned against her front wall. The wind had died down a little and the rain had stopped falling but the surface of the water was still slate-black and heaving. There wasn't a gull to be seen, gone inland for safety. She sat facing all of it, wouldn't have moved even if an earth tremor had sent the whole building down crazily into the bay, and felt the hot flush of shame creeping up her face. The crashing of the waves against the pilings beneath her was no stronger in her than the beating of her own heart. She wanted a drink.

Hallie Crane had felt real shame only once before in her life. She wasn't a person who did things she later regretted. Most of her actions were deliberate, considered, and consistent. Memories were usually pleasant. But once, just once, she had fallen into something she was so ashamed of that even now, eighteen years later, its memory could send her to bed for a day or more. When the phone call came telling her that her husband had died in the Vancouver hospital, she was at a community dance, nearly drunk. Her daughter had taken the message.

That wasn't me! she wanted to scream at the memory of it. That wasn't the real me, that was someone else.

And now, too, she wanted to tell that little school teacher in there that he had been given the wrong impression. She wanted to set things straight in his mind. She went back into the kitchen, checked her face in the mirror again, and walked into the café where he was helping himself to a handful of sugar cubes.

"You shouldn't listen to Morgan," she said. "He's given you the wrong impression about us. Probably wanted to shock you."

He threw a sugar cube into his mouth and crunched it between his teeth. "Is there some place around here where a person can go for a walk?"

When they both had their rain clothes on, she led him up the trail that climbed in a series of switch-backs up the slope of the hill behind the buildings. "Deer made this," she said, "and elk." The wet leaves of salal and Oregon grape knocked against their legs and soaked the bottom half of their slacks. When Mr. Grey hung onto a small scrubby pine to help pull himself up a particularly steep part of the trail, its roots were so shallow in the rocky soil that he pulled it right out and fell backward a few feet and rolled over against a windfall fir.

At last they reached the top, however, and she stood aside for him to see that beyond it there was only a small swampy valley of burnt snags and another, higher hill. "From down there I thought this was the end," he said, and she told him no, that it was only the beginning. "Just the first small step. It goes up and up and finally you're above timber altogether and in year-round snow and then it drops straight down into the Pacific."

The fishing camp below was nearly obscured by the fine rain which had started, and by the mist. The small handful of buildings looked as if they too, like Mr. Grey, had been washed in by the tide and left stranded between the sea and this hill. Smoke from the little café stood up in a thin white column, then spread out level and flat as if somewhere between the roof and the top of the hill there was an invisible ceiling.

Hallie sat down on a rock. No matter how hard she looked she could not see the mainland mountains through the dense grey wall of cloud. Below, the tiny figure of Morgan left one of the cabins and walked across to the boat house. "You shouldn't pay him any attention," she said. "He'll just give you the worst impression of things."

Mr. Grey sat down on the ground beside her. "It doesn't matter to me," he said. "I don't give a damn what you two do. When I get out of here I'll probably never think of either one of you again."

She could see him going through his life, wiping out the people he met as if they were only figures on a chalkboard. Or as if he were that wall of cloud, blocking out the whole world.

"There's nothing about you that's special. There's no way that either one of you have touched me or entered me or altered my life. When I leave I'll be the same as when I arrived, my life won't be changed, and there won't be a thing about my stay here worth remembering."

Hallie gritted her teeth. He may be a smart school teacher who thought he knew everything but there was one thing she knew better than he did. "You can't touch someone else without it affecting your life in some way," she said.

"Ah, but here's the difference: you haven't touched me." He broke off a branch of salal and started chewing on its tip. "You circle around me, you and that hairy ape of yours, making faces and screeching noises at me, but it's as if I'm watching from inside a bubble of glass. You can't penetrate. You can't touch me. You never will. I'll go on watching your mating dance without being affected in any way."

Hallie shuddered. "Mating dance?" He sounded as crude as Morgan. "Is that what you really think, just because he said it? Do you really think I'm like that?"

But he didn't answer. He found the veins in a salal leaf more interesting than her. He probably thought she had never done anything educational in her whole life, never even read a book. Well listen, she had. She told him about this story she once read, an old-fashioned tale in some book some-body'd given to her when she was a little girl. This girl in the story, this Proser-something, was out running around in a place something like this, pulling a bush right out of the ground just like Mr. Grey had and up out of that hole came old Pluto, the king of the underworld, riding in a chariot, and hauled her off against her will down into his deep horrible black place.

"Proserpina," he said. "I know the story, yes." He got up and started following the trail back from the edge, towards the swamp. She hurried to catch up to him.

"Then you know her old lady found her all right," she said, "but not before she'd half broken a promise not to eat a thing down there. So for the rest of her life, if you can believe it, she had to spend six months with her mother and six months down in the underworld with him."

"With Pluto," he tossed over his shoulder. "I didn't think anyone remembered those tales any more." They were walking on logs now; the ground was soft and damp, with a musty swamp smell. Burnt snags stood around like silent black totems.

"Anyway, that's what I feel like. Only I don't get six and six. I get three months, four if I'm lucky, of normal living with people treating me like a human being. Then along comes October and he starts in dragging me down."

"Morgan?" Mr. Grey stood on the edge of the little lake, a hundred feet of green scum in front of him, a log laid out on it like a wharf. He turned and his pale eyes crinkled, as if he was ready to disbelieve whatever she was going to say next.

Hallie stopped walking. "Pulling me down into his hell with him. Clawing at me and slobbering and pulling me down, living in slime."

Mr. Grey walked out onto the log, straight out over that floor of scum. "If I remember the story right, the girl didn't mind it so much. She got so she kind of liked old Pluto."

Hallie felt as if she might explode. "Nobody likes living in hell," she cried.

At the other end of the log he turned and faced her. "The whole world loves it," he said. He looked slightly amused, as if she were a child run up against something every adult understood. "As soon as a human being chooses to pay attention to his five senses he's electing to live in hell." He let her chew on that for a while, then bounced a little on the log to watch it disturb the thick surface of the lake. "If he pays attention to the demands of the senses, if he uses them to make judgments, if he listens to their reports of pain and disease, he's living in hell. There's nothing so special about you."

Hallie walked by herself back to the edge of the slope and sat down. After a while he came up behind her and she said, "All right, mister, you know so much. Is there a way out?"

He chuckled. "Sure there is," he said. He started down the hill. "I guess you were hoping I'd say everybody is doomed to be miserable and so you're pretty normal after all. D'you think that just because I'm soured on humanity I don't see its possibilities? Well, lady, like it or not, there are some happy people in the world."

"Who?" she demanded.

He stopped on the trail and looked up at her. "It'd be a lot easier for all of us if we didn't look around once in a while and see people who can smile."

"Who are they?" she said, running down to catch up and nearly crashing right into him.

He pushed his face so close to hers she had to step back. He spoke as if he were chipping the words out one at a time, once and for all. "Those who refuse to ride in the chariot!"

Hallie felt as if his breath had turned all of her into some cold rigid material. She looked into his eyes, pale, murky, trembling from the force of his words. A thin, barely visible red line ran from the edge of one grey disc down into the corner by the tear duct, casual as a lost thread. He was human. He was human. She lifted one hand and brushed a finger against his cheek.

Mr. Grey leapt back from her touch and tripped over a rock. He rolled over and over down the hill, slid a few feet, then rolled again until he slammed up against a tree. By the time Hallie got down that far he was on his feet again, walking with a slight limp down the deer trail to the fishing camp.

She'd handled it all wrong, she knew. She hadn't even behaved the way Hallie Crane normally would. That night in bed she thought of all the people she had known back home, the friendly nosy country people who had been her neighbours for nearly twenty years, and she tried to see herself as they would. Hallie Crane? You want to know how Hallie Crane would treat a little shit like that, spouting his nonsense? She'd throw back her head and laugh. You'd see her long white throat. You'd hear her deep harsh laugh. Hallie Crane has the sexiest laugh a man ever heard and that's exactly what she'd turn on that smart-alec school teacher. She'd laugh and ask him who the hell he thought he was.

But she hadn't done that. She didn't even have her old laugh any more. She'd kept her looks and her figure and her long slim legs, but somewhere along the way she'd lost her deep throaty laugh. Those people wouldn't recognize her without it. No wonder she's scared to come home, they'd say. Hallie Crane without her laugh isn't Hallie Crane.

And she knew that she would never go back. There was nothing strong enough to pull her back to that place; not friends, not daughter, not grandchildren. She didn't want to see her son-in-law again. She didn't want to see the house again, or the small farms that surrounded it. Some day, maybe, she would send down enough money for her daughter and the children to fly up and spend part of the summer with her. That would be nice. Her daughter could help out in the café, talk to the tourists, find out that the kind of life her old lady lived wasn't so bad after all. Maybe Morgan would take them fishing.

While Hallie was lying in bed planning her future she heard Mr. Grey get up and go outside. Just keep on walking, she thought, walk right on over the mountains and down-island until you find the road, then keep on walking still. You've stirred up here all that needs to be stirred. How nice it would be to wake up in the morning and find he had gone, that he had shoved out to sea in his boat and disappeared. She would worry perhaps, for a few minutes, that he was in danger or even drowned, but soon she would say it was his own choice and forget him.

Though Hallie believed a little in the power of thought, she never expected immediate results. The sound of lumber breaking, snapping like kindling, and a long scream right outside the café brought her up out of the bed and to her feet. Outside her front door she discovered a large section of the boardwalk railing had been broken away. There was no sound below but the slapping of the sea. "Mr. Grey?" she said, in case he was close by and watching her. But no answer came so she yelled his name into the dark. She felt for a moment as if she were alone, the only person left in the world, abandoned. She screamed for Morgan, who came up the slope eventually with a strong flashlight he aimed down into the water splashing sloppily around the pilings, and it wasn't until morning that they found Mr. Grey's body, back under the boardwalk and nudging like a dead fish against the rock her house was built on.

"You son of a bitch," Hallie said to Morgan. "Did you do this?" Morgan came up close and looked hard at her. The rain was rolling off his flattened hair and down his face, dripping from the end of his nose. "Do you think that?" he said.

She looked into his eyes, steady as stone. "No," she said, and turned away. She went back into the café and waited until he had fished the body out and came to bang on her door.

"We'll have to bury him," he said.

She shuddered. "We're not *that* far from civilization. It doesn't seem right."

She turned away but he stepped in and walked around to face her and wrapped his arms so tight around her she couldn't move. She could smell the smoked fish on his breath, could see the black spikes of his week-old beard. She tried to push away but his grip was too tight, his arms too strong.

"What're you going to do?" he said.

"Going home."

"Hell you are. You're home now."

"I mean down-island, back to my family. I'll fly out as soon as the weather changes. I want to get away from this goddam hole."

"You'll never go back there again and you know it."

During the following week the storm continued. Waves hit the rocks and leapt up almost as high as the boardwalk railings. The wind, coming in from the strait like a giant flat hand, bent the seaside pines and firs down almost to the ground. Morgan walked up to the café every day and tried to talk her into moving down to the boat house but she didn't talk to him at all. She rolled up Hamilton Grey's sleeping bag and folded his tent and left them piled on the stage beside the piano for the day when the RCMP would be finally contacted and come to ask questions about his death.

At the end of the week Morgan came to the door and asked if she wanted to help bury the little school teacher. She nearly laughed and said "No, but thank you for thinking of me," but instead just shook her head and shut the door in his face. Through the window of a back room she watched him drag the body out of the shed and haul it, wrapped in one of her blankets and laid out flat on a piece of canvas, up the steep slope of the hill. She ran out into the rain with Mr. Grey's books, scrambled up the hill until she caught up with Morgan, and said, "Throw these in too." She tossed the books, whose titles she hadn't even noticed, onto the canvas beside the body and hurried back down the hill before he started digging the grave.

That evening the wind was quieter, the rain silent, but Morgan still hadn't fixed the radio set. Hallie sat for a long time at the window, look-ing out to sea, listening to the intense beating of her own heart. Then she packed her suitcase and walked down the boardwalk, slowly, casually as if she hoped for a ship to appear from behind the point of land and sail in to pick her up by the time she got down to the gravel beach. But no ship came and Hallie Crane walked past the beach, gravel crunching under her heels, walked past Mr. Grey's little aluminum boat still tied to a driftwood log, and knocked lightly on the boat-house door.

Inside, she put down her suitcase and took a good look around. "The first thing you can do," she told Morgan, "is go up and bring down my own bed. I'm just here for the company."

"Sure you are," he said, and shut the door.

"I can't stand being alone for long."

"Sit down," he said. "I was making some coffee."

She smiled. "Did you dig a deep enough grave?"

"Deep enough so the rain won't wash him out, shallow enough for peo-ple or relatives to dig up if they want to see the body."

"He had no relatives," she said, taking off her coat. "He said he had no one." She smiled. She would like to have laughed, like the old Hallie, but she turned instead to the window and looked out for a moment across the little bay. "He told me there was no one in the world who could touch him, not even us."

Spit Delaney's Island

I hate to think what Marsten would say if I told him I was doing this. Nearly every day on the way home from the paper mill he sits in his car out front until I invite him in for a beer, and then he says "By gosh, I don't mind if I do" and comes in. We sit back in the only two chairs there are in this motel cabin, facing each other across the table, while he complains about all the people at the mill who wouldn't put in a decent day's work if their lives depended on it, and can't be trusted to blow their own noses without a boss telling them to. Sometimes he gets excited and yells at me and calls me stupid fool for brooding about my marriage break-up, and tells me I ought to be glad to escape from a woman like Stella Delaney. But what does a man like Marsten know about the things that I'm thinking, after what's happened to me? What does he know? Sooner or later he stands up to leave, drives a fist into his stomach to trigger one of his belches, and says "Yes sir; it's a bugger all right," which is his opinion on the general affairs of the world. I've a pretty good idea what he would say if he knew I was doing this, thinking these things, or if he found out about Phemie Porter. I know Marsten; that son of a gun would go through the roof.

I feel new at this life still. Stella and me've been separated for eight, nearly nine, months now, and sometimes I still don't know what I'm supposed to do or how to act. Nobody tells you, you're just dumped. I feel like I walked out into the middle of somebody else's play, right in the middle of it, and nobody's told me what lines to say. Not that anybody'd catch me going to a play, or to much of anything else any more for that matter, except to work every day and then back home, if you can call this place home. It's only a cabin, but I guess it's good enough, it's all I need it to be. On the edge of the village, right on the beach, it's just a few minutes' walk from a grocery store, and only the highway stretches out between me and my job at the mill where I spend all the time that I can. Inside there's this double bed with a sort of orange tattered chenille over it, a wooden table, a pile of dog-eared old paperbacks I'll never read, a hotplate, a watercolour of these stupid-looking wooden ducks trying to fly up off a phony lake, and my big oil painting of Old Number One the steam loci they sold right out from under me for those Ottawa tourists to stare at. And of course there's the view, the strait, whose tides slosh forward up the gravel slope, nudging driftwood and seaweed ahead, almost to the cabin door. And roar in my window all night. The Touch-and-Go Motel. It's a good enough place.

Not that you'll ever catch Marsten admitting it. He's a big slow-moving man with all the time in the world to live everyone else's life, and no interest at all in his own. He's worked in the yard crew at the mill for most of the twenty years I've been there, and eats his pork-and-bean sandwiches every noon in the shack with me, and tells me it's high time I got over being a Separated Man, acting as if the world has ground to a sudden stop. He's got this jowly head that seems to grow right up out of his shoulders, like a walrus, with thick sagging lips, and a pair of pale little eyes nearly buried in flesh. His body is like a walrus, too, tapered away from its heavy top. When he sits down he tries two or three times to get one knee up over the other, but never can, and always ends up sitting with his tiny legs wide apart and his elbows planted squarely on the table. "Yes sir, it's a bugger all right," he says, and calls me every kind of fool, and belches, and thinks of forty-seven different reasons why a man is better off without a wife and ought to be glad. I tell him he's a decent enough friend but I'd like it a lot if he could keep his nose in his own business for a change. Old Marsten.

"Make a joke if you want," he says, squeezing both eyes up closed and hauling a handkerchief out of his pocket to mop off the sweat from the folds of his neck. "Make a joke out of it if you want, man, but you'll be making yourself sick if you go on full of self-pity. It's time you started having some fun."

How can I have any fun when he's always hanging around nagging at me? Him and that other one, that Bested woman. Sometimes if Marsten isn't quick enough at ducking out of the cabin, he gets trapped into a second beer by the only other person who ever visits me, old Mrs. Bested, the woman who owns this motel. She comes in, whenever she can catch us, with three bottles in her hands, and sits nursing one of them between her knees on the side of the bed, her powdered face pointing out towards sea. "It's a lonely life," she says, her bit of blackmail. I don't know how much she can see; she has these eyelids that never open, the kind that would have to have been slit by a doctor's knife when she was born. She tilts back when there's something that has to be seen, but usually only stares into the insides of those lids, and sucks the neck of her beer bottle, and pouts out her lips to release the gas. That woman always makes me feel cold when she's in the room, I don't know why. There's something about her. If she gets into the cabin before Marsten has left, and gets herself settled on the bed, the two of them could be arguing there until late into the evening, and forget all about supper, and never bother to count the empty bottles that get lined up along the baseboard by the door.

"Vision is a thing of the heart," she likes to say, rolling the bottle between her hands. "A person could be blind as a bat and have vision clear as glass."

"Excuse me," says Marsten, "but that is a lot of hooey."

"The important thing is to *see*," she says. "It takes more than just opening your eyes to do that."

"And that," says Marsten, "is a load of manure."

Old Mrs. Bested threatens to pout. "I know what I know," she says, and points her chin.

Sometimes she drives fingers into her hair, riles it all up into a bush of blue-white flames. When the light catches it a certain way I expect her to float away. A good blast of wind and she could go out under it, floating, out the window like the helpless stem of a dandelion parachute.

"Have you been to see the children this week?" she nags at me.

"Is Mrs. Delaney well, up there at the house? Have you seen her at all?"

"Have you signed the papers for ever, so to speak, or is there a chance that you'll patch it up?"

"Don't you ever go out for some fun, Mr. Delaney? It's not healthy for a man to sit and feel sorry for himself." Echoing Marsten, the big-mouth. There are times when I can see myself smashing her skull in with a leg wrenched out of a chair. Just to shut up her talking.

Eventually, if she stays long enough, she'll get around to talking about her hands. They're magic, she says, and holds them up like jewels to turn in the light. "I have magic hands." They look like pretty ordinary hands to me, but she holds them up as if they had the secret of life in them.

"Sure," Marsten says, "and I have a big toe that can talk."

"With these hands," she says, "I can pull all of the pain out of your body, out of your mind. It's a fact."

And somehow she always manages to talk one of us, usually me, into letting her prove it. She stands up behind the chair, digs her hands into my neck, and explores down into the shoulders. Her thick fingers slide down under my shirt, dig hard into muscles, threaten to shake me right off the chair.

"Nobody believes in love any more," she says. Her breath when she leans close is beer-sour and hot.

Well, how could you? I want to know. Forty years have nearly managed to educate all that stuff out of me.

"Though the television seems to go on believing," she says.

Marsten roars. "Oh the tee vee!"

Nobody in my family ever used the word "love" when I was a kid. Not the way those actors use it. It was the kind of word, like "God," which would shrivel your tongue if you tried it, or make your neck burn and cringe if someone else did. You didn't know where to look. Not that it stopped me from thinking for a while there that I had a lot of it to give, but I guess Stella finished all that.

"The end of every marriage—good or bad—is cataclysmic," old Mrs. B. says. She likes words she can wrap her tongue around. "Either you die or you get yourself born again. Those are the only choices."

This to me, who sometimes wonder if I've managed it even the first time. I'm always getting this picture of myself legless, thrown up out of the sea and shrivelling, drying up like kelp or a marooned starfish.

When Marsten and the old woman start arguing about religion I just have to get outside, just far enough for the sound of the waves to drown out their voices. In the new dark, it's hard to tell where the land dies and ocean begins, except by sound. But where the eel grass saws at my ankles and rotting crabs stink in my nostrils, I spread my feet and pee into gravel.

That's what it's like around here, that's what I've got to put up with. It's a good thing I know more than I've ever told them, is all I can say. If I really was brooding as bad as they think, their stupid bickering would drive me up the wall. Sometimes I feel like telling them about Phemie Porter to see what would happen, the looks on their faces. Just to see how stupid they'd feel, after all their feeling sorry for me, and feeling superior, and telling me to snap out of it. Those two stopped looking at me, really looking, long ago.

It's because Stella got the place, that's what it is. They just can't accept that. I let her keep the place, it only made sense to me, there was a good chance she'd be saddled with that imbecile mother of hers for ever, and she couldn't very well kick Jon and Cora out before they finished high school. So I just let her have it. Why fight? I couldn't pretend I'd ever made good use of the land, or needed all those car parts I had in the shed, or laid any plans for the resurrection of the old boarded-up gas station. I couldn't think of a single reason for hanging on, it was almost a relief to take my pickup and camper and a few things and move down here to the beach.

Something happened when I was moving out that I can hardly believe. Stella kept out of the way all the time I was rummaging through the house, picking out what I wanted, which wasn't much, but when I was all set to go she comes out onto the front step and said, "You forgot your own true love," and I said What is that woman talking about? "You forgot your picture of the one dearest to your heart." Then I knew what she meant, my big oil painting of Old Number One that I operated every day for twenty years until they sold her on me, so I went back in and hauled it out to the camper. It's a wonder she didn't just let me forget it and then do what she always wanted to do with it, put an axe right through the middle. Stella always said she could take a mistress easier than Old Number One, you could scratch a mistress's eyes out, she said, but what do you do to a steam locomotive? How can you fight it? Something I didn't forget was my little cassette tape of Old Number One huffing and chugging down the track and blowing her whistle, though I'd never played it again since the day she wrecked my recorder throwing it out onto that street in the village in Ireland. I kept the tape in my pocket, always. I knew I'd get a new recorder some day, I wanted to get one of them kind I could rig up into the cab of the pickup, so I'd have it wherever I went. I'll never get over losing that loci. Spit and Old Number One, we were a team. Roy Rogers and Trigger. Who else in that mill got out of bed at four o'clock in the morning to fire up a head of steam for the day's work? I'll never get over the way they took her away from me, never.

Actually, there were two things that surprised me the day I moved out. The first was forgetting that painting I went to so much trouble and expense to get painted. The second was Jon and Cora. They went out for the day and didn't even offer to help. Didn't hang around watching. They just went out. Cora I think went over to a friend's, where she'd sit stuffing chocolate cake into her face and watching the soap operas on television, and complaining about her tight brassiere straps. Jon rammed a book up under his armpit, sniffed at us all, and went mincing down the road to wherever. I don't mind having a son that's a brain, I told Stella, but if he don't get that hump out of his shoulders and wipe that prissy look off his mouth I'll be wishing he'd change his name. Well don't worry about it, old Stella says, if I get married again some day, maybe my new husband'll adopt them and then you won't have to be ashamed. That was about the closest she ever came to being mean back then, last fall at the beginning, and I can't blame her for that one, they're her kids too. I guess I was just a bit put out by the way they didn't think it was important to stay around home the day that I happened to be moving out. Didn't lift a finger to help, or stand and watch, or wish me good luck or anything. I might as well have been one of them hitch-hikers in off the highway to use the toilet or get a drink of water.

All through the business of the separation Stella was as kind as you could expect, she was always considerate and never raised her voice to me once or did a mean thing or tried to get more than anyone would agree she had coming to her. You wouldn't think there was a spiteful bone in her body, except for her one or two comments about Old Number One and the way I couldn't get over her. What I don't understand is *what happened to her over the winter?* While I was trying to get used to this whole new way of looking at myself and fighting the urge to just chuck it all and go off somewhere new, and dreaming the damnedest nightmares, *what was happening to her?* I don't believe that if you chop all the arms and legs off a man and a woman and thrown them both into a brand-new country where they don't know the language, I just don't believe the woman would be any faster at adjusting than the man. It doesn't make sense. I can't believe that while he is lying around waiting for new legs to grow on and hoping to die, that she would decide legless was what she'd always wanted and a new language was as good as the old. It doesn't make any sense to me. I would just like to know what was happening to Stella Delaney over those winter months, between the time I moved off the place, and the time I took her out for dinner in May of this year.

I should've just kept out of it. But you get used to remembering your wedding anniversary and doing something special on it, and it's not something you can just ignore, even when it shouldn't mean anything any more, so I phoned up Stella in the middle of May and told her let's go out to supper somewhere to celebrate the first wedding anniversary we've ever spent as a Separated Couple. She told me it would probably be a big mistake, but if it was that important to me, she couldn't see any reason why not. What I shouldn't have done was let her pick the place. I'd forgotten already about that part of Stella, the part that never remembers to think how *I'd* feel in a place, and also the part that told her the way to prove she's as good as the best of them is to spend as much money.

It rained all the day of our anniversary, and blew too, but when I drove up to get her, it started to clear. All those brown sag-bellied clouds split, to let sun in, and then peeled back like gobs of gauze, leaving streaks and fluffs behind to turn pink and brownish-red over towards where the sun would set. I remember because I was nervous as hell driving up to get her, and had a good look at the sky to get my mind off it. But I knew, oh I knew the minute I saw those flaming torches outside the restaurant and the sort of old-private-house look to the place that the whole thing was one big fat mistake. You just couldn't imagine Spit Delaney going up those steps and inside and eating there, it wasn't my kind of place. But it was Stella Delaney's kind of place, she said, and went right on in so I had to follow her.

The sight of her hair all frizzed out like a pile of steel wool was a bit of a shock when I picked her up, but that was nothing compared to the way I felt when she took off her coat and there she was in tight black pants and a black top all covered with Indian fancywork and four or five different kinds of necklaces flopping around on her chest. Stella was one of those women who still wore housedresses when we were married, around the house, even when every other woman we knew, no matter what age or size, was wearing pants like a man to go everywhere even in public. She wore flowered dresses to the day I left. I don't know what happened after that. I'm scared to think. Forty years old and bony as an old nag and here she was in black pants, for crying out loud, and beads. I never said a thing, I couldn't, my throat was all closed up already from wondering how I was going to get through eating a meal in a place like *that*, with waiters flapping around in black suits setting people's supper on fire and pouring out wine for them to taste and nod over, and mixing the salads right out in plain view with hands that would look better tightening nuts. One consolation, if I spilled soup all over myself, or left the waiters too small a tip, there wouldn't be anybody from work there to see me.

Old Stella acted as if she ate there every day. You'd think the place was built for her, you'd think the waiters had been flown in from somewhere just to serve her. She always did think she could've been a lady if she'd ever been given a chance. She knew which fork to use. But I could never see her acting like that without thinking Come on lady, this is Spit sitting here, I'm the one that's seen you walking around naked in the bedroom and how lady are you then? How can you put on this act in front of someone who's seen the stretch-marks on your belly? And of course this time all I had to do was think that and the next thing I was thinking was about being in bed together and what a wild woman she could be under the sheets if she felt like it, and wondering if before the night was out she might admit she was missing it, too. You can't blame me for hoping. But old Stella didn't suspect my thoughts, she was busy acting a lady. That was the thing she knew best how to do.

She also knew how to go for the throat. The first thing she says when we're sitting down is "Have you been taking out many women to dinner?"

None, I told her. Not one. I wouldn't know how to start.

"That's stupid," she says. "You never had any trouble asking *me*, in the old days."

Well, that was because I knew who I was back in those days, or thought I did. I hadn't been hit by all the big questions yet, or lost everything in the world that mattered, or had the chance to find out how some women think.

"It's a shame that you don't," she said. "I've been inside some of the most interesting restaurants. From one end of the Island to the other. You shouldn't cheat yourself out of these things."

She ordered a gigantic vegetarian kind of thing for herself, of course—what else could I expect?—and I ordered scallops with some fancy foreign name. I like sea food. But I should've ordered roast beef and potatoes. This stuff came in a giant white shell, scallops and mushrooms buried in a white wine and cheese sauce. At least I could stir my fork around in it, and look busy, without anyone knowing how much I'd left uneaten. It smelled good, but my stomach was in no shape to receive. By the time I'd waded through soup and salad my insides were hollering Stop.

"Really, I don't know how you can eat those things," she said. She dabbed at her mouth with the big linen napkin.

"Why not?" I said.

"I mean because they were alive," she said. "It almost makes you a murderer."

I laughed. This was something else that was new. Stella in the old days would eat a horse while it was standing if she was hungry enough, and not bat an eye. "Don't be ridiculous, woman," I said. "These are only fish, and anyway what makes you think eating that plate of carrots is any different?"

Oh man, did she look holy. "A carrot was never conscious. You can't say it's been killed."

Well, I had her there. "Don't be so sure about that," I said, and who cares if the other tables all looked up from their lobsters and bleeding steaks and bottles of wine? "Listen to this," I said. "I read it in the papers."

"Please, Spit, keep your voice down." Old Stella can say something like that with a look on her face that would make others think she was just telling me how much she liked a present I bought her.

So I told her about these scientists I read about, experimenting with plants. They rig them up to electric machines of some kind, put a whole bunch of plants in a room and then pay this guy to go in and rip one of them all to pieces. Then they parade a whole lot of people, including this one guy, past the plants one by one, see, one by one, and they *recognize* him. When the fellow that ripped the one plant all to bits walked past, all the other plants went crazy.

"Ha!" said Stella, and popped in a whole carrot to show how impressed she was.

"Fear, Stella," I said. "What about that? Fear for survival. What does that say about you and your carrots?"

"I don't think everybody needs to hear you, Spit," she says, and shoots me one of her looks. "I'm sure the cook in the kitchen finds it interesting, but this is hardly the time."

It's because carrots don't have eyes, of course. If carrots had big sad eyes like a cow you wouldn't catch her eating them either. I almost enjoyed fishing out scallops from the sauce after that, and chewing them down.

I thought I had her stopped, she was quiet for a while. But all she was doing was thinking of ways to get even. "I think you just cancelled out your own argument," she said. "And since you're so good at noticing weird things like that, you must've seen about the man in the car accident."

I should've said "Sure" and changed the subject. But not me, I said, "What man?"

She had me. That look on her face. "This has happened before, but it happened again last month somewhere. I think it was in the States. I read it in a magazine. This was a perfectly healthy middle-aged man living a normal life and doing his job, and he got killed in a car accident. His skull was split open,"—she lowered her voice so the others wouldn't be offended, or bring up their supper—"and when they examined him in the hospital

they discovered that all he had left of his brain was a tiny knot of gristle."
I could tell by the way she held her fork just outside her lips that there was
supposed to be some great big lesson in it for me. And here it was: she said
of course it made you wonder if the brain is so all-fired important as it's
cracked up to be, if maybe our thinking don't come from somewhere else
altogether.

"You mean in the kneecaps?" I said. I had to.

No, she said, she meant *outside*. "And something else too. It means if a
man with no brains at all can carry on living a normal life and do all the
things that have to be done then *what is the matter with you?*" She put
down her fork and her knife and sat back.

What's that supposed to mean, I wanted to know. They tell me the lady
spider eats her mate when he's served his purpose; I guess I ought to con-
sider myself lucky.

"It means don't you think it's time you stopped acting like a kid that's
been kicked out of his cradle and started building a new life for yourself?
It means don't you think I know you've been acting as if the world came
to an end, and making everybody feel sorry for you, and going around
with this martyr look on your face? It means why don't you start trying to
find your own life in *yourself* instead of behaving as if it all depended on
everyone else, and you got cheated out of your share?"

By God, I could've told her a few things. What did she know? How
would she know what it felt like to be me? She couldn't even imagine
what it's like to be locked up inside me, locked inside this. The only thing
I ever liked about my job gone, nearly twenty years of marriage and family down the drain, everything I thought was real just turned into nothing.
And not able to tell anybody about it, just locked up inside and acting out
this play for other people, and not knowing what lines to say next. By God,
I could tell her a few things.

What I should've done right then was tell her about the dream I kept
having. That'd let her know a few things. I should've told her about the
dream and how it started on Christmas night, when I came back to the
Touch-and-Go after that horrible family supper with her and the kids and
her old lady. Christmas night old Kanikiluk walks right into the cabin and
changes me zap, just like that, into a fish, a dolphin I think or one of that

type of thing, and off I go cutting arcs through the Pacific, leaping and div-
ing and curving this way and that, all the way out past pleasure boats and
seiners and even the big foreign trawlers, all the way out to that damned
seam they told me about. Where the lava is leaking out of the crack along
the bottom, pushing the continents apart. But I never found it, I dived and
dived and looked all over the bottom with those other fish, but I never
found it and had to come back in. So I come skimming in to land as fast
as I can go, cutting through the surface, streaking up to the coast and leaping out of the waves at last and *bang* here I am beached on the dry sand
and can't move except flop around this way and that. And that's how it
ends, every time, with me on that sand, beached, neither in ocean or land.
The sun is drying me out, killing me. I should've told her that. Maybe if I
let her know the kind of dream I was having she might open up and tell
me what happened to *her* since we parted, what had made her change.

But I didn't get to tell her, because right then was when the restaurant
door opened and in stepped this woman I'd never seen before, dolled up
in the ugliest outfit you could imagine, and stands there looking around.
If I hadn't been so mad at Stella I might not've reacted the way I did, I
might not even have noticed her. What I said was "Look at that rig. Some
people shouldn't be allowed out in public."

Well, it's true. She looked as if she just stepped out of a freak show, or
a movie. She was short and dumpy, and had on an old moth-eaten fur coat
she must've found in somebody's attic, and a long skirt that reached to the
floor, and *hair*, she had it so thick and long that fourteen families of rats
could be nesting in it. And probably were. She thought she was really
something. You could tell by the way she held her head that she thought
she was something, but she was ugly. She must've been thirty-five or more,
dressed like an insane teenager.

"That's an awful thing to say," Stella said, but I waved her to be quiet.
I wanted a look at this creature.

There was a boy with her, who took off her fur coat, peeled it back off
her shoulders. He couldn't have been more than twenty, I'd say, and, oh,
seven feet tall, thin as a rake, with hair leaping out from his head like a
crown of wire. All hair and bulging crotch; the rest of him might have
been made of water pipes, wrapped in dirty denim.

And there she was, peeled out of her fur, with her tits hanging free in an old wrinkled sweater, and a plaid skirt that could've been made from a horse blanket. When she started to walk over to the corner table behind the waiter I saw she had hiking boots on, probably the only first-owner things on her body. Oh, I've seen lots of her kind around, especially in summer, they come out of the woodwork or somewhere parading themselves, but this one was the worst of the lot.

But Stella just turned back to her food. She was too lady to stare. She went on, telling me what my problem was, like someone reading a catalogue:

1. I put too much faith in things, and none in people,

2. I'm scared to think about anything in case I run into a question I can't answer,

3. I act like I believe a broken-up marriage is a sign that I'm a worthless human being,

4. I treat women as if they're all created for my benefit, but

5. I haven't got the guts to approach one now that I've failed with my first.

(She stopped here to order dessert—strawberries in ice cream—in a voice that must've made the waiter want to go out and puke, so sweet and thin and familiar. She smiled at his retreating ass, then turned back to me and went on.)

6. I never learned how to tell anyone else what I was feeling, so

7. I was always getting hurt when people couldn't guess what I felt, so

8. I figured that once I was married and had kids and a job I liked I didn't have to put any more effort into life, or try to improve, or imagine there was anything left I could try to understand, and one more thing:

9. a man who would say a woman is ugly and think he's said all that needs to be said about her has a lot of changing ahead of him.

And here I was thinking she wasn't ugly after all, my woman in the corner table with her pipe-stem boy, she was *grotesque*. Stella went on talking about things, about people we knew, about the kids and their school work, about what she figured I ought to be doing with myself, but I hardly listened. I was busy watching that woman. The boy sat barely moving, never changing the expression on his face. But she acted like a half-starved logger just come into the grub-house after a day of setting chokers. She laughed loud and coarse at the waiter doing his thing with the tray and the flames, showing spaces between her teeth, and sat with her knees wide apart in that skirt. (Stella, even in her black pants, sat so tight-together you couldn't drive a wedge.) When her food came she dug in, got it all over her hands, laughed with her mouth full, and hollered for the waiter to bring her a better class of wine. I wished my mother could've seen this. Her tongue would cluck in her mouth for a month afterwards. Me, I could've watched that woman for ever, she was such a good show.

"Is that what your freedom will turn you into?" I asked Stella. "Is that where you're headed? Liberated woman. Is that what you want to be like?"

But she didn't answer me. She leapt up from the table, snorting the way she does when she's holding back on a sob, and headed over towards the door. I didn't think a thing like that would bother her, she always used to like being teased a bit, I thought she'd take it as teasing. But she didn't. She just up and got out of there fast and left me to pay the bill by myself.

On my way out, on my way past the corner table, that woman's hand shot out and grabbed ahold of my pants, just above the knee, and held on. When I looked at her, thinking What the hell's this all about? she went on to finish chewing on something before she spoke. She looked at my knees first, then all the way up to my throat, then at my face.

"Aren't you a find," she said.

I looked at the boy but he was watching her, with a small paused-in-the-middle-of-a-chew smile on his face, like somebody waiting. He looked like someone who thought everything she did or said was all right with him, and more than all right. He had this fair, nearly invisible moustache and a few pimples high up on his cheeks, and strange clear eyes.

The woman looked around the room, as if gathering an audience, then looked up at me again. Her eyeballs were great scarred knobs, diseased probably and discoloured too, nearly yellow. But they were not hard, or cruel.

"You'll learn to walk, Mr. Man," she said, nearly purring it. "Some day you'll learn to walk."

I nearly choked when she said that. You'd think she'd been listening to the dream I never got around to telling Stella about. It gives you the creeps to think how some people in this world know things they've never been told, like they could see straight into your head. I don't understand how they do it, I don't even want to know. I nearly choked when she said that, I was so surprised, but all I did was get out of there as fast as I could go.

I'd seen the Wooden Nickel before, I'd been past it a few times since it opened, but I never went in. Who wants to look at other people's old junk? To me the place was just an old broken-down boxy house by the side of the tracks no matter how much they fixed it up and painted it showy yellow with red trim and hung up their sign. I would probably never have gone inside it yet if it weren't for Phemie Porter.

That's what her name turned out to be. Phemie Porter. She's from Back East somewhere, Toronto I think. A poet. I haven't seen her books in the window of the bookstore in the village so I guess she's not very famous yet. And she's thirty-two, not as old as I thought. The kid with the hair and crotch is Reef.

I never slept that night, after I took Stella home. She wouldn't even speak to me in the pickup and only got out and slammed the door to go into the house, so I knew that was that, it was finished, I'd clobbered myself good. So I went home to the Touch-and-Go and lay on the top of the bed until six o'clock in the morning. When I looked out the window I thought maybe I'd done some damage to my eyes or something, everything had turned purple and mauve, or lilac. The sun had just cut loose from the mainland mountains into the sky and still looked as if it had burned a wide hole out of the mountains—a wide white gap of light—but the rest of the coastal range made its jagged purple wall from one end to the other of all I could see. The strait, nearly high tide, was all that lilac colour, too, except for the bars of whitecaps and breakers near the beach. I got up and went down to the edge of the water in my undershorts and there was this body of a seal rolling there at the edge, rolling and rolling as each wave slapped it up against gravel. It was all wrapped around in strips of seaweed and kelp and bits of bark. Poor old seal's eyes were open, dull and brown; he wasn't the first that I'd ever seen like that. I don't know what happened to him, it could have been only old age, his coat was all scratched and ragged and torn. Maybe he was cut by an outboard motor, and bled to death. He'd go out with the tide, later, and then come in somewhere else down the coast.

But later I'd had a bit of sleep at last and got dressed and come out again to see if he'd gone. The tide had moved far out, beyond tide pools and sand and hadn't left him behind, so I walked out and started following the edge of the water along, slapping my bare feet in the foam-edge, heading south. I couldn't find my seal all the way around that bay, past the tourist cabins and the hotels, so I walked up the slope to follow the seawall back.

And there, at the foot of the big totem, was that woman from the restaurant, squatting on a pile of pack-sacks and sleeping bags and gear. She was dressed exactly the same as she'd been the night before, probably hadn't taken her clothes off, but her face was all puffed up from sleeping. She laughed at me.

"Yes," she said. "I thought this would be where we'd find you. Paddling on the edge of the sea."

Her boyfriend was standing up, leaning against the backside of the totem, looking at me. I didn't like the looks of that fellow, I don't mind admitting; there was something dangerous in his face.

"Excuse me," I said, and went on past. No crazy woman was going to make fun of me. What I do is my business. There's no law that says I've got to put up with that kind of thing. They were loiterers, is all, they'd probably slept right there on the beach like a lot of others I'd seen.

But she tells me oh please don't go by in a huff it was only a joke.

Then she said, "You're as touchy as my husband."

I looked at the boy. "This is your husband?"

She laughed and threw up her hands. "Heavens, no! I left my husband at home!"

I know I shouldn't have said this but I did. I thought it would be the last I saw of them. "Then what is he, your son?"

Well, she let out one roaring laugh, you'd think it was a drunken old wheezing man, they must have heard her all up and down this beach. "Reef?" she said, and roared again, flapped her knees in and out. "He's just my portable prick."

What do you say? I've heard some coarse women in my day, in the parts department of the mill and up in the camps years ago, but I could tell I was blushing this time. It was one of those times when you suddenly get a picture of yourself, as if you'd stepped out a few paces and looked back. There I was, this lanky old scrawny-necked bugger, blushing right up to the peak of my engineer's cap. Forty years old, with big feet. I'd heard things in my day and said things that would make her turn green, but here she was making me blush. I'm glad Stella wasn't around is all I can say.

That boy just looked at me, never smiled, with a bit of a sneer. Maybe he really was nothing more than what she said. There was no sign of anything else in his eyes.

"You got a car?" she said, and stood up, stamping the folds out of her skirt. "Do you drive something?" I wondered how long it had been since she'd taken those hiking boots off.

"I got a pickup," I said, "and a camper." I knew what she was after, she didn't fool me. I'd seen them lined up along the road with their thumbs out. But I don't lie. Ever.

Suddenly she grabbed my arm and pushed herself close. "Wonderful! Because you're going to take us for a drive. Up into the mountains."

"The hell I am," I said.

But I did. I don't know how it happened. I don't know how anything happens. I've always hated those hitch-hikers, dressed up in their stupid costumes, expecting other people to waste gas on them. I've watched them for years along the highway in front of the place, Stella's place now, too lazy to lift a thumb, some of them. Lying down on the gravel. I don't know how many times I've been tempted to go out in my truck, drop one tire onto the shoulder, and run over them all. I wouldn't pick one of them creeps up, I told Stella, if I thought he was dying. So don't ask what happened here, I don't know. Why would I want those two freaks in my truck? Why would I want to go anywhere at all on my day off from work?

It might have been the way she looked at the early swimmers, at the kids playing in the tide pools, and said, "Let these fish splash around in the water. People are meant to climb mountains. Take me inland, Mr. Man, take me up into the hills!"

Maybe I'm just stupid. Or maybe it was the look of challenge in her eyes. I'd never seen such big eyeballs, or so scarred. I wondered if you could get your eyeballs scarred from what you've *seen* or does it have to be something else. No woman's look had ever challenged me like that before, maybe I just couldn't stand to turn it down.

If I'd known she was a poet I'd never have gone. If I'd known I'd get a letter from her a day later with this piece of paper in it, one of these mixed-up modern unreadable poems called "The Man Without Legs," she wouldn't have got inside my pickup for even a minute. You can't trust people who write things on paper, they think they own all the world and people too, to do what they want with. It's probably a good thing I can't make head nor tail of the thing, it's just gibberish to me. Some things you're better off not knowing. Next thing I know I'll be hearing that thing is in a book somewhere, for people to read. Good luck to them if they can make more sense out of it than I can.

"I'll take you a part of the way," I told her. "I'll take you as far as Robinsons', I could do with some fresh eggs."

So we were off. I've got to admit I was curious, it might have been curiosity that did it. Maybe all I wanted to do was find out what made these people tick, this woman anyway. You see them passing by from their own worlds going somewhere, but you never know any. They kind of scare me too, most people you can size up pretty fast and know where you stand, but I always said to Stella you just couldn't tell what those hitchhikers were liable to do. How can you feel safe around people when you haven't any idea what goes on inside them? Me, I like to know what people are thinking, so I'll know what they're up to.

So the first thing I said when we started up from the coast was "Why?" The woman was sitting in the middle of the cab, beside me, with her boy by the door. All their gear was thrown in the back, inside the camper. We drove uphill from the totem past the golf course and the big inn, and through the cluster of little shops—drug store and variety store and boarded-up theatre and Oddfellows' Hall. "Why up to the mountains?"

"The highest mountain we can find around here," she said. She put her hand down over her friend's crotch, gave it a pat, then folded both hands in her lap. She peered down close to the registration card on the steering column. "Your name is . . . Albert Delaney?"

"Spit," I said.

"Spit?"

The boy smiled. I wondered what it felt like to have somebody do that to you in public, what she'd just done to him. What kind of world do these people live in anyway? What kind of people are they? Stella would never have done that if I'd promised her a fur coat for it.

"I've crossed the country, end to end," she said, "for my next book of poems."

"Scenery?" I said.

"Especially *not* the scenery. It's humanity I want. It's evidence I want, of the humanity that's hiding in man."

Then why climb a mountain, I wanted to know. There wouldn't be people up there. Not in our mountains.

"There'll be me," she says. "I'm in search of my own too, especially. What better place to find it?"

"Just drive," the boy said. It was the first thing I'd heard from him, and he didn't even turn to say it, just kept his eyes straight ahead. It was nothing more than I should've expected. You couldn't expect gratitude for the ride, or even respect, you had to put up with the insolence too on top of everything else. Burn up your gas, sit in your cab, take up your time, then spit in your eye to show what a fool you are. That boy was looking for trouble.

But not the woman. Phemie Porter. There was something else in her, I was beginning to see it. She said, "You drive like a man that knows how to handle a machine." And of course she was right. There isn't a person down at that mill who can handle a loci the way that I can, I don't suppose there's a man on this island can get as *close* to an engine as Spit Delaney. Ask around. It wasn't just accident they were able to sell Old Number One to the museum at fifty years old and still going strong, it was because she'd been cared for by me for so long. I know engines. Driving the pickup is kid's play in comparison, but still if a person knows what to look for, you can tell a man who's used to handling big machinery. Not that I'm such a fool I let this Phemie Porter win me over with that one sentence or anything. I would still like to have dumped her into the ocean for a good bath, and put some human clothes on her, and sent her back to her husband. I still wanted to tell her to act her age, and put on some makeup and comb her hair, make herself look decent.

We drove uphill through brush—fir mostly, with their limp yellowish paws of new growth drooping at the ends of the limbs, in gravelly soil and tangles of Oregon grape and salal—snaking around corners bright yellow with broom. Once in a while the brush would disappear, suddenly, to give us a view of big green fenced-in fields with Holsteins grazing, a gigantic dairy farm, and far to the west, beyond more trees, the great jagged-peaked snow caps of the nearest mountain. It was far enough off to be blue still, except for the lower slopes where sun was lighting up some patches of green furry timber.

"There's a lot of climbing in that mountain," she said. "My father used to take us up the side of every hill he could find, to ski, or explore, or simply to camp overnight. It was all part of the same thing, he said, going into yourself. When I was eleven years old he sold everything he owned, handed the money over to my mother, and disappeared into the Laurentians for a year. When he came back he was a changed man, but my mother wouldn't have him. He should've spent the money on a psychiatrist, she said, and shut the door in his face."

Then there we were, turning a corner to cross the tracks, and right in front of us was the big bright yellow building with the red trim. Along the top of the verandah was its sign: WOODEN NICKEL, with an oversize 1922 nickel between the words, and all along below were flower boxes and old wooden barrels and a cast-iron kitchen stove and a big trunk and an old wringer washing machine. The two big windows were divided into dozens of tiny panes, with bottles and jars and vases showing through from inside.

The minute she saw it she yelled "Stop!" and I slammed on my brakes automatically and pulled over, even while I was saying "It's only a second-hand store, probably a whole lot of old junk. You're better to stay out of there."

Who knows how different things might have been if I'd just stepped on the gas and gone on past it, or if I'd dropped them off there and said "See you around" and come back by myself to the cabin? I'll never know, it's impossible. Instead, I pulled over on the opposite side of the road, against the high narrow-slat fence, and we got out.

There were cars parked every which way in the gravel yard, and several along the side of the road. Some people were going in, tourists, and others were coming out. Two woman hurried out across the road, one of them holding a plate and a couple of little bottles, and saying "I need these like I need a hole in the head but I couldn't resist." The other woman laughed. She had a little change purse in her hand.

"It's a good place to throw away money," I warned her.

But oh no, she had to go in. Anything old, even junk, fascinated her, she said. "We're in no hurry, so why not take the time for a look around?"

The last time she was in a second-hand store, she said, she'd found a crystal ball. Some fortune teller's. She took it to a party, she said, as a joke. But she looked so deep into some of them they got scared, and told her to leave if she wouldn't stop. "Some of them worked up a real sweat," she said and pulled her face into a horrible shape and showed me her claws and cackled like a witch. "I . . . can . . . see . . . *ev* . . . rything," she said. I could see why they asked her to leave, but I didn't say anything. I just wasn't used to women like that, who would do a thing like that in public.

Crossing the road she hooked her arm into mine and the Crotch walked behind. I hoped nobody going by would think we belonged together. I could just see somebody from work driving along and seeing that rig latched onto me and thinking old Spit's gone around the bend, or acting like a hippie, or got himself tied up in women's lib. I could just hear them. I tried to hurry her across, but then I thought to hell with them. What do they know about anything? It felt kind of good having somebody hooked on my arm again. Fright as she was to look at, I think that woman liked me. I don't know what the other one thought, the boy. That was his look-out.

While we were crossing the gravel, a family of overweight people came out of the front door, one at a time. First the father, a huge balding man in sun glasses and a hanging-out shirt and sandals, then a short chubby lady in shorts, with her white ripply legs all exposed, then a whole line of kids in descending order, all round and red-faced and pleased with themselves. When they were all out onto the gravel yard they gathered around in a circle to compare notes or something. The old man handed sticks of chewing gum out, all around, and they dropped all their wrappings on the ground. "Excuse me," Phemie Porter said, and went over. "Are you people from the States?"

They all turned to her, identical faces chewing, curious. "Sure am," the father said, and patted his belly.

"Do you think this is a beautiful country?" Phemie says.

"Just lovely," the mother bubbled. "Just lovely."

Phemie put the toe of her boot out amongst the pieces of paper and tin foil on the ground. "Then perhaps you won't mind leaving it that way?" She said it so softly I could barely hear it.

The smiles all reassembled into scowls. Red faces got redder. The mother's hands jerked to her throat. Old Father Tourist, though, just started to laugh, that kind of forced jolly laugh some people have when they try to cover up a blunder. "Talk about blights on the landscape," he said, and nudged at his wife. The wife looked Phemie over and put a hand against her mouth. The kids all started to giggle.

But Phemie Porter just swung around and gave me a look out of those eyes and walked back up to the verandah and into the store. It made me feel sick, the way they treated her. It made me ashamed of us all, I wanted to hit somebody. But I followed her inside the building, and Reef came after. I bet those fat-assed farts would have the paper picked up by the time we came out, though. There were others who'd seen them and heard, they wouldn't have the nerve to just walk away.

Inside that place you didn't know where to turn, or where to start. Phemie Porter got all excited and tried to see everything at once. The place was all fixed up to look old, but it was tidy, not what you'd expect, and had rows and rows of old used furniture fixed up in the first room. She ran her hand over everything, tables, desks, chairs, sewing machines, as if it was all something she'd never seen before, or heard of. "Oh, look at this," she said, or "Oh, look at that." She wanted to touch and see everything all at once. The fellow that seemed to be running the place—a young blond-headed fellow doing additions or something at a desk in the corner—looked up at her excitement and then gave me a grin. He was probably thinking here was a sale for sure, nothing less than a hundred dollars. Or maybe he was trying to tell me he'd seen plenty like her before, don't get embarrassed. He probably had too, he looked at her as if he knew the type. There was a green eyeshade on his forehead, and he was wearing a pair of coveralls with engineer stripes the same as my cap. He went back to his work. At least he wasn't going to try talking us into something.

There were plenty of things to look at, I've got to admit. You could spend all day just looking. And every bit of it had been found on this island, nothing was brought in from the mainland. A whole line-up of old tobacco cans across the corner, I don't know who'd buy them or what for but they brought back some memories: Clubman, and Hickory, Troost I think, and Heine's Blend with its picture of a wooden-shoed Dutchman by a wind-mill. Old-fashioned druggist bottles of every shape. *Aqua calcic*, whatever that means. *Ferri et quinni*. I wouldn't have minded walking out with the swede saw I found hung up on the cedar-shake wall either, I don't know what for, but it looked like a good thing to have.

I glanced up once, and found myself looking back from a gilt-edged mirror. I'd forgotten to shave that morning, I was in such a hurry to get out. This face of mine looked bruised, and old. Not something I wanted to spend very much time looking at. In the background I caught the bean-pole glaring at me, leaning up near the door. One hand laid out flat on his narrow belly kept moving, slowly, in a kind of a circle.

"Oh, look at this!" she said, and dragged me back to see some old chest of drawers that was still being worked on, in a little alcove off the back corner. Someone had been taking old paint off, the good rich grain of old oak was beginning to show through in patches. "Somebody else would've slapped new paint on top and thought they'd improved it," she said. "These people know where the real value is found." She didn't try to make a les-son out of it for me, the way Stella might have (everything to Stella had a message in it aimed at me, the whole world to her was organized in pat-terns meant to straighten me out) but she did put her hand on mine and made me run my fingers over the grain. As if I'd never felt oak before.

"I dedicated my first book of poems to a man by the name of Eloff Nurmi," she said, "and no one could figure out why. He was the little round cabinet maker who built me my very own chest of drawers when I was small, something like this one. Inside it, he told me, he'd built a secret compartment where no one, not even my mother, would find it. It was the invisible soul of the chest, he said, where I could keep things that belonged just to me. But I never found it myself, and I was afraid to admit it to him, so I learned to store everything important in my own mind, and later in poems, and gradually began to suspect this was what he intended. He'd moved away long before the book came out, though, and I don't know what happened to him after that."

When I got rooting around amongst the books and roller skates and old crocks in another little back room, she came in and ran her finger down the whole shelf of books, paused at one and said "This New Land" then went on to the end and dismissed the lot. Suddenly she stooped and came up with a bedpan, "What the best people are wearing this year," she said, and turned it upside down on her head. "Things, things, things," she said, and did a turn under the new hat, then stooped to make a face in a mirror. Then she swept the bedpan off, handed it to me, and I put it down. I couldn't help thinking of all the bare asses that had sat on it, but of course that would mean nothing to her.

"My husband is a doctor," she said. "Speaking of bedpans. Deadpans. He's crazy about me. He's crazy, period, he's a shrink. I was his patient for a while, but he gave up and married me instead." Those eyeballs took in everything in the room, came back to me. "He intends to retire early, he says, so he can follow me when I go off like this, and find out what I'm after. But he'll never retire, and he'll never follow me, and he'll never be able to see.

"Things, things, things," she sang, scooping up a handful of cutlery out of a tray and letting them clatter back again. "We're surrounded by thousands of things and what do any of them mean?"

"Money to the guy that sells them," I said. And of course the boy in the coveralls was watching us, he must've thought he had a couple of loonies in there.

"There is no truth in things," she said, "except as they bring out the truth in a person. Tell me a thing that you love and I'll tell you a thing about you."

"Old Number One," I told her.

"What? Old Number One? What's that? Do you mean yourself? Then you are a man who is trapped by your own limits."

I didn't bother to correct her, it would only confuse things.

"Tell me this, then," she said. "If I was going to buy you something from this store, anything at all, what one thing would you want it to be?"

I should've said tobacco tin, or swede saw, or just anything at all. I should've said a book, or anything. But oh no, when she said that, I got this idea. "If there was a tape recorder around here I could give you your answer to that other question."

"A tape recorder?" she said. "There's not going to be a tape recorder around here, not in a place like this. They sell old stuff, these things are nearly antiques."

Of course if she let it drop at that I'd've kept quiet and that would be the end of it. She could buy me a picture or something else if she wanted to, if that was her way of paying me back for the ride. But she didn't let it drop, she *asked*, and of course there wasn't a tape recorder for sale in the place. Just to borrow then, she said, I couldn't believe the nerve she had, was there one we could borrow for five minutes. It turned out there was one, a little black plastic one, in that back room where they scraped the paint off old furniture. Phemie Porter made it sound as if lending that thing to us was an honour any storekeeper would be glad to break his neck for.

"Now what is it I'm going to hear?" she said.

I got scared. I'd been carrying that cassette around in my pocket for nearly a year, not playing it, just feeling it there and thinking maybe I'd play it again some day and maybe I wouldn't, considering the trouble it already caused me. But I never expected to be playing it for a stranger, like her, in a public place. I wished I'd kept my big mouth shut.

We sat on the edge of the verandah, up at the end by the flower boxes, and I put the machine on my knee. Reef stayed down at the other end, leering. Along the edge of the road the family of Americans was leaning all over a white Cadillac, having a picnic. They took food out of a big paper bag that sat up on the hood and went back to lean on different parts of the car to eat and throw back mouthfuls of tinned pop. When he saw us the father let out a single snort and turned his back, to show what he thought. Other people, coming in, paid us no attention at all.

"I think there used to be a little train station somewhere around here," I told her. "See that track going by? You keep your eye on where it disappears in the bush and imagine what you hear is coming from down there."

I pushed the button. There was nothing for a minute, then a voice: *I don't know where you'll be when you listen to this, but this is one way I can be sure of being heard, you're bound to listen some . . .*

I pushed the Stop button. That was Stella's voice. What the hell was going on? I ran it ahead a foot or so and pushed the Play again.

not enough, not enough at all, Spit. A man who . . .

I shut it off again. I couldn't believe it.

"What's the matter?" Phemie said.

"She taped over it." I just couldn't believe it. "She taped over it." I could feel the sweat breaking out on my forehead, and my upper lip. Everything got confused.

"Who?"

"Stella. She got ahold of it somehow and taped over it." If I had her there, if I could get my hands on her. My shaking hands.

I ran it up to halfway in case she'd run out of message for me and there was still some of the loci left, but when I turned it on again there she still was, talking: *Some day you will have to learn how,* she said, *you'd never learn it being married to me and that train. Maybe your freedom will help you to . . .*

Freedom. I wanted to bash her with freedom. I wanted to strangle her with freedom. If she'd been there I would've pushed that tape machine down her throat sideways. I would've made her eat the thing. I could hardly see for the sweat that was getting into my eyes, stinging.

"She must've done it back then before I moved out," I said. "While we were working out the settlement. She must've known I would give in and play it some day."

People had stopped to watch us, to listen. The tourists were all facing our way so they wouldn't miss a thing. Reef had come over closer and squatted, his wrists draped over his knees. He had long, long hands that hung down limply. I imagined those hands touching her. I remembered them peeling back the fur in the restaurant. I imagined them running up her arm, up her leg. It doesn't make any sense—I shouldn't have been thinking that, I should have been screaming about Stella, or throwing that machine over into the bush, or taking the cassette out to stamp it into the gravel. But I didn't feel like that at all. I felt like putting my head on her shoulder, or crying. I had to haul my handkerchief out of my pocket and mop the sweat off my face, and around my neck, the way Marsten does.

If I were making this up, if I were making up lies about myself, that is not how I would end the episode at the Wooden Nickel. Not like that. That was too calm to be the end of anything. If I was making it all up to work out the way it should, I would say I threw that little machine into the brush, and went yelling after it to stamp it to pieces, grind it under my heels. Then that family of fatties starts to laugh, see, like this is all a good show just for them and I yell something at them. I yell something obscene and violent and threaten to gouge out their eyes if they don't shut up their faces. The owner of the store comes out too, and yells what am I doing with his recorder, but I tell him to go back in his hole in the junk and drop dead. Reef tries to quiet me, he comes over and puts one of those long narrow hands on my arm, tries to steady me into silence, but when I look in his eyes I see the hatred that's been building up all day. He despises me. He would like to kill me. Without moving a muscle in his face, without changing his expression at all, he brings up a sharp bony knee and gets me hard in the crotch and I go down, puking into the salal, and he kicks me. The pain, the sickening pain, is everywhere inside me, ripping me open. I even think I may die there, on the ground. It isn't until later when I have got back up onto my feet that Phemie Porter comes over, dragging her skirt through the brush, and crossing the tracks. *That woman is wrong*, she says. *In all those years of marriage she couldn't see it but she's wrong.* Everybody is standing around in the gravel and along the road and on the verandah of the store, watching us. Like a movie.

It isn't true, though. That isn't the way it happened. Maybe a few years from now when I remember that day at the Wooden Nickel I won't be able to tell which was true and which I've made up. It won't even matter. I will probably remember the made-up one clearest, so that when I drive by the store in my camper I can think that at least I offered that fellow who runs it a bit of excitement, a story he can remember. And I will probably think that, for him and the others who work in there with him, I offered a bit of myself, I exposed something.

They're not likely to remember two people sitting on the verandah. A dumpy woman dressed up in those crazy clothes, with too much hair, and a lanky scrawny-necked engineer who needed a shave, the two of them staring at the little black plastic box of a recording machine as if there was a beast in it. And they won't remember that the woman put her hand on the man's arm, and held on for a while, and then told him she could imagine the sounds of a steam loci easy enough, that she didn't need a tape for it and neither did he.

She told me this: "You've already got everything in you that you need."

"What is it?" I said.

"When those tourists were laughing at me," she said. "For just a split second we touched, we overlapped."

I could've told her that was all a load of manure, the way Marsten would've. I could've told her she didn't know a thing about me. But that wouldn't be true. She did know. She knew plenty about me, and that's what I'd guessed about her from the beginning.

But maybe I shouldn't have run away. Maybe I should not have left them there at the store and got into my pickup and driven home. There was a lot left I could offer. I could've told her all about the Doukhobor colony that lived across the road once, behind that high picket fence. A religious colony that didn't believe in marriage. Maybe she'd have got a poem out of that. I could've told her about them, and about the mountain she was going to. I could've told her what to expect there, the distance to the timber line, and what she would find in the alpine meadows.

But she scared me off. She said, "Come on up with me, Spit Delaney, come walking with me on the mountains. Learn to see. Don't go back to your puddles."

As if I could.

It's something to think about, though. When Marsten sits out in his car waiting to be asked in for a beer I'm tempted to tell him, "Can't ask you in tonight, Marsten, there's a woman waiting for me, up a mountain." Or when he gets nagging at me to quit brooding, to get back in the swing of life. What is the matter with him? Don't people look at other people? Can't they tell when other people start to change? But I know him, he doesn't have an idea what anyone else is like. He just wants someone to talk to, and some place to drink beer, and he probably likes being able to argue with old Mrs. Bested who owns the Touch-and-Go Motel. Her magic hands haven't done any good yet, and of course they never will. But she thinks she's doing something, or tries, nearly every night when she comes in. She hasn't looked at me either, really, in months. And she's probably forgotten what those magic hands of hers are after. It's all just habit, we go through, we act out. And they don't know a thing about me. Not a thing. They haven't noticed yet that there have been a few nights when I haven't come straight home from work, and a few nights when I've gone out late and not come home until far into morning. They don't notice a thing.

Sometimes I'm tempted to tell them "I knew a poet once, for a while. She invited me up into the mountains with her." But they'd only say "Sure, sure," and go on with their arguing, and talking about magic hands, and drinking their beer. Or say "How did a poet get into the mill?" which is as big as they think my world ever gets. No, that isn't what they would say. They'd just look at me (Marsten squeezing his eyes into a squint, old Mrs. Bested leaning back to peer through her slits) they'd just look at me as if I had left my brains behind me somewhere on the road, and maybe roll a few sounds around in their mouths waiting for me to add more, something that would make sense to them, something that would fit closer to their idea of what I am like. It just doesn't enter some people's heads that others might not be what they seem. So I'll never tell them about the poet, and anyway she may have come down off that mountain long ago now, and gone home.

Though maybe not. I could go up there yet, to see. I should, to see for myself. She just might still be there. The most she could've found up there for company would be a timber cruiser or a half-crazy old prospector or a party of university students looking at rocks. Still, I like to imagine her stumbling into a camp of wild and desperate soldiers laying plans to set the island afloat and liberate us all from something. They tell me the mountains on islands in other parts of the world are just swarming with these secret armies and escaped convicts, with passwords and smuggled-in machine guns and whispered meetings. Not us, as far as I know, but I still like to think of her coming into a group of them, being caught by their lookout. They would kill the Crotch right away, of course, but she'd become one of them, and even more than that, she'd become a leader, too, in no time at all. Maybe she's up there now, somewhere, plotting my freedom for me. I just may go up yet, to see for myself.

In the meantime, I've still got the poem she sent me, the day after the

Wooden Nickel, postmarked at the little village just up beyond it. It's handwritten, not typed, scribbled out in her writing. Sometimes when I read it, it starts to make a kind of sense to me, if I don't try too hard, but if I look up from it for even a second the meaning just disappears and it all looks like gibberish again. But she's in there, somewhere. She's in there somewhere looking at me clearer than anyone's ever seen me before. If I could understand, if I could get inside those words with her, I think I'd be able to know what it was she saw when she looked at me, what it was that made her believe I could manage, that I could survive and go on. But I won't tell Marsten about it. I know him, the son of a gun would go through the roof. Or die laughing. I wouldn't tell him a thing.

ABOUT THE AUTHOR

Jack Hodgins' fiction has won the Governor General's Award, the Canada-Australia Prize, the Commonwealth Prize (Canada and the Caribbean) and the Ethel Wilson Fiction Prize, amongst others. He has given readings, talks, and workshops in Australia, New Zealand, Japan, and several European countries, and has taught an annual fiction workshop in Mallorca, Spain. *A Passion for Narrative* (a guide to writing fiction) is used in classrooms and writing groups across Canada and Australia. In 2006 he received both the Terasen Lifetime Achievement Award and the Lieutenant Governor's Award for Literary Excellence in British Columbia. In 2009 the Governor General appointed him a Member of the Order of Canada. His most recent novel, *The Master of Happy Endings*, was published in 2010. He and his wife Dianne live in Victoria. More information is available on his website: www.jackhodgins.ca.

RECYCLED
Paper made from
recycled material
FSC® C021757

Marquis Book Printing Inc.

Québec, Canada
2010

Printed on Silva Enviro 100% post-consumer EcoLogo certified paper,
processed chlorine free and manufactured using biogas energy.

100%   PERMANENT